A Lantern of Love
A Novel in Three Parts

Della Campbell MacLeod

Contents

A LANTERN OF LOVE
A NOVEL IN THREE PARTS

BY

Della Campbell MacLeod

A LANTERN OF LOVE

PROLOGUE

I

AT the far end of the long room hung an old gilt mirror. In this was re-flected a portrait that hung directly opposite at the other end of the room. The portrait was also in a gilt frame somewhat tarnished.

The mirror needed re-silvering. There was no wiping the haze from its face. Mammy Linda bewailed the distance to Nuaw 'Leens every time she rubbed over the long glass. The portrait, too, was very old and had a quality of mistiness that made it adorably soft. Its reflection in the mirror was even more tender and illusive. The face gained new values in the mirror. Somehow it seemed informed with—if not spirit—memory.

The room smelled of beeswax. When the floor was polished and Mammy Linda's dust-rag had gone carefully into each crevice of the carved rosewood furniture, she took the cover off the old blue Chinese jar out of which floated a cloud of scent, a potpourri Iliad of the flower garden just outside the long French windows.

Even the tiny child at the old negress's heels felt the spell of the room. She tiptoed after the black woman, like an acolyte attending a priest. Behind the child followed a grey kitten.

"See!" The baby would walk to the mirror and identify the kitten in the glass with the kitten behind her. "See?" she would ask Mammy Linda as if to explain to her that the kittens were the same kitten.

Mammy Linda would nod her turbaned head and mirate greatly over the discovery. The kittens being disposed of, the child would turn to a more complex problem. She knew only a few words and these were of one syllable. Her vocabulary was far behind her vision. Mammy Linda sensed this.

The old negress saw in the mirror a baby girl two years old, with a thatch of red-gold hair, dressed in a low-necked dimity slip. The child's wide-set blue eyes gravely studied the reflections in the long glass.

Mammy Linda waited for her to make the discovery afresh every morning.

"See!" would finally come the announcement as the child turned to the old negress, pointing to the reflected portrait. "See?" she would touch herself, then indicate the reflection of the lovely wilful face in the tarnished gold frame. *"Me."*

At first Mammy Linda shook her head and pointed to the baby reflected in the glass. The child would stamp her foot and try again to make herself understood., She touched herself, then pointed to the reflected portrait.

"See?" she questioned, pantomiming what she did not know the words to explain. *"Me."*

And Mammy Linda understood at last.

II

THE child and the grey kitten pattered after the turbaned old negress as she set the drawing-room in order every morning. And the child and the kitten trailed after her when she went to the attic.

The attic fascinated the baby girl just as the drawing-room did. It, too, was full of mystery. The grey kitten chased a mouse one day and the child followed. Mammy Linda found her at last in a remote gable where were stored portfolios of yellowed music. She turned the leaves joyfully and tried to make the old negress understand what she had found. The little girl cried when Mammy Linda tried to take her away from the music. The scene ended in the portfolios being brought down to the drawing-room.

The child would turn the old dog's-eared pages of music as other children pore over Mother Goose pictures. After a while she gave up trying to make Mammy

Linda understand.

Then she tried to tell Bob. He shook his head. He told the child's mother and father that they ought to know what she was trying to say. The child knew her father and mother could not understand.

III

THE river flowed just below the flower garden. The little girl thought the river was alive. She could hear it growl far underneath as she sat making a playhouse in the roots of the old oak-tree on its bank.

The child was as sensitive to color as she was to sound. People were white like day and black like night. Most of them on Palmetto Grove Plantation were black like night. The only white people she saw were her father and mother and Bob.

Her father and mother never finished what they had to tell each other. The child knew she belonged to them, but she did not feel that they belonged to her.

Bob seemed outside somehow, just as she seemed outside even when her father and mother held her in their arms between them.

Mammy Linda and the grey kitten and Bob (when she thought of him) made up the little girl's world.

It was a very beautiful world, gay flowers in the garden and butterflies that could not be caught; the sun shining strong and white over the white cotton-fields; and the laughing black people—and the river that growled sometimes.

And set about the plantation, like the gilt frame of the portrait, were dark cypress-trees draped with swaying grey moss which somehow seemed to make the sunshine brighter by day and which certainly made the dark night blacker. Especially when the hoot owls started calling:

"I co-ooks for my-se'f; who co-ooks for you-all?" Mammy Linda told the little girl that this was what the old owls were saying. The child had never seen an owl, but she knew they stayed in cypress-trees: just as she knew cooks stayed in the kitchen and were always black. Her fantastic imagination pictured an owl as a feathered nigger that flew from tree to tree, hooting:

"I co-ooks for my-se'f; who co-ooks for you-all?"

PART I

NEW YORK

O Lady, we receive but what we give, And in our life alone does nature live.

COLERIDGE

CHAPTER I

New York, November, 1917

MY LOVE:

I DO not even know your name. I have seen you but four times in all my life.

The first time was eleven years ago. I had walked in on my rich cousin Jinny Foster at Southampton the night before. She had a houseful of smart guests. I arrived in the midst of them just before dinner.

Tom Foster saw me first and told everybody I was Diana Cameron, a little cousin of his wife's from the South that they hadn't seen since I was knee-high to a grasshopper. Jinny came down the stairs just then. There wasn't anything she could do but make the best of my inopportune arrival. She was annoyed and ashamed of me; she was for sending me to bed at once. Tom wouldn't hear of my not coming in to dinner with the others.

Jinny seemed to feel happier about me before the evening was over. The elderly man who took her in to dinner kept looking at me. He said something that made her look hopefully in my direction and smile. Then the great artist Gauze, the star guest of the evening, told Tom he'd love to paint that little honey-colored thing in the pongee frock as she looked when she stood in the door arriving.

After that Jinny got awfully cordial, and laughed about my ridiculous clothes and made all the others laugh when she told them how I had been brought up.

There was nothing to do but take me along on the picnic they had planned for the next day. We went in sail-boats to an island. I was still tired from my long journey, and not very happy, feeling I had made a mistake in counting on my cousin's hospitality. Nobody noticed me to-day.

The great artist did not recognize me in Jinny's brilliant red coat and hat. (She was annoyed because I had no wrap or sport hat.) He asked Tom where the little honey-colored girl was this morning. Tom pushed me forward.

"You're all wrong in that color," the painter burst out irritably. "Hideous!" Every time he looked at me he shuddered. I knew as well as he did that the color, which accentuated Jinny's flashy good looks, washed me out entirely. The coat smelled of jacqueminot rose scent, which also depressed me.

After the haughty white butler and his assistants had served the picnic meal people began to pair off. I found myself alone. I strolled along the cliffs and climbed far up on the rocks and sat behind a boulder and was sorry that I had come.

Sorry that I had come to Jinny; not sorry that I came to New York. I only wished I had stayed in New York longer than the two days I stopped there on my way to Southampton. I was sorry I had not gone on with Suzanne Souchon to Paris. I refused to let my thought turn backward to Bob and the South. I was running away from all that forever.

I had thrown Jinny's coat off and forgotten about Jinny and her friends. I was recalling what Palozzi had said about my voice; how happy Suzanne was that the great teacher agreed with her about it.

The salt air stimulated me; made me glad I had hard work ahead waiting for me. The sun shone warm on these sheltered rocks. The buoyant, sparkling air seemed full of energy. Suzanne had said I could accomplish anything if I would work.

The surf dashed against the rocks far below. I could no longer see the blue cliffs across the bay. A mist blotted out the mainland. The clear blue sky had faded to sodden grey. The wind was rising. The mist thickened. I could scarcely see the waves that now dashed angrily against the rocks below. The air had grown cold. I gathered Jinny's coat about me and retraced my way along the cliffs. The beach was almost obliterated by the fog, but I sped toward it to join the others.

The boats were not where I remembered. I quickened my pace, calling. No answer. I found the landing. Nobody was in sight. After so long a time, when I was quite exhausted trying to overtake them, for I supposed Jinny and her friends had gone farther down the beach, I realized my situation. They had gone and left me. I had been forgotten.

Waves dashed high. The fog rolled in thicker. The wind blew harder. I was in a panic of fear and cold. The woolly coat and hat were damp from the fog. Even my hair was as wet as if I had been in the rain.

It did not occur to me that they would not come back for me. I stayed near the landing, every now and then hallooing so they would know where to find me. The fog was now so thick they could locate me only by sound. The wind was terrific on the beach, but I would not leave it for fear I might miss the returning boat. I started to run back and forth, exercising my arms to try to warm up.

It seemed hours that I battled with the wind, running up and down the beach. The tide was coming in; the waves rolled nearer my feet.

At last I heard a motor-boat. I called and ran as near the water as I dared. I called again. It sounded down the beach. I ran in that direction still hallooing. Every now and then I would lose the sound of the chugging engine. The boat seemed going away. I put up my hands and hallooed. A voice out of the fog answered. The engine chugged again when the wind fell, and I kept hallooing.

At last through the fog I could see the outline of a motor-boat near the shore. After an interminable time it made a landing behind a point some distance from where we landed this morning.

"Here I am!" I called. A man was knee-deep in the water securing the boat. He did not seem to hear me. I ran as near as I could, for the waves still rolled high on the beach, and called again: "Here I am!"

"Hallo!" he answered, wading ashore, his arms full of rugs and indeterminate things. A lantern waved in his hand. I ran to meet him.

"Oh, you've come for me!" I heard my joyful greeting while he was as yet only a shadow in the grey fog. He lifted the lantern to find me.

"Where are you?" he asked. Then, when the light caught me: "And **what?**" in amazement.

I saw he was not one of the picnic party. Roughly dressed as he was, I knew he was not one of Jinny's white servants. Something in his voice made me think of Bob even before I saw his face.

"They forgot me," I said. "I thought you were one of the picnic party that had come back to get me."

"They will come back for you, I'm sure," he comforted heartily. "This is a pretty stiff squall. Nothing to do but wait for it to blow over. No boat can stand those seas." He was leading the way from the beach. "Could you help me with the lantern?"

I took the lantern. "Those rocks just ahead," he directed. "Let's investigate them."

The rocks jutted out into a shelf. Underneath was a cave of sorts. The rocks made at least a sheltering roof.

"We'll be protected here," the man said, putting down his load of things from the boat, "when the rain starts."

He unstrapped a pack wrapped in tarpaulin, and fastened the waterproof up as a curtain on the side from which the wind blew strongest. I held it while he secured it to the rocks,

"Now we can have a fire," he said.

The lantern cast a flickering light by which we could scarcely distinguish each other. We went out for driftwood, I carrying the lantern. The man found a log and rolled it up the beach and to the edge of the cave. Against this he laid a fire.

I was shivering, cold to the bone. He was trying to light a match. I made a wind-shield of my hands to keep it from going out. My teeth were chattering.

"Haven't got a chill, have you?" He took my cold hands in his lean, warm ones. We looked at each other across the kindling blaze.

"Oh, no!" I protested.

"Where's your coat, child?" I had thrown the coat off. I preferred the cold to Jinny's jacqueminot rose scent that seemed heavier than ever in the damp air. He reached for it to put around me.

"It isn't my coat," I said. "It is scented with a perfume that makes my head ache."

"It is rather an exotic fragrance," the stranger agreed. Then he looked across the fire at me. "And you are not in the least exotic," he smiled. "Fact is I thought you were a spirit down there on the beach—the spirit of the wind." He had laid down Jinny's coat, and handed me a rug. "How's this? ... Hungry?" I nodded.

He opened a kit from which he took a saucepan. Into this he poured water from a thermos bottle and placed it over the blaze, which fought against heavy odds in the wind. At last the water boiled. He poured it over malted milk tablets, and handed me a cup.

"I never know my luck," the stranger explained, "so I have to go prepared. A squall like this often makes me put into strange ports," he smiled, "like this one. But until now I've never had a charming companion to share my malted milk and chocolate and crackers."

Both of us were ravenously hungry. Together we finished up the last crumb of everything in the kit. He asked if I minded his pipe. The tobacco smoke threw a blue-grey veil that seemed to draw us closer together. I had a sudden ridiculous feeling that this unwalled, wind-swept cave was home; that this stranger I had never seen before was less strange than any one I had ever known in all my life; that the winds howling about us were the winds of chance that had blown us to each other.

I tried to think of Suzanne Souchon and Palozzi and the work I was going to do. I was fighting against the peace and happiness that seemed closing in on me. Less than a fortnight ago I had dedicated myself to Art; vowed never again to put myself in a place where a man could hurt me. Already I felt panic-stricken that even the scars I meant to cherish always were gone.

The stranger was spreading out a lot of blue-print drawings from a portfolio that was damp.

"I am charting the tides, measuring the currents in these waters," he said, "for the Government's new hydrographic survey."

He was telling me about the tides and tracing them on his maps. For the first time I felt I had taken a perilous step in leaving the back-waters of Palmetto Grove and Bob. He saw I was troubled.

"Don't be worried." He put away the blue-prints. "They'll come for you as soon as a boat can get out."

"You think so?"

"If you live around here," he began.

"I live in Mississippi." He looked at me and I could not keep my eyes from his.

"The night is dark," he observed quietly, "and you are far from home."

"Yes," I agreed, and threw a handful of wet trash on the fire so he could not see my face.

The wind billowed against the tarpaulin as if it were a sail. It had started to rain. Nearly all the wood was burned. We sat in silence.

"I have a little sister," the man said at last. He rose and went out in the rain and fetched more wood. His corduroy clothes were wet. And yet he insisted on bringing still more wood.

An old book in a parchment binding had fallen out of the portfolio. The man said he always carried it with him.

"Confucius was a great philosopher," he smiled, and then he read aloud:

Chung Kung asked: "What is love?"

The Master replied: "Without the door to behave as though a great guest were come."

I wondered what the curious words meant. He found another passage and read:

The Master said: "What a man was Hui! A dish of rice, a gourd of water in a low alleyway; no man can bear such misery. Yet Hui never fell from mirth. What a man he was!"

He put the book back in the portfolio and shut it.

"Shall I sing for you?" I asked him. I was sheltered from the wind and rain that beat in on him.

I sang and he sat, tall and dark; strong and tender-eyed; mysterious as Lohengrin, familiar and dear as Bob—across the fire, smoking his pipe.

When I awoke I was alone. The sun was shining. I ran down on the beach. Across the waters skimmed a sail-boat. The elderly man who took Jinny in to dinner last night stood up and hallooed to me and waved.

The boat was landing. I wrote on the sand near the cave:

"Thank you. Good-bye." I fastened my handkerchief on a stick and left the tiny flag flying.

My common sense counselled me not to linger, The rescuing party did not discover the motor-boat.

I could not bring myself to speak of you to Jinny or to the people I met at her house.

CHAPTER II

I SPENT the summer with Jinny, and she was glad to have me after Crœsus showed such interest in me. Crœsus was the middle-aged man who noticed me at dinner the first night. He was a multi-millionaire who had made his money in pig-iron.

He had a yacht and was a fine catch. Jinny devilled the life out of me to marry him long before he ever spoke to me of his hopes. Socially he was a great card and it was a feather in Jinny's cap when he kept on asking to come for the week-ends and holidays, when everybody else was begging him to come to them.

Gauze, the great artist, had made my stock go up still higher with Jinny. He was trying to paint me. Jinny asked him to stop at the house and he accepted her invitation. Everybody openly envied her entertaining such a lion.

Gauze had a terrible temper. He would fly into great rages at me because he said I never looked the same long enough for him to finish a sketch. Jinny and her friends thought I was getting better-looking, improving every day, but Gauze did not.

"Get back into your feeling that night when you arrived," he would command me. He seemed to think I ought to be able to recapture the expression when I slipped into the pongee frock in which he had first seen me. Finally he threw down his brushes in disgust. "Each day you grow farther away from my ideal," he said. "Now I would never know you to be the same person as the little honey-colored thing I am trying to paint."

He packed up and left in high dudgeon on the noon train.

I would not have recognized myself as the same girl after two months in Jinny's household. She would not let me wear any of the things I had brought from the South. Lovely new clothes were specially designed for me by Rollins. Jinny gave them to me.

My hair no longer hung in long braids below my waist. Celeste, Jinny's French maid, had taught me how to arrange it beautifully on my head. Jinny had taken me to the specialists who took care of her hair. They raved over the color of my hair and its luxuriance. It only needed to be properly looked after, they said. They shampooed it with delicious-smelling herbs and camomile and polished it until it shone like satin.

I was accepting everything from Jinny and with each gift I was losing a little more of my independence. Jinny was glad to do all this. She never grew tired of telling me. She expected me to return it, I knew, by doing the things I could do for her.

Crœsus asked us all to go for a six weeks' cruise on his yacht. I did not want to go. I offered to stay at Southampton with the servants and help look after Aline, Jinny's two-year-old baby, who was always ailing, while Jinny went on the cruise. She got furious at that. Aline had a trained nurse, she reminded me. She said that I knew Crœsus was only getting up the party for me. That everybody else knew it. We had a scene, but it ended in my going.

Crœsus somehow always reminded me of the Wolf in Little Red Riding Hood. I don't know why. It wasn't that I did not like him. I simply had nothing in common with him or with Jinny or with Jinny's friends. But I was caught up in the whirlpool of things that engulfed them, and I had no time to call my own.

Jinny had planned to stay on for the winter in New York, so Aline could be near the specialist who was treating her poor little spine. I was to stay with her. Tom Foster's political duties called him back to Washington. We were late in coming into town from Southampton and this was my last free day before I settled down to hard work in my singing lessons with Palozzi.

Crœsus was giving me a luncheon at the Plaza and taking us all to the opera later for the first Saturday matinee of the season. I did not want to go, but Jinny did. She overrode my objections as selfish after all she had been doing for me. Finally I said all right I would go, and I honestly meant to go.

Jinny went ahead and the car was sent back for me. Just as we turned into Central Park at Seventy-Second Street, the car collided with a truck, and the chauffeur told me I had better take a taxi, as our automobile was badly damaged. I left him with no other thought than to get the first taxi or bus that passed.

I do not pretend to know why my feet took me flying across the park, instead of down Fifth Avenue to the Plaza; nor why I hurried to a Western Union office to send two telegrams. One was to Crœsus, the other to Jinny. The messages were to say that I could not possibly get there. No excuse.

I shivered at the thought of the scene I should have to go through with Jinny later, but something stronger even than my dread of a quarrel with her claimed this afternoon. I had one dollar left in my purse, and I was ravenously hungry. I spent forty cents of it for lunch at Child's and then gaily and plan-less boarded a down-town car.

The posters of a play caught my eye. The theatre was somewhere below Herald Square and the play was called "A Gentleman from Mississippi." I bought a fifty-cent seat, the first row in the top gallery, and climbed up, up to it.

My interest was on the stage, but suddenly after the curtain rose, even while I was most absorbed in the scene, an overwhelming something surged through me. It was as if some heavenly current, a delicious tide of warmth and welcome flowed through my heart. My eyes followed the current. In an aisle seat in the first row of the first balcony you were just sitting down.

A curtain of grey mist blotted out the stage. I heard the wind rushing in from the sea; the waves breaking against the shore. A driftwood fire blew this way and that. Across it you sat, smoking a pipe, and the blue-grey smoke was curved like a scarf held above our heads.

"The night is dark," I heard you saying quietly, "and you are far from home."

Now I was realizing for the first time what it was to be far from home. I was not homesick for the Mississippi cotton plantation where I was born, but for that wind-swept cave that had sheltered us together through the stormy night.

A dark young foreigner sat next to me. We two were the only ones in that row. When the curtain fell on the first act I leaned back and closed my eyes.

"But don't cry"—he turned his serious eyes on me. "I think it vill end 'appily."

That was the first I knew that tears were rolling down my cheeks. Mysterious tears, where did they come from? Not from any reservoir in my being that had ever functioned before. What did they mean? I had a vague sensation that they were melted rainbows, the fulfilment of some apocryphal prophecy long expected by my heart.

You could not have seen me. Even in the shadows when the curtain went up again I could barely distinguish you. But somehow I did not need my eyes to see. What made you look up, your eyes hunting the darker shadow in which I was concealed, and turn back disappointed to the stage? You were bewildered. I could sense that. Then you took out your watch, a great old-fashioned gold one, put on your grey overcoat and rose to go out. It was the end of the second act.

Again I leaned far back in the shadows. The solemn little foreigner remonstrated: "But it is not a sad play. There is no reason to cry."

Real tears are the only expression of real joy. April rains were devised to take the strain off the year when winter goes and spring is arriving. I felt like a January garden bare to look at, but full of quickening flowers.

CHAPTER III

IT was three years before I saw you again. I was still in New York, but now working for my living, singing, and not to the audiences I had planned to sing to either!

Tom Foster and Jinny were now living in Washington. Even at that distance Jinny kept tabs on me, and I knew she thoroughly enjoyed hearing or seeing that I was having a pretty hard struggle. But I was making a living, such as it was, and supporting myself.

I rented a room from Miss Fortescue, a worldly old spinster, on East Sixtieth Street, and we had most of our meals together at her smart club. She was making a fight to keep up appearances, too, and I saw the same people in her house that I had met in Jinny's. They were all friendly enough and everybody knew my story— Jinny told it—and they all helped me in their futile, silly way, to sing here and there and everywhere a programme needed to be padded out, or a dull dinner party had to be offset by a musical programme.

My cousin, John Bardston, who breeds thoroughbreds on a farm in the bluegrass region of Kentucky, called me on the 'phone early one morning. Couldn't I come have breakfast with him and do some shopping for Daisy, his wife, while he went down to Wall Street? Daisy wanted the things sent to-day.

John ordered the breakfast, explaining that he kept on stopping at the Holland House because he liked the baked apples they had there for breakfast. Something made me turn toward the dining-room door. There you stood, the morning paper in your hands.

Our eyes met, in involuntary recognition. The next instant I saw you could not place me. The confusion was only for a fraction of a second. I felt the color surge up into my face. After all, I had been too surprised to bow to you.

"Some one you know?" John observed my confusion.

"No," I said, "oh, no."

"I would have sworn," he said, as he poured cream over his prized baked apple, "that each of you recognized the other."

The head waiter personally conducted you to a table near the front windows. He deferred to you as if you were the President of the United States.

John hunted for and finally found Daisy's letter and turned it over to me. She wanted a silver brocade evening gown and some sort of a gold arrow, she said, for her hair, and a turquoise blue taffeta petticoat, blue with a sheen on it. I read and re-read the letter. The words would not register in my mind.

Again I was swept around and around in a current of exquisite warmth and well-being. My back was toward you.

"That chap who thought he knew you" John observed as he helped me to Irish bacon and watercress, "is still puzzling over how he made his mistake."

"Is he?" I asked weakly. "How do you know?"

"He's racking his brain"—John made his report with the detachment of a well-trained spy—"trying to figure out how two red-headed—"

"Chestnut sorrel," I corrected, "for me, please."

"In the shade, maybe," John conceded. "But with the sun shining on it as it is now—I call it—"

"Please don't!" I bagged.

"I won't," he agreed. "But I say, Di, you have grown into a ripping beauty. Never would have known you, 'pon my word. What a sheen!" He surveyed my hair. "Kentucky Belle hasn't such a coat. I've fed her a hogshead of molasses and a ton of carrots to get it."

"I've really changed, John?"

"Never would have known you," he repeated. "You've got a new gait. Why, you look as if your father might have been a race-horse and your mother a pheasant."

I had on a little hat of marvellous pheasant feathers.

"That chap behind his paper over there"—John suddenly switched back to you—"is trying to figure out how two red-headed people happened to marry." John studied my face. "That's my theory," he drawled on, "of how the world conflagration is going to start on the last great day."

"He thinks we are brother and sister" (that's what I wanted you to think). "You're my first cousin, and we've always been told we look alike." John smiled dubiously. "I probably remind him of some one he has seen."

"And he recalled some one—"

"Yes," I welcomed his explanation, "he is rather like a man I met once."

John was laying out yellow-backed bills on the table for Daisy's finery. He laid out an extra hundred and pushed it toward me.

"That's to get a pair of satin slippers for those silly, expensive, tissue-paper feet of yours. Accept them from 'Kentucky Belle.'" (That was a yearling colt he had just sold for a hundred thousand.) "Have Daisy's things sent special delivery direct. I've got to catch the noon train."

Then to the waiter. "Call the lady a taxi."

"No, a hansom," I corrected.

John put me in the hansom cab. It stopped just in front of the window where you sat. "Aren't you kissing me good-bye?" He pulled me back to kiss him.

Over his shoulder I lifted my eyes and again met your bewildered brown eyes.

John started down Fifth Avenue. (It was the last time I ever saw him. He was killed the next Kentucky Derby day, riding "My Luck," the pride of his heart.) I drove away, the freshet of three years ago again inundating my heart. You were still in the world. That was as far as my dream went. You were real and still alive.

You knew you had seen me, somewhere, but for the life of you, you couldn't remember where!

I knew you would never associate me, as I look now, with the wind-blown girl who held the lantern for you, picking up driftwood in the fog, so many years ago.

CHAPTER IV

AND yesterday, two years later, our paths converged again.

I had sung at a charity bazaar at the Waldorf, and slipped away early, stopping at a Japanese florist's shop at Thirtieth Street. I buy all sorts of things there that do not interest me in the least, to hover over a miniature Japanese garden that I do want most desperately.

It is an embryo estate after my own heart. A house and a garden; with a temple and a lantern and an ancient, ancient cedar-tree, warped and twisted and human as a wise old Buddhist priest. I hung over it, following, for the hundredth time, the tiny worn path I know so well, across the red lacquer bridge, over it on up the hill, going slowly to get the line of the tree, and the cottage with its straw roof and the tea-house, farther up; all the potential enchantment encompassed in such an estate. Oh, for the price that would make it mine!

Little slant-eyed Yuki waited expectantly near. I had to buy something as a sop to him.

"These have but just opened." Yuki held a bowl of Chinese lilies before me. "They will bring luck."

The bowl, flowers, rocks, and all, including the water, he explained, was "saled" at one dollar and seventy-five cents—just one hundred and seventy-odd dollars less than the earth, heaven, and water arrangement that I want so much. Certainly, he babbled on, since I lived so near, it could be sent, without in any way disturbing the arrangement.

Yuki's English is limited. Instead of my name, he took, as usual, the number of my room and the name of the quiet hotel where I live.

Outside, on Fifth Avenue, a soldier in uniform was standing. Ostensibly he was observing the antics of a pair of waltzing white mice in the window. I turned suddenly—what was the use brooding over the garden any longer—and my eyes met the quiet brown eyes of the soldier. It was you.

And since we are prisoners in a world where convention keeps guard, our greeting was no greeting, but a look of recognition. I hurried out of the shop, with only one feeling, to run away, to hide my joy that you were still in the world. The sweet world where you and I could meet, did meet, every dozen years or so, if all the meeting meant was the sight of you; the blessed assurance that you were still in it, and as alone as I have always been.

Oh, my Love! My Love!

And when the bowl of Chinese lilies came, the garden I desired so much came with it. It was sent up to my room while I was at dinner. I called up the shop. It was closed. The next day was Thanksgiving. All day I had the garden, but I dare not take liberties in a place that did not belong to me. It must go back the first thing the next day. I went in person to tell Yuki to send for it.

But Yuki protested that it had been paid for and directions left for it to be sent to me. Impossible, I replied. He had confused an order. I had bought only the sacred lilies.

Yuki was insistent. It was a gift. There was no mistake. He could not remember who had bought it, so many customers were being served at that late hour. But it was by way of being a Thanksgiving present, he recalled that much. He could not take back a gift that had been sent as the honorable garden had been sent.

"How was it sent?" I pursued.

"It was the sacred lilies that brought you the gift of the garden!" he replied cryptically. "Did I not say such would 'appen? And very much you admire that garden, always. Is it not true?"

Why deny what he knew so well?

"I get these directions to send the garden" he volunteered the information in a tone of finality. "To the young lady who stood looking at it so long, and who then bought the lilies. It was not five minutes after you depart."

But who it was who buy the garden and pay for him, his dishonorable memory, he swore, had lost every trace of recollection of the gentle-mans. "Gentleman," I repeated.

"I remember nothing clearly. This august T-Thanksgeeving h-holiday has erased all from my non-observant mind."

You must have sent me the Japanese garden! With its cottage just big enough for two lovers, its fairytale stream with goldfish swimming under the red bridge;

with its lanterned nooks and its temple, set behind the ancient-of-days cedar-tree. And you were in uniform!

Oh, my Love! Maybe you are already on the sea bound for France. If I only knew your name!

CHAPTER V

ALL day a song sings in my consciousness and I cannot catch the words. I know the melody, and yet I grope for it in vain when I try to set it to music.

The mysterious, haunting, elusive air is hidden in a mist. I feel near it, but it eludes me. One minute I think I know all the words; I am sure I can find the chords on my piano. Then it is gone again like the butterflies I chased in my childhood.

I almost whisper the words; the soft pedal muffles the music. I can't get it, and I cannot let it alone. I seem to be searching in a fog. The song is something about a lantern, I know that much.

The widow of a famous general has a room near mine. She is a lovely little wraith of a creature. She smiles at me when we go up and down in the elevator. She comes as near being an acquaintance as I have in the hotel. She seems to know nobody in the house either.

To-night she tapped timidly on my door. "Please forgive me for intruding," she begged.

"My apology must be I could not stay away from your music. I can only catch a strain of it now and then in my room." She had clasped her tiny hands together like a child asking a favor. "Would you let me listen to all of that song?"

This is the first thing I have ever tried to compose. I was embarrassed, overcome with shyness. It was very difficult to tell my secret to a stranger.

She was as agitated as I. Her eyes shone as I told how I had tried to catch the melody, to find the words, to capture the haunting thing that sings just ahead, just above me, out of my reach. What she had heard was only the ghostly refrain of the lovely lyric that eluded me.

"What does it mean to you?" she whispered.

I shook my head. "I don't know," I told her; "if I could only see it—feel it distinctly. Somehow it seems set in a fog."

"To me it brings back the Taj Mahal, India's 'white wonder,' " she said slowly. There was an expression almost rapt on her face. "Love's supreme monument to human affection. Above the crypt containing the heart-dust of Shah Jehan and the fair queen of his youth, Mumtaz Mahal—"

Her words were a recitative that fascinated me. "—Hangs a light, that illumines the shadows of night in that tomb of love—a lantern of love." "Tell me," I pleaded, "what is a lantern of love?"

"In the beginning of life it is a hope," she said.

"In the end a memory. It is the beacon for the love that is to come; the blessing from the love that has gone."

The General's widow feels now, she said, with him gone, as if all the world were a desert and life a sandstorm; that people are but whirling atoms swept by the winds of chance. But that his memory is her lantern of love, always turned to reflect the past.

She stood beside the piano. My fingers wandered over the keys. Suddenly I caught the air again, and the words. I struck the chords confidently, and the lovely, sobbing, soaring melody sang itself.

Over and over I sang it for her. At last she stooped and, as light as a butterfly's touch, kissed me on the cheek. "Good-night!"

I played softly on—hoping to find the end of the song. The verses I had sung, I knew, were but as steps up a stair. And the summit, the end of the song, was not yet.

A lantern of love! Could its light reach you in this world's sandstorm of molecule people and infinitesimal things?

I wonder!

CHAPTER VI

BELOVED.

LAST night in my dream I crossed the tiny red lacquer bridge in the Japanese garden you sent me and there you were waiting, and we went on up the hill together and sat down under the ancient cedar-tree (four hundred years old and ten inches tall), and you told me what I am telling you now: I love you!

Last night it seemed that these three words had never been used before. "I love you" sounded dewy, untouched; an emotion that no mortals save ourselves had ever felt or put into words.

When I write, "I love you," in the cold light of day, it sounds as old and looks as age-worn as mummy dust. But whispered on the other side of the red lacquer drawbridge of dreams!

How different!

I love you!

CHAPTER VII

YOU did not send me the Japanese garden, after all. I might have known from whom it came.

I would like to tell you about Crœsus.

And to tell you about Timothy. And to tell you about myself.

There is little to tell you about myself. I came to New York when I was seventeen, expecting in due course of time to sing in the Metropolitan Opera. Quaint, isn't it? The idea was put into my head by the French opera singer in New Orleans who was my teacher for two years. I think she really believed I was destined for a great career. Suzanne Souchon was her name. She is now a world-famous opera singer in Paris.

I came to New York with her. She introduced me to Palozzi. He agreed with her about my voice, that it was a contralto of pure gold, and I was to have lessons from him. I think Suzanne must have given Palozzi the impression that I came from people of great wealth. She knew that Bob, my uncle and guardian, was a cotton planter. I spent the summer with the Fosters, and began my singing lessons in the autumn.

It was at the Fosters' I met Crœsus. I never liked him, but Jinny dinned it into my ears, morning, noon, and night, that Crœsus was rich, rich, rich, and that I was poor, poor, poor!

It was about Crœsus that Jinny and I at last had the quarrel that ended in my refusing to accept anything from her. But why retrace in detail those early years?

Cut off from Jinny's hospitality and easy-going generosity, I soon realized that independence was costing me more than I could afford. One needed to have more gold than a golden throat to afford lessons from Palozzi. What with his lessons, and the accompanist he recommended, and the specialist he insisted on my having to take care of my throat, I needed a gold mine to draw on.

That was the first year the boll weevil struck Palmetto Grove. Bob wrote to ask me to wait a little longer for my usual allowance.

Palozzi shrugged his shoulders, and the accompanist mentioned her rent due and living expenses, and the specialist sent his bills and mailed others in case the first had been lost, and still the allowance did not come.

Bob had to write me finally that all the Southern banks were in a bad way and that they would loan no money on land or the cotton crops. And I owed Palozzi, and I owed my accompanist and the specialist, and for my room rent, and for my meals at the club.

I tried to explain the situation to each one. It was new to me and it seemed so simple. I did not know then that the old, old story in New York is debt, and the promise everlasting is, "I'll pay you as soon as I can."

When I announced I had to go to work all the friends I had inherited from Jinny and their friends interested themselves to help me. And all the rich women at the club got busy. No Southern girl, properly introduced, ever utterly failed in New York. It is still trying to make amends to us for the Civil War.

And everybody conspired to give me even a better time because I was young and helpless and Southern and had to work. But looking back I see, kind-hearted as they were, I have had to sing for every supper that has ever come my way.

I sing at club meetings and Dixie societies, at Kentucky breakfasts and Missouri luncheons, and in private houses where there is a programme to be padded out. I sing for my rich friends' charities, and I sing for their private entertainments, and for this I am paid, and I am always in debt and always tired and always lonely.

Alice Grant is vulgar but kind-hearted. She is a Western woman who has had two divorces already and who always has an affair on hand. She is Jinny's best friend. Alice has a certain honesty, a good humor, and she is not altogether selfish.

"What do you get out of the life you lead, child?" Alice asks me every time she borrows money from me to tide her over until the first of the month. "You can't keep on batting around like this in New York. What's the idea, anyway? You trying to understudy Mariana or whatever her name was in the moated grange?

"You were born to wear sables and pearls with your meerschaum coloring. Feet, sensitive and high-strung as yours, have to be kept satin-shod."

Alice lit a cigarette and studied me. "Say, come off your perch and be sensible, Mariana. Take Crœsus. There's always Reno if you can't stick him—Reno and alimony."

She waited for my reply.

"You don't even get what I'm saying, eh? My mind can't even reach yours by telephone!" She laughed, and shrugged her shoulders. "Oh, well, Mariana, I suppose there are no telephones to moated granges such as you live in!"

Mammy Linda, out of my childhood, flashed across my memory. She would class Alice as a jimson-weed, just as she used to call Jinny a tie-vine.

"Of course I know," Alice continued, "that you and I weren't made of the same dust—but what I want to know, Mariana, is what do you get out of this hall-bedroom life you live?"

What do I get out of it? This, that I never tell them. The right to dream of you. This is my confession, only for you, my Love.

There are times when I have felt that I could not go on. Times when my bankbook will not balance; and when my strength is spent past the point I am able to give in trying to balance my social account; to cancel the obligations that must always go with receiving even what is meant as simple hospitality.

Then Crœsus comes along. He knows the minute my spirit starts to lag.

"Your voice will not last always," he warns. "I shall be content to have you marry me for my money,"

Oh, Crœsus, Crœsus! You pauper! You haven't anything but money!

Then there is Timothy, who came from California to build bridges all over the world. Timothy thinks he can never love any one but me. I am older than Timothy, and a hundred years wiser when it comes to understanding why I am not the one for him.

But there are times, my Love, when Timothy's giant strength and youth tempt me more than Crœsus' gold does even when I am deepest in debt; times when I am dead tired in body and in soul, and when all the tides that I like to believe bear you to me, and me to you, seem reversed and to be carrying us away from each other, forever and forever. Then Timothy looms up as all I have in this poverty-stricken world and it takes all my strength not to let him come; when it takes all my courage not to cry out to him—

But it is always the thought of you that steadies me.

The Japanese garden did not come from you. Alice Grant called up to-day to thank me for giving my services to the Charity Bazaar. She told me Crœsus came in late and looked everywhere for me.

"When I told him you had sung for us for nothing," she said, "he asked permission to send you some flowers in the name of our guild as an additional contribution to the cause."

Alice felt my disappointment at the other end. "Don't tell him I told you," she begged, "but in case unexplained flowers arrive—"

Yes, I might have known! But among the flowers on sale at the Charity Bazaar, there was no Japanese garden!

Crœsus has never sent me flowers except orchids, that leave me as cold as diamonds do.

Crœsus up to this time hasn't even had the perception to divine I was born in October and adore chrysanthemums. Of course you did not send me the garden.

CHAPTER VIII

Has this been thus before? And shall not thus Time's eddying flight Still with our lives our loves restore in death's despite?
DANTE GABRIEL ROSSETTI

I WAS born on Palmetto Grove, a Mississippi cotton plantation. My earliest recollections are of vast cotton-fields stretching from the tawny river boundary on one side to a background of shadowy cypress in the far distance.

Deer-Lick Lake marked the boundary of the Palmetto Grove fields to the north. On the south a big unnamed bayou separated it from Roseneath, the Foster plantation.

Until I was twelve years old I had not set foot beyond Palmetto Grove, unless it was to pay an infrequent visit to Jinny Adair, an orphan cousin, ten years older than I, who lived at Roseneath with Cousin Clara, her aunt, who kept house for the Fosters to whom the plantation belonged.

Mammy Linda never liked Jinny. If she could she would have kept me entirely away from her.

"She's a tie-vine, dat li'l' Jinny gal," Mammy would say. (A tie-vine was a parasitic vine, hated by the field-hands.)

"She's my cousin," I would reply.

"On her ma's side, yes," Mammy would agree. "But a distant cousin, and her pa wuz an Adair, and all de Adairs is jimson-weeds."

Jimson-weeds were dank, coarse weeds (commoner even than just plain weeds, Mammy declared) that grew where old pig-pens had been.

Our own family Mammy Linda always proudly referred to as "Grand Jook Jesmuns."

From time to time various indigent intellectual gentlemen stopped by Palmetto Grove and lingered indefinitely, ostensibly to teach me; in reality because the kind-hearted hosts saw the situation and delicately did what they could to remedy it.

There was room for anybody who stopped by Palmetto Grove. The house itself was big enough for everybody in the world, I used to think.

It was a long, low structure with far-stretching wings and an ell. It has been in the Cameron family since the plantation was cleared and reclaimed from the virgin forest by my great-grandfather.

He journeyed from Virginia to this trackless wilderness with his Italian bride who could speak no English. He was the family's great exquisite, destined for a diplomatic career and sent on the grand tour after finishing his studies at Oxford and in Paris. He had planned to bid for a post in the Orient, and was on his way to the Far East when he met his fate in Florence, losing his heart to a young Italian prima donna. She "reciprocated the attachment" is the way a later and less emotional historian wrote it down in the family archives.

They were married and proceeded to China on the honeymoon. The Orient did not appeal to the young bride, except as a perfect place to shop, and as she had given up her career for him, she argued and convinced her husband that it was up to him to show an equal renunciation for her. The honeymoon trip to the Orient resulted only in a fine collection of Chinese things which they brought back with them to Virginia where they expected to live on his ancestral estate with the rest of the large family. The young bride was frank enough to say she wanted to leave Italy to get away from her family.

Unfortunate to relate the relatives of her husband did not appeal to the young Florentine any more than her own family in Italy had done. The snobbish Virginians in turn considered an opera-singer no particular distinction or addition to the family. In fact they regarded her as somewhat of a millstone about his neck, in that the training bestowed on the quasi-diplomat left him high and dry since she would have none of it, and it was the only profession he knew.

There seemed to be no place for the strangely mated, infatuated young lovers in Virginia, so they set out in coach and four, with wagons and slaves and much Chinese furniture, to the wilds of Mississippi.

The fair Italian was a strange and barbaric creature to the end of her days which were not prolonged after the birth of her first child, a son.

The young husband followed her six months later, an authentic record of a broken heart truly (this was the medical verdict pronounced when he died).

An old-maid sister journeyed down from Virginia, took charge of the plantation, banished the Chinese furniture and all the "trash" (as she considered the various collections) from the Orient to the attic, substituting the best colonial, and reared the boy, sending him in due time to the University of Virginia, and seeing to it that he spent his summers in his father's native State.

When this youth reached the age of twenty-one, after he had looked over the long list of Virginia's eligible daughters and been duly presented to them by his relatives and theirs, he strolled off one day and married an adorable little Irish nobody-at-all. His maiden aunt promptly shook the dust of Palmetto Grove Plantation from her high arched feet forever, and went back, serenely contemptuous of her nephew and all that concerned him, to a nobler, fairer stream, the pedigreed James.

The next event of importance on Palmetto Grove was the birth of twin boys, my father and Bob. "The Kathleen girl," their mother, died before they were grown, and her husband, with prompt gallantry, joined her, the world having ceased to interest him with his love gone on before.

The next record was that of my father Roderick. He married Diana Latournelle of Louisiana. Bob, his twin brother, also adored her. They fought a duel about her, but she brought about a reconciliation, and as time went on, so the story goes, she who had refused to be the wife of Bob became his devoted sister.

The family in Virginia, now nearly extinct, sent high-flown letters welcoming a daughter of the Latournelles into the family. And no doubt she replied duly, for she was a beautifully bred and punctilious lady. She was my mother. Bob continued to live with them at Palmetto Grove.

Though the memory of my mother is not very vivid, I can recall the atmosphere of quiet happiness and order that prevailed in her time. And I remember how the house was overpoweringly sweet with Cape jasmines when she died. To this day I cannot bear the scent of a gardenia.

My father ran true to family form. Like his immediate forebears he proceeded to get his affairs in order and then he followed his love, leaving me an orphan with Bob as my sole guardian. Mammy Linda was custodian of my dress and deportment. Both tried to do their duty by me.

Bob's idea of bringing up a girl child, I fancy, was not to interfere with her. I was allowed to do as I pleased. I had no young associates. Even that early, music was a passion with me. I sang, and rode horse-back over the fields with Bob, and felt no need of other children to play with. At night Bob would read the Psalms (which I adored) and from old calf-bound volumes of Virgil and Homer and Marcus Aurelius while I strummed away at my five-finger exercises. I could hardly read three-syllabled words in English. I knew no Italian at all, yet—

I do not know how to write this strange thing I am about to tell you. It was something I could not speak of to any one when I was a child.

Amber and coral and jade—these colors would suddenly enfold me, and beyond and around them came a flood of crystal light. It was as if I, enwrapped in these colors, were in the centre of a bubble. This exquisite adventure had a way of disappearing suddenly as a soap-bubble melts.

I trembled with ecstasy when I felt it coming, and when it left me I was desolated. For the coming of these colors always meant the coming of a tide of marvellous music, beautiful, heavenly melodies in strange words, that I understood perfectly—so long as the bubble of light lasted. My throat was but the passageway of notes so crystal clear, so round and true and pure, that the very glory of such singing was too much for me.

I was singing old Italian operas from the yellow portfolios that had belonged to my great-grand-mother, the Florentine singer, whose grave is under the cedars beyond the garden. So long as the colors lasted, every note was familiar and I knew every word.—But when the bubble of light faded, try as I would, not one note could I play, nor one word of the strange language could I translate.

If Bob ever suspected anything out of the ordinary, he did not speak of it to me. Mammy Linda seemed to come pretty near understanding. She had all the negro's childlike acceptance of the supernatural. Perhaps she, no more than I, could put it into words. Mammy Linda knew that the portrait of my own mother did not interest me. She knew I adored the portrait of the Florentine opera-singer. I was supposed to wear a gold locket containing the photographs of my mother and my father. I did not like to wear it. One day Mammy Linda showed me a curious wonderful glob of clear green, strung on a Chinese chain. I gasped at the sight of it, I trembled with delight at the feel of it.

"It's jade," she said; "it belonged to yoh gre't-grandma, dee singer. Dey left dis out when dey tuck all t' other jewels ter de safe-deposit bank, when yoh ma died."

Bob said of course I might have it. I wore this talisman for years, until I finally lost it at the convent in New Orleans.

Mammy kept my ribbons in a sandalwood box, that I know must have belonged to the Florentine singer, and I found a fan in a crumbling box in the attic that had the same fragrance.

Sandalwood is the only scent I have ever been able to use.

Even when I was too young to understand why, the family portraits used to perplex me. I still wonder how it happened that the men straight down in the family all looked the same, tall, rugged, austere, direct harebell blue-eyed Scotchmen, always the same Puritan gentleman, who in turn chose a mate as unlike himself as possible and loved her with all the savage passion of a Puritan. The wives all Catholic, the husbands all Scotch Presbyterian, God-fearing, Bible-reading, priest-hating Calvinists, who grimly agreed to a Catholic ceremony as a courtesy due the lady in the case, equally grimly agreeing that the children, such offspring of this marriage, should be brought up in the Catholic faith, all the while knowing that no son or daughter of his would ever bow a knee to Rome, no matter what environment or training might be used to bias the child's belief.

I wondered even as child how each man absolutely reproduced himself in his son, and even that young I knew and secretly exulted because I knew that I, the first daughter under the Palmetto Grove roof-tree, looked like the ancestress who has always seemed nearest to me, the Florentine.

What was beauty in her was homeliness in me. She had wonderful dark red hair; my hair was an indeterminate carroty color. Her skin was white and velvety as a Cape jasmine petal; there were veins of coral underlying it. My skin, where the sun did not touch it, was the same, but my face was freckled as a turkey's egg. Her eyes were pools of blue-grey lights, fringed with long bronze lashes. My eyes were changeable as my hair. Some days they were blue, but most of the time they were grey, but my eyelashes were almost as long as my hair. The Florentine singer's throat was long and round, the color of cream roses. My throat was sunburned and slender and longer than hers. She was beautiful, and I was like her, but I was not beautiful.

But at times that became more infrequent as I grew older—when the miracle enfolded me—I knew I had my great-grandmother's heaven-given voice. My own voice I recognized as something entirely apart from the divine power that came to me with the amber and coral and jade in the crystal light.

At thirteen I was sent to the convent in New Orleans where my mother was educated. The vacations I spent on Palmetto Grove with Bob. Jinny Adair graduated from the convent before I went there. She made a great pet of me. She was spending most of her time at Roseneath, the Foster plantation. She and Tom Foster were married the next year after she left the convent. That was the year he ran for the legislature, starting his political career that afterwards took him to Washington.

I missed Jinny greatly when I went home during vacations after she married. She sent me letters about her gay social life and in each she said I must come stay with them as soon as my school days were over.

On my fifteenth birthday, Cousin 'Toinette (on my mother's side in New Orleans) came to take me with her to the French opera. It was there I heard Suzanne Souchon sing. A door of heaven opened to me that night. Her voice then was just coming into its perfection. The whole world is now at her feet.

And one day I met the singer. She was a friend of my mother's old friends, the Mandevilles, on Royal Street. They invited me for Sunday dinner. Bob was in town and Suzanne Souchon listened to me sing, and told me, what I knew, that my voice was her voice, and she offered to teach me. She said my voice was a gift from God, a jewel song in itself, priceless. She told Bob and I told him I had to leave the convent. He was glad enough to hear me say how I hated it there. I am sure it was his feeling about Rome made it thus easy for me to begin my operatic training so early and so unhampered. Both of us ignored Cousin 'Toinette. We knew what arguments she would use to oppose my leaving the convent. I was only fifteen.

CHAPTER IX

I STUDIED singing for two seasons in New Orleans with Suzanne Souchon as my teacher.

Seen in retrospect that period of my life now seems as unreal as an act of an almost forgotten play. The time somehow always seems to be spring-time, and the stage settings, wistaria.

To this day, wistaria, with its heady, heavy fragrance, brings back to me memories of Anthony Willing, and all the old happiness and misery that went to make up my first romance when I was sixteen.

I boarded the second year with Madame Monterey, down on Royal Street, in order to be nearer my teacher, who lived at a little French hotel not far from the opera house. The Monterey house was full of lovely old furniture; the courtyard brimming with blossom and scent was enchanting, the cooking delicious. I sat at Madame's table with her worthless Creole husband and her two silly old-maid sisters.

Oh, the gossip and the chatter of those creoles! From the youngest to the oldest all seemed to be obsessed on the subject of love and marriage. They read the paper only to see who was engaged or who was married or who had a baby.

I soon came to know the scandals of the street and the principals by sight. Fitz-Gerald, "the Irish Gentleman," as they used to call him, was drinking himself to death, and incidentally going to the devil because of a ballet-dancer.

"Fine gentlemans they are," Madame told me, "Fitz-Gerald and his frien,' Mees-tair Anthony Willing." Mr. Willing was ill, she explained. Drink would also finish him. She sighed and shook her head. "It ees a pity he falls not in love."

John Bardston was a senior at Tulane that year. His mother was my mother's half sister, but his people lived in Kentucky, and I had not seen him since a visit they made to Palmetto Grove when I was a tiny child. Madame Monterey and the boarders arranged a romance about us, inviting John regularly for the noon Sunday breakfast, after which we all used to go to the matinée at the French opera. John was even then desperately in love with Daisy Gardiner whom he afterwards married. He told me all about it the first Sunday. (They thought he was proposing to me.)

One day, as I passed down the long upper gallery going to my room, I saw a strange man sitting in the sunshine. He turned eagerly to me.

"Are you going to sing this afternoon?" he asked quite simply.

"Does it disturb you?" I asked.

"I can hear you there in my room," he said. "You have saved my life."

This was my first meeting with Anthony Willing. Somehow I felt that the Prodigal Son in the Bible must have looked like him; must have had the same quality of human appeal. There was no mire upon his sensitive face. I had never seen such loneliness as looked from his grey eyes.

In a few days he came downstairs to dinner. All traces of his illness had disappeared. He radiated strength and vitality.

"Ah, there I see he is!" Madame exclaimed. "It makes great happiness that Meestair Willing is once more recovered."

Naturally he came to our table to speak with Madame when he had finished his dinner. Madame welcomed him as joyously as if she had not been going up to see him every day, kind-hearted, motherly soul that she was.

"You have not yet met ze new y'ong leddy yet." Madame waved to me with her napkin. "I present you, Meestair Willing, to Mees Diana Cameron, of Palmetto Grove Plantation, who have arrive to stody music."

Anthony Willing drew up a chair between Madame and me. Madame was now dispensing the dessert, a sweet omelette, and in the excitement of serving it at the exact right degree of perfection and sending it post-haste to the various tables, she left us alone.

Anthony Willing suddenly reformed Fitz-Gerald used to wait to tease me about spoiling his boon companion "If he keeps up this gait," he said, "there's nothing can save him from being our next District Attorney, God help us!"

I knew it. And yet Anthony Willing and I seldom met. No one but Fitz-Gerald suspected our interest in each other. Fitz-Gerald had a rival now for the notorious little ballet-dancer's affections, and he was seldom at meals, and even more rarely sober.

Oh, those stupid boarders! They thought Anthony was staying at home to be with them. He would play chess assiduously with old Colonel Dubois in one end of the long drawing-room after dinner, while I devoted myself to Madame's stupid old-maid sisters, Mademoiselle 'Toinette and Mademoiselle Celeste, and their everlasting fancy work at the other. But somehow it always happened before the evening was over that he was beside me. We had nothing to say; each fled at the other's approach, and yet we lived only for moments like this when chance threw us together.

I detest cards. To keep out of a game one night, I pretended to read Mademoiselle 'Toinette's future. At the far end of the room, Anthony checkmated or was checkmated by the Colonel. I could feel him gravitating toward me. Long before the game was lost or won, he had persuaded the Colonel into joining us.

"The Colonel wants his fortune read," Anthony announced as they joined the group around me. I shuffled the cards and dealt out the Colonel's future and made up an elaborate romance for him. Madame, in the meantime, her game of cards finished, unearthed a planchette and the crowd drifted to her. The board was spelling out a weird mixture of French and English which they about it interpreted to each other.

Anthony sat down on the table, pushing the cards aside to make room for himself· "Read my fortune," he begged. I spread the cards.

I told him he was going to marry a Spanish girl from South America; that she had dark eyes and hair like a raven's wing.

"No," he stopped me, leaning so near that I was overcome by the tidal wave of his presence. "The girl I love has hair that is never the same color two days in succession. Some days it is brown like a thrush's wing, bronze powdered, and other days it is streaked, tawny gold, and seen in the sunset light it is red like the Queen's carnival robe."

"Oh," I heard myself say, "it isn't like that at all. It is carroty, sorrel, molasses candy—awful colored hair to love—"

"And her eyes"—he ignored the interruption and made a bold pretense of reading the cards in case the others might suspect—"are never the same color twice. Some days they are grey like a dove's breast, and other days they are like larkspur, and again they are moss-agates, full of green jade lights."

"The cards say the girl you are to marry"—I ignored his eloquence—"has dark eyes."

"But the girl I love," he whispered, "has eyes as blue as the peacock on your fan."

"You mustn't." I had a desperate longing to flee away from him forever; to make him go to some dark-eyed senorita, to give back my peace, instead of this wild tumult that engulfed me.

"Forgive me," he whispered. "I didn't mean to tell you—yet."

The Montereys gave a picnic one Sunday over the lake at Covington. I duly set forth with John Bardston. And I clung to him even though I didn't hear a word he was telling me about Daisy. Anthony and I had barely spoken to each other for weeks. But after lunch we found ourselves walking through the yellow jasmine-scented pine woods together.

The high tide of spring lifted us beyond the need of speech. He told me he was twenty-seven, and I said I was sixteen, and he told me he loved me.

New notes came into my voice. Suzanne Souchon predicted grand opera. She was to sing in Covent Garden in the summer. I laughed secretly at her idea that a career allured me. The French opera company was preparing to disperse, the season being over.

Suzanne, now that her work was over, gossiped as vivaciously as Madame's boarders. No one knew that Anthony and I loved each other. Suzanne was keen to find out about Fitz-Gerald. She knew the ballet-dancer and his infatuation for her.

"They all are bewitched," Suzanne said. "Even the fine young gentleman I often see walking home with you. He called on her in her dressing-room las' night, I hear."

She could not tell if he were really interested in "ze person" herself, but certainly he had come to see her and they talked deeply in earnest.

My heart fell like a plummet and sounded depths of misery new to me. I would not believe it; I could not. I told myself there must be some explanation.

Bob arrived the next morning on business. He left word for me to meet him downtown for dinner. We went to Antoine's. It seemed that the evening's developments were stage-managed by Fate.

For before our dinner was half over, in walked Anthony Willing and the notorious little ballet-dancer. A table had evidently been reserved for him, for they passed through without seeing us, and went directly to a more intimate nook in the rear.

Five minutes later Bob had promised me that I might go to New York. Before the coffee came he had agreed to a grand opera career.

As we left Antoine's we met Fitz-Gerald, intoxicated, coming in. His bloodshot eyes swept the room. He hesitated a moment when he saw me, but drunk as he was, he was too much the gentleman to ask me what he wanted to know—if I had seen Anthony with the dancer.

I did not go back to Palmetto Grove with Bob. Instead I left with Suzanne Souchon the next day for New York. I would take Jinny Foster at her word, to come any time to stay with her. She was at Southampton for the summer. It was my first taste of society. In August, Crœsus invited us to go with him on his yacht for a six weeks' cruise. I returned with Jinny to New York late in the autumn and started my singing lessons under Palozzi.

Years afterwards, when I thought I had forgotten the affair, the story was finished. I was singing at a private house in New York. Old Colonel Dubois was there and took me in to supper. He grew reminiscent of New Orleans and finished the story of the ballet-dancer.

Anthony Willing was trying to save Fitz-Gerald from the woman, and finally did so.

"And did she marry him?" I asked. "He never loved but one girl," Colonel Dubois continued, "and you should know who she was." Unemotionally I told him my side of the story. "Child, child," he said sadly; "but youth is cruel and unforgiving. And you soon ceased to care." I confessed as much.

"Willing was killed out hunting in North Carolina," the Colonel said, "that autumn. Whether it was an accident—"

He left it unfinished.

CHAPTER X

THERE is another man in those years when I waited and you did not come. It is Peter.

Jinny Foster, after the specialists could do nothing for Aline, her little daughter, reluctantly gave up her dream of living in New York. Tom Foster felt that her place was with him in Washington. He had been reëlected to the Senate, and had definitely decided on politics as a career. Roseneath, his plantation next to Palmetto Grove, had been turned over to an excellent manager, and Cousin Clara continued to live in the big house and keep it in readiness against their return. Jinny declared life was too short, at best, to spend any part of the year on a Mississippi cotton plantation. After they moved to Washington and bought a house there, she was even less inclined to return South, for she soon became one of the most popular women in society.

In the meantime I had remained in New York, still singing industriously for my supper, also in order to continue the habit of dinner and breakfast. The operatic dream had long since been abandoned. Cotton was less than five cents and the boll weevil had not been exterminated. Bob wrote infrequently. There was little about himself, but much about myself. He was worried most because he could not send me any money. I invented triumphs to deceive him. I told him I was making more than enough for my needs. I could read between the lines in his letters how much he wanted to see me. He said he would not be selfish enough to ask me to give up my glorious prospects to come back to Palmetto Grove, but that maybe some day I could be spared from my engagements long enough to run home to see him. Run home to see him! But the years drifted on and I did not go home.

One day I received a wire from Jinny Foster in Washington. Could I come down to sing at a big dinner she was giving and to stay a week? I had barely time to dress for dinner when I arrived.

Black Tilly brought me a message from Aline, now a hopeless little cripple of five, to ask that I come to the nursery for her to see me before I went downstairs.

Peter Wentworth was in the nursery. He had brought Aline a bull pup. Her frail arms were neck-laced about him and the puppy. She reached up to include me in the embrace.

"Diana," she did the honors, "this is Peter, and the new puppy he brought me. His name is Jupiter." If I had not seen him first with Aline, Peter Went-worth would never have appealed to me in the least. Downstairs with Jinny's society friends he was simply a man of the world; a distinguished diplomat he might have passed for, the type of man careful to be seen with only the right people always.

Jinny told me about him after the others had gone. He was a brilliant editorial writer on a big newspaper, and poor. He supported a lot of helpless sisters some-where in the country. He was a member of all the smart clubs; he went everywhere; he was the special pet of more than one rich society matron. The picture Jinny drew was that of the cynical society man. I could not reconcile her description to Aline's friend, the Peter I met in the nursery, who showed such a different self to the ador-ing little crippled child.

It was Aline's Peter who came to be my friend. He never pretended with me. Aline somehow seemed to know the combination to his heart At her touch the real man stepped forth. He told me about his early struggles, how he had supported his family since he was fifteen; how in the early days he was always hungry, always hounded by the spectre of poverty, the pressing need of money. He confessed one day quite simply that it was this early fear that still stalked him. I cried over the picture he drew of himself at seventeen, working in a printing office, burning up with fever, yet never daring to stop. "And always lonely," he added reminiscently; "Good God! How lonely!"

A few days later I heard Jinny and some of her pitiless society friends taking an inventory of the men in their set. Peter Wentworth, when his turn came, was duly dissected. They all agreed that he was stingy. He sent no flowers to the women whose hospitality he accepted; he gave no dinners; he did nothing to pay his social debts.

A pain went through my heart Why should Peter Wentworth, I asked myself, hang on to these trivial society people to whom he meant nothing more than a good-looking, distinguished man, an ornament to any dinner or dance? Why should he accept their entertainment or provide entertainment for them? I thought of the half-starved boy, hard-pressed always for more money than he could make, and my heart yearned to comfort him.

I do not know whether or not I ever loved Peter Wentworth. But certainly he was the dominating interest in my life for several years. I could never understand why he felt it necessary to keep up any social position. He loathed the cotillions, but he never missed one. The dinners were equally a bore to him, yet he always went to them. He said it was necessary to his work for him to keep in touch with people. But more and more he turned to me. It came to the place where he used to come to spend an evening and neither of us would speak. That was the winter the Fosters went to California and I stayed with Aline in their house in Washington. We kept only two of the servants, the cook and Black Tilly. Aline and I had a peaceful two months together.

On Christmas Eve it was snowing hard. Aline had a cold. After an early supper in the nursery she dropped off to sleep while I sang to her. Peter was out of town. I went down in the living-room and lay on the sofa in the firelight, feeling very forlorn and lonely. The Fosters would soon be returning. I must be getting back on the job in New York. I wondered if there were many people in New York who had missed my songs the two months I had been away.

I found myself taking stock of my life. Christmas and birthdays are apt to bring the feeling that one's books should be balanced. Here I was drifting to ward twenty-five and I had accomplished none of the things I set out to do.

What would my voice come to, after all? I had no home; no ties. I knew Peter Wentworth cared for me, and that I cared for him, for the Peter Aline and I knew, the real Peter, lonely and homesick for a family fireside and a little child's love. Why not take the real man, ignoring the Peter the society world had so long held as its own?

I could hear the sleigh-bells outside on wagons delivering belated Christmas shopping. Could not Peter and I build us a nest somewhere; could I not give him all—and more—the world had given? Fundamentally was not all that mattered the real Peter's heart, and did I not know that to be generous and appreciative of the finer things he had missed in life?

Then the front doorbell rang. I heard voices on the steps. Peter, himself, big, brown, flecked with snow, came in. My heart leaped to welcome him, as I turned the light on. He was alone, yet a moment before I had heard voices. To whom was he talking outside on the steps?

"Oh, that"—he warmed his hands at the blazing hickory logs—"was only a beggar. A patriarchal old gentleman who asked me to give him a quarter for a drink. He said he was a Confederate veteran and that it was Christmas."

"Of course you gave it to him."

"I did not," Peter replied, taking both of my hands in his big hand still tingling from the frost and snow outside. "That was what you heard. He did not seem to think I heard his reasons for asking a quarter—that he was a Confederate veteran and it was Christmas."

"But maybe a quarter," I argued, "would have blotted out the humiliation that he is a beggar on Christmas Eve."

I do not recall the rest of the evening. "And I thought you loved me!" Peter kept saying over and over.

"No—I almost loved you."

So Peter Wentworth went out of my life I haven't seen him for years.

CHAPTER XI

LAST winter I was the voice behind the scenes in a big Broadway success. The star of the play could not sing a note. The part she played was that of a woman with a marvellous voice. The play promised to run a second season.

Several weeks before Easter, one cold, sleety Wednesday, I found, on reaching the theatre for the matinée performance, the two weeks' notice posted. I was no more surprised than the other members of the company. A story got around that the star and the manager had fallen out. He took his revenge by closing the play. There was a second company on the road, and it was rumored that after Easter he intended to bring it to Broadway. My props were swept from under me, for I liked the work and the certainty of a salary every week.

I had halfway promised Alice Grant to come for dinner that night. I sent a wire to her that it would be impossible for me to get there. After my last song was over, I hurried away from the theatre. A cold, wet snow was falling. An east wind came from the river. I struck out for Fifth Avenue with its jonquil lights and leisurely crowds. The wind tinned me into a cross-street, one of the East Thirties. I walked on without design and finally drew up before a door over which was a sign: "The Tappahannock Tea-Room."

I was hungry, and I had to get my dinner somewhere, so I went in. The place was warm and homelike. A blazing fire crackled on the hearth; rush-bottomed chairs and old-fashioned rag rugs were scattered here and there; blooming red geraniums were ranged in the windows. The menu card announced Virginia cooking to be the specialty of the kitchen. A beautiful woman, with sparkling brown eyes and grey hair that belied the youthful face beneath it, was embroidering by the fire, near which the table I chose was placed.

"You are from the South?" she looked up to ask when I gave my order. She directed the colored waitress to bring some spoon-bread with my order. We drifted into a conversation with the easy friendliness of Southerners. She told me she was from Virginia, and asked from what part of the South I came, and if I lived in New York, and what I was doing.

In fifteen minutes I knew her name was Lura Hicks, that she was widowed, with an aviator son now training to go to France, and that business was booming with her. And she in turn knew I was a singer; she had heard of me through my singing at the Dixie Society affairs which she said she was too busy to ever attend. Her face lighted with keener interest when I told her I sang in the Broadway play. She had heard me sing in that. She loved my voice. She had seen the play several times solely to hear the star, as she thought, sing.

Since I was a singer perhaps I could help her in the matter of finding a soloist for her church as substitute for the one they now had and who was leaving soon on a six months' leave of absence.

"Our soloist is going to California," she said. "She has been left some property and has to go West to see about it, but she wants her place when she returns in the autumn."

She mentioned the salary. It was the identical amount I was receiving at the theatre. I told her that I would gladly take the place, if she thought I could fill it, as my work at the theatre would last only two more weeks. She said she didn't see why I could not fill it, but that she was only one of the committee to decide. She went to the telephone and finally came back and announced that she had made an appointment for me to sing for them at eleven the next morning. Still the name of the church did not register. When I finished my dinner and started back to the theatre, it was with the understanding that she would call for me and take me to her church in the morning. I walked back toward Broadway in a very different frame of mind from that in which I left the theatre a few hours earlier. Meeting Lura Hicks was like going home, somehow. We were friends without knowing the first things, each about the other. I went to bed wondering idly what kind of church her church was, that it could pay a soloist such a salary. It seemed the dominating interest with her, and yet she bore none of the hall-marks by what I had come to recognize "a consecrated Christian." She looked more like a lady in an opera box. She was "joy made manifest" if I ever beheld it. I had heard of certain advanced modern churches holding their services in theatres. I concluded Lura Hicks, in spite of her homely rag rugs, her rush-bottomed chairs, her old-fashioned red geraniums, must be some sort of a religious radical.

I sang for Lura's committee the next morning in a beautiful church with a pipe organ worthy of Saint Cecilia. Still I did not know what "denomination" the church was until I was notified a few days later that I had been elected substitute soloist. I looked with incredulous eyes on the letter-head. It was a church that even I, confirmed non-churchgoer that I am, had accepted from hearsay as anti-Christ, a church whose faith, based on power to heal all manner of disease, I had heard made a joke for years. Protestant churches, I knew, hated this church as Bob hates the Pope and Rome. Nevertheless I made up my mind to sing for its members in return for the salary they offered to pay for my services.

The experience might be interesting, even amusing. Since it promised work for the spring and summer, it was a port in the present uncertainty. The final argument for it was Lura Hicks herself. She was homelike and human as a rag rug made from familiar family garments; as cheerful and heartening as a hickory fire; no one who could dispense cooking as orthodox as hers could be far off the track spiritually. I had not met anybody like her in New York. I looked forward to the first service with curious interest.

The Sunday services were Greek so far as I understood the philosophy they tried to expound. But I was tremendously impressed by the congregation. It was like singing to the Metropolitan Opera House. Every seat, even up to the highest balcony, was occupied. There was scarcely standing-room in the back of the church. I took part in the services automatically, leading in the hymns and singing a solo that the music committee selected for me.

When I was not singing, I sat behind a screen with the organist, feeling much as if I were at a theatrical performance given in a language I did not understand.

On Wednesday evenings the services were shortened to give the audience the opportunity to testify to the healing power of this new faith, which, they claimed, was very old religion scientifically employed. I heard unbelievable testimonies of miraculous healings, "protections," and "realizations." The speakers did not impress me as fanatics, yet I cannot say that I was more convinced than I would have been at an experience meeting of so many Munchausens.

My friends ragged me about my new job, and hunted up old jokes about it, and put aside new ones, thinking that I would contribute my quota from seeing the original performers. At first I pretended to be amused, but even then I could not say why I felt a distinct resentment at every gibe thrown at Lura's church. She had not once spoken to me about the tenets of her faith. She was so busy living her religion, she didn't have to preach it.

One Wednesday night, in the midst of the testimonies, an unheard-of thing happened. Some one laughed out loud; then another tittered. Even I, to whom the church meant nothing, was aghast. The Reader raised his hand for silence. The speaker concluded her experience and sat down. The absolute silence was the greatest rebuke the offender could have faced. Then the invitation was repeated from the pulpit for those who had been benefited to speak. The meeting continued.

When I came out on the street, Alice Grant's chauffeur came up to say their car was waiting for me. In it were Jinny Foster, Alice Grant, and Dolly Wayne. Jinny called out even before I got in that they were to stop for Crœsus on the way downtown. Jinny had come down from Bar Harbor where they were spending the summer, and had run into Alice and Dolly at the Ritz. The latter had come in from Southampton for the night.

"It was too late to get you for dinner," Jinny said. "You had gone when we called up your place. Miss Fortescue told us you were at this church, so We went there ... I never heard such nutty speech-making in all my life."Dolly tittered.

"I couldn't keep my face straight," Jinny continued, "but when Dolly laughed out loud I confess I was scared cold."

"Who is it you have to see in East Thirtieth Street?" Jinny demanded, when I told her I could not go with them to the Delmonico roof.

I evaded her question by saying I had work to do to-night.

"If it's work, why aren't you going back to Miss Fortescue's, where you live, to do it?" Jinny persisted. "Who lives at this East Thirtieth Street place anyway?"

"No one you know." "One of your new friends, then?" pointedly. "Yes, one of my new friends," I replied. "What's the idea, Mariana?" asked Alice Grant. "You trying to drop all of us?"

Jinny saved me the necessity of a reply. "What's got into you, Di? It's not this fool new religion, is it?"

"I don't know, Jinny," I said truthfully. "You'll have to forgive me, but I've— I've got to get away from all of you to-night—"

"I believe it is beginning to take" giggled Dolly Wayne. -

"They were like people from another world," Alice said, "with that peace—"

"They do belong to another world," Jinny interrupted crossly. Then she began all over again her arguments and her persuasions for me to come along with then.

The chauffeur drew up before the old red-brick house where Lura Hicks had told me she lived. I had never been there. She was not expecting me now. I did not know that she would be at home.

Jinny must have sensed some of this, for the car waited while I rang the bell.

"Your friends may not be at home, after all," she called. "Then you'll have to come with us. Crœsus expects us to bring you."

I rang again, desperately. Far off I heard footsteps.

"I say, Di," Jinny leaned out of the car to call ingratiatingly, "of course I know it means a good salary, this solo position, but don't sign your soul away to that church. Take 'em as the jokes they are!"

"Good-bye, Jinny!" I held a curb bit on my tongue. "It will probably be a long time before I see any of you again."

Then Lura's little black maid-of-all-work opened the door.

It was a long time before I saw any one from Jinny's world again. For the next day I moved down to the quiet little hotel near Lura where I have lived ever since.

CHAPTER XII

Heaven is a place with many doors and each may enter in his own way,

HINDU PROVERB

December 1, 1917

I HAVE been singing in Lura's church (as I have come to call it) for a year now. The soloist whose place I have been filling returns shortly. And Lura is getting her affairs in order to go to France, where her boy is in the Aviation Service.

I dined at the Tappahannock Tea-Room with her to-night to say good-bye. She came nearer to talking to me about religion than she has ever done before.

"I tell you this," she said, "not that I think you are ready for it now, but if ever you face a blank wall, physically, financially, or spiritually—"

She stopped.

"Was it ever like that with you?" I asked.

Lura Hicks laughed.

"Was it?" she repeated enigmatically. "Suppose you had a family to support and nothing to support them on—a Virginia family used to comfort and ease and plenty. Suppose everything was suddenly swept away and you, without capital, experience, friends, or trained servants to assist you, had to start running a big boarding-house: that you had to, because it meant a roof over your heads—

"Suppose it was suddenly put up to you, who didn't know how to do anything, that you had this chance when you had never so much as put your foot in such a place before. A cheap boarding-house full of cheap boarders, cheap food, cheap servants. And not one boarder that could be counted on to pay his board. Suppose things were so desperate that there was no food for the family, except what the boarders left on their plates, no heat except—"

Lura could laugh now at the hideous memory. "—There was only one servant finally, a faithful old soul we had brought from Virginia. She fed the furnace for weeks by hacking out the underpinning of the house, the rafters and beams in the basement. The structure couldn't have stood three weeks more of cold weather, when the scene shifts to Atlantic City.

"—Another cheap boarding-house and all the debts carried forward from the former venture. There was one profitable boarder, an eccentric, rich old lady who took a fancy to me one day on the Board-Walk, who went home with me, and rented the front parlor.

"Things seemed to be working out. I was nearly paying my expenses on her, when one morning, while I was out marketing, she attempted to clean some gloves with gasoline, set herself afire, and burned up as neat as ever, without scorching a thing in the room!

"Of course, after that the other boarders left, like the rats they were, most of them omitting the final formality of settling up.

"It was Wednesday night, I remember, and I had to get out somewhere. The Board-Walk was hideous to me. I turned into a small lighted church because it looked cool and quiet. And the service I heard that night changed my whole life. The reader was a man without a palate. He nearly drove me wild, but in ten minutes I had forgotten his physical defect. I knew I was listening to the Truth, and that it was the Truth Jesus meant when he said he came to bring life and to bring it more abundantly.

"I cannot explain in words what was to me a spiritual revelation. But I can truthfully say from that day to this I have never worried about my own petty affairs, boarding-houses or what-not. I have been busy about the Father's business and my own needs have been supplied. The Tappahannock Tea-Room runs itself a great deal better than I ever ran my cheap boarding-houses."

Lura Hicks laughed and opened her arms to me. "Good-bye, Diana Cameron," she said. "Each of us has to work out his own salvation. But you remember this: 'Love never faileth.' "

The soloist has returned. . . For over a year now I have rested on the security of a salary. I shall have to start out again.

Oh, how I hate the thought of those Dixie dances, and Ohio luncheons, and the

Missouri dinners! Clubs! The thought of them is almost a physical.

There is nothing to be had in the way of solo work in any other church. I have canvassed them all.

I haven't been out of town even for one day for over a year. Perhaps a vacation would do me good. I thought once of going South to spend Christmas with Bob. But somehow I do not want to go back to Palmetto Grove.

Mammy Linda is long since dead. Bob doesn't need me, and I seem to have lost the old affection I had for the plantation as a child.

My childhood seems very far away. There is but one thing that could allure me back home.

Sometimes there sweeps over me a great wave of nostalgia for the miracle that used to come to me when I was a child.

If I could only feel once more myself, wrapped in amber and coral and jade—in the bubble of crystal light!

But I know that that is gone forever. Gone with the old miracle which transmuted my voice into the voice of an angel, easily singing songs that she understood, in a language unknown to her.

Perhaps, after all, it was only a dream! I wonder if it is true, as I remember—that once I could—Of course, it could not be true.

The thought of Christmas on Palmetto Grove does not appeal to me. Bob will probably have a houseful of his friends—there was always a houseful in the old days—to spend the holidays with him.

CHAPTER XIII

OUT of the dear sky came this cable to-day from Bermuda:

Reservations for you on Carlotta. Ticket by special delivery. Come for Christmas. Next boat.

It was signed "Tink."

Later the special delivery letter arrived, enclosing a return ticket to Bermuda.

I met Tink and the Commodore two years ago when I spent an Easter vacation in Bermuda. Our friendship was the suddenest it has proved as strong as it was sudden. This letter explains that they have decided that the Christmas present they want most is a visit from me; they enclose the ticket as their Christmas present to me.

It is sleeting In New York. The only thing I have to hold me is a ridiculous feeling about leaving the Japanese garden. Why should that hold me? It was not from you. And yet I met you under that cedar-tree one night, even if it were a tree bought with Crœsus' money.

It has sleeted all day. The sun is shining in Bermuda, and the boat sails to-morrow at eleven.

Yuki is to keep the honorable garden safe against my return.

PART II
BERMUDA

All things which participate in anything which is common to them all move towards that which is of the same kind with themselves.

. . . Accordingly, then, everything also which participates in the common intelligent nature moves in like manner towards that which is of the tame land with itself, or moves even more.

MARCUS AURELIUS

CHAPTER I

On board S. S. Carlotta December 7, 1917

Two days out from New York. The ungentle Gulf Stream is crossed, double-crossed if I am any judge.

Just out of the New York Harbor we ran into a gale, going seventy-five miles an hour—and not in our direction. This little boat, they say, makes only one mile an hour in a storm. Last night she must have travelled it going round in a circle, a very vicious circle. When she did move forward it was something like an imitation of George Cohan in his early days, when he used to make his exit from the stage walking on his left ear!

I am a good sailor, but as a whirling dervish I am a failure. I went to bed only after I was banged black and blue trying to stand up. Being pitched from porthole to door, and back again, with the sport re-versed so the washstand could get a crack at me, finally made the stuffy little berth seem a sanctuary.

The day was bad enough, but last night was hideous. The storm raged and shrieked. Rain blew in the porthole, even with the window shut and the storm shutters tightly closed. I was dead tired and soon fell asleep.

Then the real demon sport started. Things in the stateroom came to life and started a chase. My squirrel muff with its satin arm-loop resolved itself into an elephantine cat with a bristling tail. It fled terrified before my brown walking-boots. These in turn reverted to long-horned Texas steers that hooked wildly at everything in sight. The well-bred black satin slippers I wore at dinner the first night out went suddenly insane and joined in the chase, yelping at the heels of the brown boots. The crystal buckles on the slippers resolved themselves into two eyes of baleful, greenish light that searched the uttermost corners of the tiny stateroom for what they might intimidate and devour. A jar of cold cream on the washstand shook itself out of its place of security and went crashing after the other things.

From top berth to sofa, from door to porthole, back again and under the bed, only to emerge the next minute flying off in another direction, they kept the chase up. I leaned out and tried to catch some or all of the mad things, but I soon gave up, beaten. The business of staying in the berth was all I could manage.

Then through the misty darkness I saw that my blue Chinese bedroom slippers were tenanted by an ancient Chinaman with a flowing pigtail. He umpired the game, smoking a long opium pipe that smelled of steerage cooking.

Oh, what a brute of a night!

Beyond the Gulf Stream lies Bermuda. All the afternoon going up the harbor from St. George's, the sea has been a turquoise cup: the sky an inverted bowl of blue larkspur.

We came in on a tender long after the captain had abandoned any hope of docking until morning. No one met me.

The drive around the harbor from Hamilton to Paget was a series of bouquets. First that reached my nostrils was cedar shavings when we passed the shop of the Boer who makes furniture and souvenirs.

Then came the curve, the mango marsh, and the scent of the sea, which I had not smelled so long as I was at sea.

"And oh, the smell of that jasmine flower"—(only I have never seen a jasmine in Bermuda) or freesia or whatever it is that comes to life down here at night. One gets it only in driving and along the sea. It was mixed with freshly ploughed ground and flavored with absinthe—not absinthe really, but crushed fennel that grows in crannies along the rock-walled roads, and in the corners of the Portuguese "patches."

The fishing-boats were huddled in port for the night, and the "White Swan" tea-house of pleasant memory was cuddled down in its curve like a snowy bird with head tucked under its wing until morning. The lights of Hamilton, reflected in long fingers of gold, quivered in the dark mirror of the harbor.

Then up, up, up the road to the heaven-kissing hill to the white icing cottage where the Commodore and Tink live.

They had heard the boat would not get in until the next morning. Even so they did not know that I was on it.

Never was such a welcome. We just sat and looked at each other and said over and over again that it was absolutely unbelievable that I had come to spend Christmas with them.

It still seemed a dream. When I told them it was sleeting in New York when I left, I felt that I wasn't to be relied on. I may have thought it was sleeting, but it couldn't be true, if this peaceful spring night of warmth and fragrance were true.

"It's all a dream," I heard myself say; "I'm not really here. Don't believe anything I say."

"Damme," said the Commodore, "but you've got to have a drink." All the drink I wanted was a glass of cold water, and a tub of hot water.

I went to sleep in a little four-poster cedar bed that smelled like the heart of Lebanon. On two sides of my room French windows were open on a scented garden. Oh, the sybaritic bliss of a bed, clean and cool and soft, a bed that stood still.

A night-bird somewhere out in the tangle of the garden softly and softly, over and over again, sang one note.

Utter weariness. Peace. After four nights of nightmare tossing, I drifted slowly, deliriously slowly, off to sleep, lulled by the night-bird's note. It sounded like "You," "You," "You-u-u."

Oh, who are *you* and where, my Love?

CHAPTER II

***Bermuda, December* 10**

CLYTEMNESTRA, twelve years old, done in bronze, was standing in the morning sunshine. It was not her noiseless padding in that wakened me, but the scent of the flowers in the vase she set on the table beside my bed.

There were three stalks of narcissi, a kind of indeterminate family as if a jonquil had married by capture a paper-white narcissus, and these were their children, yellow and white mixed, with the spring odor of each intensified by the union; several sprays of pink snap-dragon, two of wall-flowers, flanking three old-fashioned cinnamon roses, the whole enveloped in a ballet-skirt of maidenhair fern.

"It is a bouquet," Clytemnestra informed me gravely. I'll say it is a bouquet!

Then she pattered out and pattered in again with a tray of ambrosial morning food which I ate to music. A red-bird was giving a Biltmore morning musicale in the peach-tree that hangs over the water-tank just above the garden on which my windows open. It was a one-man concert and a gay affair, the conductor and soloist being one and the same. In his brilliant scarlet coat he out-Sousa-ed Sousa, and challenged bird or leaf, tree or blossom, to match-me-if-you-can!

Then Tink came in and sat on the edge of the bed, and we told each other again that it could not possibly be true that I was there.

"But you did expect me." I pointed to the dressing-table. (My own dressing-case, bags, and trunk had to be left with the customs-people on the wharf last night) There sat an enormous bottle of the un-scented eau de cologne I like best—that is to be had only in Bermuda, because it is made here by a chemist from an old French formula handed down in his family, and he is not commercial enough to advertise or exploit it on the market elsewhere—and a big box of "Poudre de toilette et de beauté," pink as pale coral and smelling of Liberty's shop and London.

"They were provided against your coming," Tink admitted; "but we were so superstitious about it, we pretended to each other that there wasn't a chance in the world that you would get here."

Tink and the Commodore drove off for a morning in town and left Cheri-Moia, the tiny grey kitten, to amuse me.

The peace and quiet of this place!

Tink and the Commodore lead the quietest life in the world. He is white-haired and thirty-five years older than she, and they are first cousins and wildly in love with each other.

Bermuda is a coral formation, and when a house is to be built, the architect selects the location and digs out enough white coral to build it, and there it is! Then more of the white coral rock is burnt to get lime for the cement and to whitewash it outside and inside. The roofs are of the same white rock cut into tiles, and double-daubed and whitewashed in order that the rain, the only fresh water to be had in the island, may be absolutely pure when it runs into the tanks where it is kept for drinking purposes.

The effect of these houses is charming beyond words. No photograph gives the faintest idea of their quaintness. Tink says they make her think of the cakes that members of her family used to try to ice at home, and which always ended with: "I knew all the time I ought to send that cake to the caterer!"

Kodak pictures of this cottage invariably come more or less a likeness to an angel cake, a loaf effect at that, no matter from what angle it is taken. It is only a rented furnished cottage. Tink and the Commodore have added cedar furniture, books and pictures, and hung the whole house with chintz. There is a sun parlor with a great stone fireplace for cool days.

In one corner of the garden in front of the house is a green chair. I am sitting in it now. From here one gets a view of the harbor spread far below. The little sail-boats drift like white butterflies over the blue waters down there.

The water is never the same shade of blue half an hour at a time. It runs the heavenly scale of blues from aqua-marine to azure; from lapis-lazuli to amethyst, from turquoise to sapphire, from palest forget-me-not to all the glinting bronze-powdered blues and greens of a peacock's breast. The little boats dip along and are finally lost behind this fairy island or that one; like a snail's silver trail in a garden lies the path of each on the water.

Cheri-Moia is being given a lesson by her mother, the Bride (that's her name)—oh, but it's a blot to write it!—in the gentle art of how to catch a "chick-o'-the-village" bird for her luncheon.

Cheri-Moia is built like a little square piano, covered with the softest grey fur. Her mother, the Bride, must have looked exactly like this when she was a tiny kitten. Cheri-Moia's teeth are tiny briars carved of pearl; her mouth is red coral. She is a most enchanting young cat, a very Cleopatra siren of kittens;—but she shall not crunch that innocent bird, so long as I am in this island to prevent it!

BERMUDA

CHAPTER III

In a deserted garden Bermuda, December 12

WHY is it that a rose is the one flower in an abandoned garden that holds on longest to the hope that *they* will come back; the one flower that refuses to run to pot? Is it feminine vanity, or the indomitable determination to remain a rose, fragrant and satinpetalled to the end?

Two years ago this garden in which I am hidden away (ostensibly to be sketching a copper-colored Bougainvillea spilling down the hill above, but in reality to write to you) was a dream of beauty and order. Violets bordered the brick walks; begonias stood at attention presenting arms of pink blossoms; prim white lilies made a procession of devout nuns always on their way to Mass. Geraniums and narcissi and heliotrope and all the annuals beloved of English gardeners were tucked in this corner and that one, neat as children in Sunday pews, chin up, elbows down, eager to please.

That was the first winter the Americans who own the cottage failed to come down for the season. Two years have passed. Some say they are afraid of the submarines, others that there is illness in the family. The house remains un-aired, the garden uncaredfor.

Coming down from the cottage above, I had to fight my way through the old path, now grown up with brambles. The stone steps are entirely closed by the unpruned Spanish daggers that used to guard its portals like two slim sentries.

Now, there is nothing left to guard. Not a violet in bloom. Here and there I find a scraggly, anæmic vine that once was a violet plant The paw-paw-tree has had its top blown off, and the broken shaft stands, a monument to better days. Once there was a jolly regiment of jonquils always doing drills there by the gate; now not one remains. True, there are still "match-me-if-you-can" hedges, but out of all proportion, with their old rare variation of colors now slumped into one indifferent maroon, bordered carelessly with white, put on any sort of fashion. Written all over the hedge is the sloven's excuse: No one will see me, anyway.

The lantanas are like men one sees on the ship three days out after a storm, in collars one suspects, and in clothes one knows they have slept in.

Only the rose has stayed a rose. The wind and rain of yesterday that left these other flowers bedrabbled and frowsy, with mud spatting on their faces, was but a shower-bath to the roses. This rose vine under which I am sitting looks as if she might trip down the hill to the sea at dawn for a dip in the salt spray, every morning.

There are five red roses and innumerable buds on the branch that hangs over my shoulder, and each is as perfect a rose as one might find in Gulistan, tenanted by nightingales.

It comes to me that this deserted garden is like life, and these flowers, gone to rack and ruin, like human beings. How many men and women there are who present arms in perfection, true to type, so long as there are those to see, to care, but who, left to themselves, let go pride and form, through lack of heart or because of the effort required; who slump lower and lower, until they lose all faculty of blossoming, all form and dignity and character—to be lost finally in the rabble, the hoi-polloi of life.

How few of us there are who, like the rose, can hold to our individuality, our fineness, our exquisiteness, with no one to see or care!

This strange thing we call the heart, that we accept with a point at its base and a cleft in its upper boundary, may it not be that "garden enclosed" within us, of which Solomon speaks? The garden that is made ready by dreams for the beloved one's coining, but which, when the expected one does not come, and the years roll on, we lose interest in and let the flowers die of neglect or go to pot through selfishness or laziness.

My love, the garden of my heart shall never be given over for a home for slatterns. No matter what effort it costs me, I shall keep up its taxes, and make it stand at attention. Its roses, whether you come or do not come, shall keep their satin cleanliness and fragrance, not because they were for you, but because they are roses and must remain true to type—roses to the end.

CHAPTER IV

Bermuda, December 14

THE cedar flames were leaping and crackling in the big stone fireplace. We had been driving all the afternoon. Now supper was over. The Commodore lay in the long swing seat, smoking peacefully. Tink was hurrying to get her Christmas mail ready for the next day's steamer. I was playing with Cheri-Moia and her fool mother, the Bride.

"Terence has heard you are here," the Commodore remarked apropos of nothing, "or he has come up the hill, seen you through the window, and fled."

"He's come, seen you through the window, and gone." Tink stopped writing to repeat

The Commodore sighed. "Terence is a damn fool," he said tenderly.

Terence Woode, it seems, is the one person in Bermuda who is even more averse to people who call and are called upon than the Commodore and Tink. They had told me about their friendship with him, and warned me that I must not feel hurt if he fled like a wild rabbit at my approach. They had told me his story. How he lived like a hermit crab alone in a lovely old place, "Cedarwoode," now denuded of everything since the death of his mother five years ago broke the entail and scattered the things that had made it a home. Terence is poor as a church mouse. (Poor because he refused to accept a fortune that everybody except himself thought he was entitled to. It was willed him, but he would have not one penny of it.) Terence is proud as Lucifer's peacock, and between him and a crowd of well-off relatives there is a great gulf fixed. Just who fixed the gulf, Tink has her own suspicions. She is sure Terence had his share in it with his wicked pride and his shyness.

The Commodore has a way of knowing, the minute he sets eyes on a person, whether that one is to mean anything in his life or not. He has reduced the process of elimination of people to a science. He happened upon Terence one day and liked him. And Terence liked the Commodore. And Tink liked him, and she determined that Terence had to behave like a human and be friends.

Even so the friendship progressed cautiously. But for over a year now, three years after they met him, Terence and Tink and the Commodore have been devoted friends. He comes to spend several evenings out of every week with them, provided they are alone. If he sees a strange person through the windows, the night swallows him up again.

There was a sudden call up from the kitchen. Clytemnestra burst through the door excitedly: "Aunt Felicity says hurry," she breathlessly addressed her mistress. "Mr. Woode is at the door. He is giving her the paw-paws he brought for you. He says he has to get back home."

Felicity, the cook, Clytemnestra, her first aide, and Georgas, the yard boy, had their instructions anticipating this event. They were not to tell Mr. Woode, if he should ask, that there was a stranger in the house. If he appeared and started to disappear because of certain reconnaissances of his own, he was to be detained forcibly if necessary.

Tink gave one leap through the door and was downstairs in the kitchen. There were protestations and strenuous efforts to escape. I dropped down on the floor in the corner.

"Don't say a word," the Commodore commanded hoarsely.

"Really—really now, my dear," came the fine voice of a gentleman being forcibly hauled upstairs by a lady twice as large as he—"I can't come in. I only stopped by to leave the paw-paws. There's a man at the ferry waiting for me."

"There's a man here waiting for you!"

"Don't be a fool, Terence," the Commodore greeted him.

Then how it happened, I don't know. I rose up and held out both my hands to the stranger and he put both of his out to me, and we were friends.

What an evening we had! Cheri-Moia left me and climbed on Terence's shoulder, a familiarity she has never taken with me, and she listened with the rest of us while he told about his early life on the lower islands, Turk's Island, the Bahamas, and many more the names of which I cannot spell.

He told strange, horrible stories of voodooism and conjuring; spells laid to ensnare the fancy, disorder the brain to insanity, or to cause death. How these savage rituals and conjuring magic are still being employed to get rid of persons wanted out of the way. And I, born on a Mississippi cotton plantation in the very heart of the black belt, know that all he said was true.

Terence is sixty-five years old and looks forty-five. In Turk's Island, where his early youth was spent, he was the pet of an old African slave, who had been a king in his own country before he was stolen and sold into slavery. From this old savage he had learned the magic rites and ceremonials of Africa. A fortuneteller in Guadeloupe had taught him to "lay the cards" to read the future before he knew his alphabet. He has promised to "lay the cards" for me, but only after the new moon. Fortunes told when the moon is waning, it seems, are not to be counted on.

In the lower islands music plays a large part in the ceremonials of magic. The call of the blood is the "Bamboula," a devil dance.

"If I had my fiddle," he said, "I'd play it for you—"

"You left one here." Tink produced a violin from somewhere under the table.

Terence tucked it under his chin, closed his eyes. Then crept forth an air so insistent, so seductive, so Imperative, that the fire-lighted room, hung with chintz, and cushioned with pillows, and rugs and easy-chairs and all the comforts of civilization, vanished, so far as I was conscious of it.

Whatever the others saw or felt, I was transported to a warmer, more languorous land, in which marshes stretched into swamps, and trees grew, not upward into dignified trees, but as bushes and jungles, slimy-fingered, reaching, not up to the sky, but back to the marsh from which they sprang. There was a full moon and a path that led down, down to the depths of this dank, dark forest, and at the end of the trail a great fire leaped.

And down the path I could see them go answering the Bamboula's invitation to the dance, tree-frogs and beetles, lizards and bats, and all the creeping, crawling, sinister things that go to make the sacrament of the black soul appeasing its gods. The fire in this forest was not a healthy, warming fire, but a hungry, crunching flame that called for victims. Ugh!

Terence said he'd have to get me a jumbi-bead, which negroes down that way believe to be a talisman against the evil eye.

Terence asked me to sing for him.

"How did you know Diana sings?" Tink asked him.

"I'm waiting." Terence smiled at her and turned to me.

I heard myself singing "The Lantern of Love." It was the first time I had thought of it since I sang for the General's widow.

"Is that all of it?" Terence asked quietly when I stopped.

"All I know," I replied.

"It is n't the end, though," Terence said.

"I never heard that song before, Terence," Tink said. "How do you happen to know it?"

"I never heard it before either," Terence said. "But it brings back to me—"

He did not finish. He simply walked out into the night without the formality of a good-bye.

"What in thunder got into Terence to-night?" the Commodore asked Tink. "I never heard him talk like that to a stranger."

Terence a stranger? I'm sure I've known him—somewhere—sometime!

And his eyes—why—his eyes—

Where **have** I seen those eyes before?

CHAPTER V

***Bermuda, December* 20**

TERENCE sent us flowers before breakfast next morning. For Tink there was a great romantic bunch of red roses; for me a personal bouquet of white spice roses, flanked with a brave array of "little red soldiers," a variety of native heath that grows in upstanding spikes, up and down which prim little soldiery red blossoms parade.

Georgas brought the flowers and the message. "Mr. Woode was happy because he was caught and brought in last night."

"But that does n't mean," Tink observed shrewdly, "that you will ever see him again."

Instead of waiting for him to return, we went to see him. An ancient negro is always cutting grass and sharpening a scythe on the lawn at "Cedarwoode." Tink explained that the grass-cutting occupation was only a camouflage: that the old grass-cutter's real business is to warn Terence when visitors are approaching, giving him time to escape, in the event the callers insist on seeing for themselves that Mr. Woode is not at home.

Father Time spoke truly. Terence was not at home.! The house was double-locked back door and front. We proceeded on our picnic without him. Our objective was St George's. We were going to the end of nowhere to do our Christmas shopping.

We turned into the south shore road along the sea. The word "blue" is to me the most beautiful music in the English language. But it takes Bermuda to make one appreciate the heavenly symphonies of beauty that can be worked out in blues.

The water was like melted peacock breasts, as it lapped the pink coral beaches. We drove under oleander hedges for miles, not oleanders in their glory, which comes in the springtime drenching the island with almond breath, but under oleanders blossoming in spite of December, here and there a spray scattering its aftermath of scent, with that of the sea, sparkling beyond

We stopped to see the "Devil's Hole," a hideous cave where devil-fish and angel-fish and an ancient turtle all live together in a bottomless pool and earn a livelihood for the quaint old man who takes the gate fee, a shilling for as long as you care to watch them.

The Commodore sat in the trap outside smoking, and waited for us. Tink livened up my horror of the place by observations on the sinister sharks that swam below, leaping hungrily at the bread she threw them.

"Now those morays," she said, indicating the huge spotted monsters, "are shyster lawyers (the negroes really do call them 'sea-lawyers') They make their living by persuading widowed angel-fish to invest all their insurance money in schemes that never eventuate. Then the angel-fish have to open tea-rooms where one can never really get what one wants, strawberries and cream around Christmas-time, but where one has to take paw-paw preserves and bread and butter and weak tea, just because it is for charity, anyway!"

Tink is adorably foolish. She doesn't belong in a house at all, but in the gayest painted van of a gipsy outfit, the Queen's own car! She is built on voluptuous lines, all curves and dimples. Her hair is black as a raven's wing; her skin is like a pomegranate that has ripened to perfection in the sunshine; and her heart is like a cedar fire, full of warmth and comfort, of substantial service and of fantastic dreams! She can tell you all about vacuum cleaners if the matter in hand requires one, but if I should come into possession of a magic carpet guaranteed to do Arabian Nights stunts, Tink is the first passenger I would ask to try it out with me.

We drove along Harrington Sound, stretched like a sash of broad blue ribbon down the centre of the island, and left it for the white road that brought us to the causeway leading to St George's. Here again the sea changed its blue, to quivering waves of fainter, finer color, aqua-marines, tipped with seed-pearls.

We tied the horse and gave him his oats just on the other side of the causeway, and found a path that led through a mangrove thicket to an open spot with a rock table waiting for us so close to the water we could use the sea as our finger-bowl. The Commodore spread the rugs. I unpacked the basket while Tink busied herself with an alcohol cooking apparatus. She was doing things with butter and eggs and tomatoes and little new onions, stirring and tasting and excitedly slapping the top on again, all the while directing us where to find the chicken, which thermos bottle held the soup, and where to find the coffee. Tink's "lob-lolly" was the last word in gipsy ambrosia. We lingered over the banquet.

St George's is the oldest town in Bermuda, the most wistfully lovely, the most peaceful in all this peaceful island. The streets are always deserted, the shops empty. Where do the people who live here keep themselves? Perhaps we arrived and departed during the siesta period of the day. Even the shops seem to be dozing.

No one could blame the people for staying at home if what lies behind those lovely old faded pink and cream walls is as charming as one pictures it Lustre cups and old pewter gleam through the fan-lights over this door and that one.

Every house is walled in with British exclusiveness. The native flowers alone fail to conform to this spirit of retirement Over this bisque-colored wall drips a Bougainvillea, with its cascading fountain of purple blossom, and across the street a vagrant pigeon-berry vine loaded with jewels of topaz nods back to it the time of day.

"This looks like an elopement, if you ask me," Tink observed, pointing to a delicate tiara of white blossoms and tendrils of tender green lifting its head over a raspberry-ice colored wall. "Juliet—and look at him!"

Across the narrow street from another garden a gorgeous passion-flower swayed and actually seemed reaching out to help the Juliet vine escape.

"She'll never make it," Tink babbled on. "The old lady, her mother, is down there in the garden holding tight to the tail of her skirts. There's going to be no scandal in that family!"

We shopped wildly and bought ancient before-the-war gifts for each other for Christmas and as souvenirs of the day.

We made a pilgrimage to the old church to see the silver communion service sent out to it by Queen Anne in—the year doesn't matter.

We lingered over the quaint epitaphs of the departed governors of the island. More than one distinguished general, with all the letters in the alphabet testifying to the honors bestowed on him by his sovereign, met an ignominious death—if this garrulous marble headstone and that one is to be trusted, from an over-generous meal of green turtle soup.

"Well, no one dies of green turtle soup as they make it in Bermuda," Tink remarked, "without having had his day. He dined at least once before he departed hence."

Going home we stopped at "Walshingham," where Tom Moore lived when he spent his year in Bermuda. The house is deserted now, but romantically interesting with its tiny-paned windows, which time has turned pink. The sea comes to the very door. We had tea in the fairy dell back of the house where the famous calabash-tree still stands. It was under this, if we take the Irish poet's word, that many a flowing bowl passed.

Tom Moore wrote several impassioned love-poems to a beautiful girl who lived near by. She did not smile on his suit Perhaps she did not value his genius as the trait most to be desired in a husband.

I asked a quaint old lady, whose grandmother—or perhaps it was her great-grandmother who lived near here in Tom, Moore's time—whatever became of the "fair Nea." Her Early-Victorian reply was: "She married a gentleman in St. George's who didn't drink!"

So we came home through the soft Southern twilight, the stars so near we could almost reach up and get a handful—home and to bed to sink forty fathoms deep in sleep brewed of sea air and twelve hours of sunlight and April showers.

CHAPTER VI

Bermuda, Christmas Day

BELIEVE me, Beloved, a damask cloth on a mahogany table, candle-lighted and holly-wreathed up to its chin, isn't a patch on a pink coral beach, sun-lighted and south-wind-swept, for a Christmas dinner.

And this was a Christmas dinner, culminating in a plum pudding that might have lighted up a baronial hall. We have just drained our ***demi-tasses.*** The table was spread down there on the sand, under a jutting rock in case an uninvited April shower should descend upon us.

Tink is writing letters home, the Commodore is propped against a rock smoking his everlasting pipe and talking to Terence, while I am hidden on this jutting grey stone promontory, far above them all and far out at sea, writing to you.

Tink and I have been swimming in this sky-blue, electrical water, soft as softest satin, all the morning. It is more peacocky blue than ever to-day; there is a high surf.

We met an angel-fish face to face. She had on a tea-gown of blue with an overdress of yellow net fastened with a coral jewel where her neck should have been. She was gone like a flash!

"Tink," I shrieked, "did you see that?"

"The angel-fish?" Tink came up out of the forget-me-not bank of eddying water, blowing like a porpoise. "Yes, I saw her. She's hurrying on to St. George's, she told me. She promised to meet a gentleman down there and she was late!"

Who wants any stimulant better than the salt spray and the sunlight? But just the same we did not scorn the Commodore's orders, to drink our cocktails as soon as we got out of the water. We got back into our clothes in pink and yellow caves, and then had dinner.

I sent Bob a "Merry Christmas" card a week ago. He will probably not send me that much of a greeting.

When he does send me a postcard these days it is written by some one else. He is gradually forgetting me just as my memory of him has grown thin.

This afternoon belongs to you. Christmas comes but once a year.

God save the King!

The days have sped by. One afternoon we went uninvited to see Terence. He showed us over the sweet old empty house where he lives and gave us tea. There is an enchanting walled garden at the side of his house, in it a great poinsettia-tree that they call here the "Christmas bush." It was aflame with the most glorious red star-flowers.

Terence does not mind me. He even seems fond of me. He says I am like some one he has known and been fond of. Out of the clear sky he told me he had an older sister, who married a rich American years ago. She died, leaving two children, a boy and a girl. The girl married not long ago. The boy has lived all over the world, and is a famous hydrographic engineer.

"He is still a boy to me," Terence explained, "but he must be over thirty. All I know of that branch of the family is from occasional letters from him. He is now in France, serving his country. I think it is my sister, his mother, you remind me of, though I was only a small boy when she went away."

Last night was Christmas Eve. Terence came and brought his other fiddle. Tink and the Commodore had piles of gifts for him. I wanted to give him a present, too, but I didn't dare. I was afraid he would take it as a liberty and disappear. He had promised to come for Christmas Eve, but we did not count on him. An army officer called just about dusk to bring some gifts, and the Commodore prevailed on him to come on downstairs to supper. Before we were half through, Clytemnestra gravely announced that Mr. Woode was upstairs.

The question was what to do with the handsome Major? If Terence saw a stranger he would fade away as all gossamer things do in the sunlight.

"I'll go up and speak to him," Tink said. "You may have to go out by the kitchen, Major; we can't have Terence frightened away."

Tink soon returned. She had actually told Terence of the stranger at the supper-table, and he was not a bit agitated. He had had his evening meal. "Hurry and go on up," she whispered to me; "he has presents for you."

I bolted upstairs. Will you listen to this? Terence had brought me two gifts. One, a jumbi-bead from a real jumbi-tree on Turk's Island, guaranteed and handed down as a talisman against all sorts of evil influence and bad luck. The other—

oh, listen well to this: a little old Confucius, benign and beautiful as Buddha. Oh, the wisdom and the patience and the kindness on his weather-beaten old Chinese face!

"There were two of these little figures," Terence told me. "They were brought from China by one of my ancestors two hundred years ago. The other one, the little Chinese wife of Confucius, my sister took with her to America. I was to keep the one, she the other. I give mine to you because you remind me of her somehow. She is long since dead. The little statue she took is no doubt lost."

He produced an old parchment book. "It is the wisdom of Confucius," he explained. He indicated the tiny, dignified figure, with a whimsical smile: "He wrote it."

Time suddenly turned back. I was comparing this old parchment book with the one from which you read to me, about Hui and the dish of rice, and the alleyway in which he lived and kept his mirth.

"Put them away quick!" Terence's ear was cocked toward the dining-room. "And do not speak of them to any one!"

Cheri-Moia climbed on Terence's shoulder and cuddled there, laying her grey face against his, softly purring. And I wasn't even permitted to thank him! Speaking of it—you-touch-'em-they-vanish-things! Terence is the human prototype of that mimosa-tree in the Far East, so sensitive it registers the approach of a strange human being ten miles off, and promptly closes its leaves!

My sense of humor was all that saved Terence from the scene he dreaded. There I sat, the old book slipped under the cushion of my chair, Confucius wrapped in the corner of a silly lace handkerchief, held dose in my hand, and the jumbi-bead slipping down, down in my bosom, its heathen surface pressing hard against my heart In the peremptory in structions from Terence to hide it quickly and say nothing, I had dropped it in the laces of my low-necked gown, and it promptly dived beyond reach of being rescued for the time being.

The British Major came up with Tink and the Commodore and departed, as befitted an officer of his rank, by the front door. Terence was too full of Christmas to realize he was meeting a stranger.

The new moon, a thin sickle of silver, hung over the harbor. Terence said the time was propitious. He would "lay the cards" for me. There were magic formulæ to be observed, the cards shuffled and double-shuffled, and the solemn moment came, and I must make a wish. Then Terence began his double-shuffling and dealing all over again. Now I must cut three times. He spread them all out. He pointed and beamed. Terence is a born giver of lovely presents.

"You are going to get your wish," he said. "You cut the very best card in the deck."

It was long past midnight; we had all gone to bed. But there was no sleep on me. I crept back to the sun-parlor. The smouldering cedar logs made the place smell like a temple, purified with sandalwood incense. Oh, the beauty and peace of the star-lighted night!

Hamilton, across the bay, lay like a city of enchantment, built of white icing, frail and quivering, reflected in the mirror of the harbor. It was as ethereal as a dream. Just then I heard music. Shall I ever hear music this side of Paradise so far removed from earth and things earthy? It was soft-stringed instruments, and throaty, mellow voices, in the distance sang:

"Oh, little town of Bethlehem, How still we see thee lie."

And this drifted into:

"While shepherds watched their flock by night, All seated on the ground."

I crept back to bed, but not to sleep. All night the island was vibrant with this angel serenade.

It was the Christmas waits. Bands of negro musicians sang and played from midnight until the dawn of Christmas morning of peace on earth, good-will to men. The night will always stay in my memory with Ariel music, played from waving bamboo stalks and from behind hibiscus hedges—with one specially celestial band stationed in the star that hangs over the garden just outside my window, the Venus star that uses the water-tank as her mirror.

Christmas Day is nearly over. The whole affair has been a festival of color. Now there are half a dozen rainbows arching around the heavens. The sun is setting. They are calling me to go home.

God save the King!

CHAPTER VII

Bermuda, December 31

WE are just back from Terence's party. We had promised to go, rain or shine. There was no shine all day; just a soggy drizzle that developed into a howling rain-storm when we Were halfway to "Cedarwoode."

It suddenly grew pitch dark. The carriage lights were no help at all. Tink drove straight ahead like one of these blindfolded mind-readers looking for the key a selected committee of citizens has hidden in one of the official record books at the city hall—straight ahead into the inky shadows of the cedar road leading to Terence's house. We went down into ruts and hung on the verge of gullies; the storm got madder and madder. The wind howled and the cedar boughs slapped us in the face. The carriage lamps suddenly conspired and went out altogether.

A faint pin-prick of light shone straight ahead Was Terence there? Was the house still there? Or had the party been postponed? We raised our voices with one accord and whooped. Then Terence whooped back and rushed out with a lantern and goloshes—or did he call them tarpaulins?

I grabbed a basket and a thermos bottle at Tink's direction, and fled to get the "collation" out of the weather. Terence gathered up the other basket and we reached the steps at the same time. Tink and the Commodore were hitching the horse.

"Wait a minute," Terence said, plunging into the candle-lighted gloom. He struck a match to the fire already laid. The next moment rosy, leaping flames lighted the two long drawing-rooms from one end to the other. And nobody was really wet at all. We ranged ourselves about the fire to let our tweeds get the moisture off. Nobody was caring what the weather did outside.

There stood the table all decked out like a bride in the centre of the splendid old cedar-raftered room. A white damask cloth came down to the floor. Terence's mother's forget-me-not and gold china was on it, and in the centre a willow-pattern stand held nuts, and around these was a whole regiment of "little red soldiers." Tink had red roses at her plate, and there were white ones at mine, and from these a chain of white-rose bridesmaids tripping around the four sides of the table.

And such silver! Old spoons, thin and fine as Terence's nose, and a wonderful old silver teapot done in repoussés of roses, and candlesticks of the same design with dunce-cap snuffers.

The fireplace, big as a New York bathroom, was built three feet up from the floor. The kettle was boiling. We opened our baskets and added our contribution to the party, creamed chicken still boiling hot in the thermos, and anchovy sandwiches, our fruit-cake and crystallized sweets. Tink had remembered that to-morrow would be Terence's birthday, and the Commodore brought him birthday greetings in a bottle.

Terence was so touched he could not eat. It was the first party in the house since the death of his mother, five years ago. He pointed to a little shrine at the far end of the other room. On it was her photograph, and under it a vase of white roses.

There was a whine at the door and a Scotch terrier, who spends all his free time with Terence, came bounding in joyfully, and a little later through the broken pane of the window a big black cat meowed and walked in and took her place gravely by the fire. It would not have surprised me at all if an angel-fish had been announced in a mother-of-pearl coach with a lobster-faced coachman on the box and a couple of crab outriders. Or for a red-bird to have come strutting in out of the wet night asking for a nip of Scotch to drink Terence's health!

Dear Terence, if you were my relative you would not be living alone in an empty house, cooking for yourself on a smoky oil-stove, with only the affection of a stray cat and the devotion of a dog that belongs to some one else, to cheer your dreary evenings.

Oh, stupid families that snap up old plate and go to law over Chippendale and satinwood, and leave unappraised as valueless a human heart so fine and rare as Terence's!

(A pang went through my heart I don't know why I should have thought of Bob. Bob has everything he wants and all the people he needs at his beck and call at Palmetto Grove.)

Terence handed me an old blue-velvet case containing two daguerreotypes. One picture was of a handsome, gallant youth in blue broadcloth, a splendid waist-coat and frills; the other was of a tea-rose-faced girl with curls over her ears.

"This is my father and mother," he said, "taken during their honeymoon. The next morning after they were married, my father observed something bright and shining under the bureau. He stooped to see what it was and found a new-minted silver coin, a one-and-a-half-cent piece. He handed it to his bride.

"'Keep this as a talisman,' he said, " 'and you will never be penniless, my dear.' "

Terence held out a tiny silver coin to me. "My mother kept it until her death," he said, "and it is your other Christmas gift from me."

Beloved, I could not say a word. Tears streamed down my face. And Terence, who is terrified at the prospect of a scene, darted off for his old violin. He stationed himself in the semi-darkness of the other room and played softly, "Believe me, if all those endearing young charms" to his mother's picture, and he kept on playing—

Orpheus built the walls of Thebes by the sound of his lute.

". . . For an ye heard a music like they are building still, Seeing the city is built To music: Therefore never built at all, And therefore built forever."

Tink's lovely face was illumined by the firelight. The Commodore, in a great chair in the corner, blew meditative smoke-rings, his eyes closed. The first notes of Moszkowski's exquisite old "Gavotte" came tripping across the polished floor.

"It's a party," Tink whispered. "People are coming in." I felt it too.

And they continued to arrive, more guests with every note. Across the years they were conjured back by the spell of a fiddle, older than the oldest memory of them all.

It was a real-lace party. The room was full of dying lilies-of-the-valley and tulle skirts on darling ladies that waltzed with splendidly romantic-looking young men, to the seductive strains of "The Beautiful Blue Danube."

"The air is heavy with proposals," Tink whispered to me, "and there are more of them engaged this minute than will ever be married."

"How could they have ended life," I asked her, "as anybody's staid and sedate white-headed old grandparents? They must pass the time in Paradise whooping over the idea that they died of old age!"

Tink touched me, then put her finger to her lips. In the twilight of the other room Terence's violin coaxed and pleaded with a familiar lovely air that one minute he could catch, only to lose it the next.

"It's your Lantern of Love," Tink told me. "Go on in there and sing it for him."

I crept to where Terence stood in the shadows and started to sing. He caught the air and played it with exquisite sympathy.

Amber and coral and jade! After all these years I felt the miracle of my childhood, trying to reach me! Oh, to be enfolded in those colors once more! The old feeling of crystal light! . . . It faded away.

Terence, his rapt old face close to the sobbing violin, played on; gradually the sadness fell away; the melody soared to triumphal heights.

"Sing," he begged. "Keep on."

"I cannot," I replied. "The end has not been given to me."

"It will be," his voice was prophetic I felt that the end of the song was hidden in the heart of the bubble of crystal light, in the amber and coral and jade of my childhood.

Would that old miracle ever enfold me again?

The fire was now only a great bed of glowing coals. We gathered close around the hearth. Terence joined us. The Magic Carpet had called for the guests and spirited them away.

"It's the weirdest, most wonderful evening of my life, Terence," Tink said; "these rooms are not empty, but furnished; I feel it, and full of people."

The black cat rubbed against Terence's knees and hunched her back. The candles were guttering almost out The last log was crumbling to ashes. It was nine o'clock. Time to go home.

Oh, Terence, what a love of a party!

CHAPTER VIII

On board S.S. Carlotta, January 4, 1918

TERENCE came before breakfast to say good-bye, and to bring me a farewell bouquet of "little red soldiers" and white roses.

"He's out there on the steps, waiting to have a word with you," Tink came to tell me. "He did not ask for us."

I carried Confucius out with me. "See," I said, "your gift goes with me as a personal companion. I shall take him with me everywhere I go. The jumbibead is his black slave." I showed him Confucius' stateroom in my purse, and the jumbi's quarters. I told him I would take the old Chinese book wherever I went I need both philosophy and wisdom.

The little silver coin I showed him, in a separate compartment in my purse. "I need luck, too—"

Terence did not wish to be reminded of his gifts. He was planning a quick exit, but something was on his mind.

"If by any chance"—he got it out at last—"you ever happen to see anything in the newspapers, about my nephew who is in France, I want to ask that you will take the trouble to send it to me." He gave me a slip of paper on which he had written his nephew's name, Stephen Abercrombie, his division and company. I put it away, making him the promise.

"Sometimes their photographs are published in the Sunday papers," he said. "I don't know my sister's son, but—I have often wished—"

Terence was gone.

The trip down was bad enough, but returning has been beyond all words. The boat has been under the surface as much as above it, and a storm has raged for three days. The Gulf Stream was an inferno. My stateroom leaked; it was freezing cold; rats squealed and fought under the berth. No one could eat anything. I can stand my own discomfort; but the physical suffering of the others has been unbearable. The walls are like tissue-paper.

It is comparatively quiet to-day, but we have run into a blizzard; snow and sleet and an icy wind.

The only time I have been able to sleep was a little while last night. I had a curious dream that did not seem to be a dream at all.

The stateroom faded away. The chilly air grew soft and warm. I stood on the pebbly beach of a stream and two familiar figures came in a sampan which I stepped aboard and was rowed to the other side; then I got out and went up a path I re-membered and to a gate, and there you stood with hands outstretched to welcome me. And I put both my hands in yours and we went up the hill together. Our feet seemed not to be touching the ground. My sensation was wings. Soul, heart, body, just fluttering, happy, wings. I do not know the words in which to record the wordless speech of our tryst. My five mortal senses seemed to have vanished because there was no longer any need of their crude offices.

Once on a day when I was poorest I went to an exhibition of sculpture at a Fifth Avenue jeweller's. There was one piece, done by an Italian sculptor, I shall never forget. It was two exquisitely virginal nude figures, a man and a woman; each aloof and alone. The one point of contact was the heads, lost in the swirl of her hair. Only a great poet could have expressed the idea of spiritual oneness so simply, so eloquently. The title of the piece was "Unity."

You and I sat under the ancient cedar-tree in the Japanese garden—And there was not two of us, but one—And suddenly the light of the dream, if dream it was, shifted. The Japanese garden seemed somehow to be Terence's garden at "Cedar-woode." And this gradually faded and merged into another garden, full of spring flowers, wistaria and jonquils and "bridal-wreath" bushes of white. It was the old garden of my childhood at Palmetto Grove. And Bob was in it, and Terence, and you and I were there.

"All three gardens belong together, can't you feel it?" I was asking you.

Grey fog was everywhere; and the sound of the sea dashing against a shore; the wind was blowing against a tarpaulin. I smelled wood smoke from a driftwood fire, across which you sat, smoking.

Then I woke up.

The ship was quiet. We were in the harbor at New York, and a blinding snowstorm blanketed the world. A buffalo-nosed tug was trying to pilot us to the wharf.

CHAPTER IX

New York, January 7, 1918

I WAS trying to decide where Confucius would like to live in my room. He did not like the desk; I felt that strongly. And even more so I felt that he would be out of place on the piano.

Just then Yuki arrived with the Japanese garden. He has taken great care of it. There is a new plot of fresh green grass on the hillside. The change has helped the goldfish. Even the lacquer on the old red bridge has a new sheen on it

Yuki's round eyes rested on Confucius, then wandered back to the garden.

"His honorable house, see?" he pointed to the tiny thatched house just this side of the path that leads to our ancient cedar-tree.

His house! Of course. Now Confucius lives on his own honorable estate which occupies a table to itself before a window that commands a view of Saint-Gaudens's "Diana," on the Madison Square Garden.

"Solemn is the son of Heaven," but satisfied. I feel it.

And my spirit, too, is steeped in great content.

I went out in the storm to-day to get a pair of rubbers, and came back without the rubbers, but with a pot of blue hyacinths. I read the old book Terence gave me. I need the wisdom of Confucius.

This is where I opened it:

The Master liked to talk of poetry, history, and the upkeep of courtesy. Of all these was he fond of talking.

The Master said: "Courtesy, courtesy," is the cry; but are jade and silk the whole of courtesy? "Harmony, harmony," is the cry; but are bells and drums the whole of harmony?

I love the high-sounding stateliness of Confucius. It is like ceremonial music; echoes that come from some far-off court of the spirit—where "the upkeep of courtesy" is practiced.

January 14

BILLS are piling up, waiting to have a word with me. The tiny balance I had in the bank may be already overdrawn. I don't remember about that last check I drew.

I've got to sing, sing, sing, to catch up. But my vacation has made me feel equal to anything.

I must get to work at once.

January 28

WHERE do these people come from who keep up the Dixie societies in New York? They are strangers to me, yet they hire me to sing because I come from Mississippi.

The Kentucky breakfasts are still going on, and the Missouri luncheons and all the dull club meetings that I hoped never to be a part of again. I am on their programmes once more, and glad to get their checks.

Palozzi heard me sing at one of these affairs, and waited to speak to me. He is more enthusiastic than ever about my voice. He says he has never heard a contralto that entranced him so. He vows I can yet make the Metropolitan Opera if I will but begin my lessons again. He woke all my old ambitions to be a great singer. I promised I would come back to him.

I shall have to keep up my outside work in order to afford him and the accompanist.

He declares I can make a fortune doing phonograph records.

He scolded me for throwing away my golden throat on these deaf nobodies, until I was in the seventh heaven of ambition and pride.

Rollins is making me a lot of new and beautiful clothes.

"I will teach you to sing"—Palozzi walked up and down the floor excitedly—"as God's favorite angel in heaven must sing!"

Is there anything more beautiful, I wonder (sitting alone here in my eagle nest of a room), than a blue hyacinth against a window, on the other side of which is a swirling snowstorm.

I shall be a great artiste yet, with the world at my feet!—But I shall sing only for—you.

CHAPTER X

New York, November, 1918

MY LOVE:

GOOD-BYE. You are not for the likes of me. Nor is there anything else for me. I am a failure.

I cannot sing, but I can see, clearly at last. See what the ending would be if I could keep on, as I have been trying to all these years. But I cannot keep on.

I am sick in body and in soul. And tired. My thumbs are down to Fate. I am beaten, and I know it

It is not hard to leave New York. I have wanted to stay here because somehow it seemed that here was my audience, my public, and here somehow I seem nearer you. The few times I have seen you have been in New York. I have clung to the dream that here our paths would some day converge.

But to-night I see clearly. You were only the hero of my dream of the love that might be, and you dissolve into thin air and nothingness, as my dream of being a great singer fades into nothingness.

The year has been a complete failure. My voice is quite gone, and you are—gone; even the Japanese garden where once I met you in my dreams is gone. The day I came home ill, a week before I was to sing for the Metropolitan Committee, I found the garden on the floor where the wind had blown it off the table, a shapeless mass. The ancient gnarled old cedar-tree was blasted and splintered as if lightning had struck it Out of the wreckage Confucius alone emerged with a charmed life, untouched.

Perhaps it is better that it should be blown away with the rest of my dreams and hopes.

Good-bye, I am tired and thirty. And the tides have carried you away from me—forever. The lantern of my love seems to have been lighted in vain.

Mississippi—you will not be passing down that way, I know. Palmetto Grove Plantation is "off the main line" in every sense of progress and relation to life.

Good-bye, my Love.

CHAPTER XI

(***News item from the Cottonport, Mississippi, Bulletin November** 30, 1918*)
Miss DIANA CAMERON, who has won fame and fortune as a singer in New York, passed through Cottonport yesterday, on her way to Palmetto Grove Plantation to visit her uncle, Robert Cameron, Esq.

This is Miss Cameron's first visit to her old home since she went to New York nearly twelve years ago, to embark on a career that has brought her recognition as one of the great artistes of the Musical World.

Miss Cameron's marvellous voice is an inheritance from an Italian ancestress, who in her generation had the world at her feet, and she bids fair to transcend the talent, to surpass the triumphs, of her distinguished great-grandmother.

I'll keep the clipping always as a joke.

The only person who spoke to me in Cottonport was an old man at the livery stable, who spat tobacco-juice and asked me if I war n't Bob Cameron's niece. I replied that I was, and asked if I could engage a team to drive me down to Palmetto Grove.

He spat again and said he thought not: that I might be able to make some arrangement to go with the mail-rider in his sulky.

I'll go through life wondering if it were the old man in the livery stable who gave me the "write-up."

PART III

MISSISSIPPI

Not by running out of yourself after it comes the love which lasts a thousand years..., Remain steadfast knowing each prisoner has to endure in patience till the season of his liberation.... When the love comes which is for you it will turn the lock easily and loose your chains.

CARPENTER

CHAPTER I

Palmetto Grove Plantation January, 1919

PALMETTO GROVE is like a negro who, knowing nothing of time, is left untouched by it; from whom no toll is taken in grey hairs and wrinkles.

The plantation is just as it was twelve years ago, but the house somehow seems to have settled down, to have spread out, like a rambler rose fallen from its support The whole place seems infinitely more desolate, set in these unending fields of dead cotton-stalks, than it used to be.

As far as the eye can reach dead cotton-stalks, brown in a sea of chocolate mud. The trees are leafless, and the long grey moss that waves from every branch gives me the melancholy feeling one gets passing a house on the door of which are funeral ribbons.

The mud cuts the plantation off from any communication with the outside world. I rode through twenty miles of it with the mail-rider in his springless sulky cart The livery-stable man at Cottonport (the nearest town and railway station) steadily refused to send any sort of team or car out to pull through such glue as plantation roads are now. The mail-rider brings the mail twice a week to the Deer-Lick store three miles below Palmetto Grove.

We reached the plantation, after five hours, late in the afternoon in the face of an east wind and lowering grey clouds. The tombstones in the little graveyard behind the garden were the first thing I saw as we turned into the plantation gate. Not a sound on the place, not a human being in sight. The mail-rider said the negroes were huddled up in their cabins out of the cold.

Bob came to the gate to help me out, little dreaming who it was. He gathered me to him with the same love that kissed me good-bye twelve years ago. His joy at seeing me was pitiful.

"You haven't written very often these last five years," he said, as we went into the house together. "But I have all your postcards, sister."

"Neither have you written very often, Bob," I replied.

He pointed to his right hand. It is twisted and bent and crushed out of all shape.

"It's nothing," he declared, "but rheumatism and malaria and a cypress-tree that fell on me. Nothing to worry over or to mention to you, but it curtailed my output as a correspondent."

He changed the subject, explaining that he had lived alone so long now that he was afraid I'd find it pretty rough and not want to stay long with him.

The house is so changed I would never have recognized it. There is no longer a drawing-room. The long beautiful room I remember as a child, with its gilt mirrors, its rosewood and blue satin furniture, the portraits on the walls reflected in the mirror of the polished floor, the whole smelling of beeswax and rose potpourri from the old Chinese jar, is gone. The door was locked when I tried it. Bob had passed into the room across the hall with my bag. The mail-rider was at his heels giving him local news of the high water, and what So-and-So thought about the prospect of an overflow. They did not miss me.

The bareness of the place, its openness, was strangely unfamiliar. I noticed a barrel at the far end of the hall, and walked to see what it held that it should be in such a place.

My hand was vigorously pecked by a sitting hen. In the wide-open double doors beyond loomed a huge and billowy figure, a negro woman, with her hands on her hips, in her mouth a corncob pipe, the fumes of which sickened me.

"Who are you?" I demanded, for in the old days negroes of her type stuck to field work and lived in the far quarters, away from the servants of the plantation house.

"Ise Mandy," she challenged my tone with her own. "Doan skeer dat hin off. De rats eats de aigs up, so I sot her in heah ter git her away frum' em. She oughter hatch now in a couple ur weeks or so."

"Take that pipe out of your mouth," I commanded. She turned and waddled out, still puffing it serenely. Bob, coming up, read the expression on my face.

"She's better than nothing," he apologized, "and niggers ain't what they used to be, honey."

He put his arms about me, and drew me into the room that is now his sitting-room, bedroom, and office. The mail-rider had gone out to see about putting his cart up for the night. Bob put his hands on my shoulders and drew me to the fading light at the window.

"Let me have a look at you"—he put on his glasses; "let me see if being a great and famous opera singer has changed you very much."

Poor old bleary blue eyes. They surveyed me with tenderness and pride and adulation. The irony of the moment was almost too much for me. I realized for the first time that however much of a failure I may have been in New York, on Palmetto Grove Plantation I was to be accepted as a great artiste, who has had the world at her feet.

Bob patted my hair and lifted my chin just as he used to do.

"If there are ghosts," he said, "I know one will walk to-night up through the garden. The ghost of the Italian girl, your great-grandmother, who gave up a career for love, to die and to be buried here." His eyes followed mine beyond the garden to the white headstones. "Maybe she will walk to-night to see you who caught her mantle, who inherited her gift. She will come to hear you sing, eh? And—and"—he bent nearer "and you look—I swear I never saw the resemblance before—like that old portrait of her up there. See?"

He marched me under the portrait to compare me with the wilful, lovely, glowing woman who looked down from the tarnished gold frame.

"I had to bring all the portraits in here," he said, "when I turned the old draw-ing-room into a commissary."

The mail-rider entered and produced Bob's mail. This left me alone with the portrait. I was glad to escape Bob's searching, near-sighted eyes. I stood looking up at the Florentine girl. I have her tawny, red-streaked hair, her throat—

"She gave up a great career, they say"—Bob turned back to refresh my memory of the family history—"for love, and only lived two years. It was very sad."

The mail-rider's "You don't say!" as he came over to have a look at the lady, made me walk to the window to conceal my emotion.

And there, on the other side of the garden, she was buried. I was thinking how infinitely sadder my own story was. The Florentine girl had a voice; she had a great love. I stood in the twilight envying her, dead, buried in these mud flats, because her brief career held both life and love.

CHAPTER II

THE plantation seemed desolate enough in the twilight when I arrived, but the first night was infinitely worse. I've never seen, never felt such blackness. It is like being alone on a desert island a thousand miles from mainland. I walked down to the river in the twilight. It is like a sluggish stream of bad coffee. But far underneath I could almost fancy I heard it growl.

I am afraid of this stillness, this blackness, this sinister stream of death that menaces, threatens, that may rise in a night and sweep us all away.

The stillness settled down over the place with the coming of night, but the night itself was vocal with noises that frightened me. Rats overhead scampered and squealed; a melancholy dog howled on the front gallery the night long; from the cedars in the garden came the hooting of screech owls, weird, and as insistent as the steady dropping of water; from the far-off cypress-trees the hoot owls of my child-hood still called: "I co-oks fer my-se'f; who co-oks fer you-all?" and the last touch in this orchestra of discord was a badly played accordion, to which a high-pitched, metallic voice sang over and over, and yet over again:

"Je-sus, feed us on bread and wine— Je-sus, feed us on bread and wine— Je-sus, feed us on bread and wine"—

Just the one line over and over, until I felt my overstrained nerves must give way. I lay sleepless, wide-eyed, until the grey dawn came, bringing another lowering, east-windy, threatening winter day.

"But I have no dogs now, sister," Bob replied to my question at breakfast. "The niggers all keep hound-dogs to hunt' possums. It must have been one of them you heard howling. Mandy's music didn't keep you awake, did it? She lives in the cabin out in the back yard.

"You'll get used to these country noises in a night or two.... But I warn you— plantation life isn't what it used to be. Everybody's moved away from around here. I gladly welcome the mail-rider when he comes to spend the night. So you can imagine what an angel from heaven you seem like, descending on me like this.

"Stay with me a little while, kitten."

CHAPTER III

Palmetto Grove Plantation January, 1919

BOB looks much older, his hair is quite white, his gout has not improved with age, and he does not see well even with his glasses. I am almost glad of this, for he cannot see how white and thin I am, nor the despair in the "two sad grey eyes" that greet me every time I look into the mirror.

I have not told him my story, nor why I suddenly changed my plans and came home to him. He knows I was ill with my throat.

I told him I came hoping the change of air would benefit it. My throat, that refused to yield to the treatment of the New York specialist, is entirely healed I feel that I could sing now if I had the heart to do it. But my disappointment at not being able to sing for the Metropolitan Committee at the time appointed weighs heavily upon me.

The situation here is depressing and hopeless enough in all truth. New York, even in its worst stages of discouragement, was never like this. There one always has the chance of the tide turning; here, one knows, things will always be the same.

There is a tide of life in New York, even if one may not be moving with the current; here one is caught in a backwater that deadens and stupefies.

Outwardly the place is very much as it was twelve years ago, but only outwardly. It reminds me of a bridge from which all the underpinning has gone; of a house, gutted by fire, but presenting the same front to the world All the old servants I remember are dead and gone. I miss Mammy Linda more than any one.

Bob has felt the futility of trying to train the field hands into anything resembling house servants. Instead of Mandy adjusting herself to his habits, he has had to accept and make the best of her ways.

There is scarcely a pane of glass left in any window in the house; the blinds are either off or without catches to keep them closed. There is only one fireplace that does not smoke; this is in the room Bob occupies. My own room upstairs is as open as a sleeping-porch. There is no way of heating it, with the top of the chimney blown off. Bob says there is not a negro on the place who could repair it, and that the nearest place we could get the necessary bricks is Cottonport. He makes some excuse, equally as shiftless, when I remind him that the doors are sagging or completely down.

"There's no use trying to do anything now, sister," he argues, "with the river rising every day; any morning we may wake up with it in the house. That's why I had all the furniture carried to the attic eight years ago when we had the big overflow. No use to invite disaster by ignoring the river. It's rising, honey."

I know it is rising. I can see it, and hear it, and feel it. It is like some mud-colored beast of the jungle this river that rushes by, and creeps nearer toward the house every night.

I know its history of old. How many a time it has licked out a tongue and gathered in a whole plantation, houses, people, and all; then, like the harlot in the Bible, wiping her mouth, declaring, "I have done nothing," it flows tranquilly on perhaps for another ten years or so. It is like living on the edge of a live volcano, yet Bob takes his chances with an equanimity I cannot understand.

The river is already over the low places in the fields. The roads are impassable. Everything, everywhere, is waterlogged. The old flower garden is a morass. I have made only one attempt to walk in it. It is a tangle of shrubbery, dead leaves, desolation. The graveyard beyond is covered by a winding sheet of yellow water.

It is all depressing beyond words. The stark-naked flatness of these unending cotton-fields with their picked brown stalks; the mud, the negroes, the mules—mules everywhere, around the house, and even under it—are getting on my nerves. There is no beauty or peace outside the house or within it.

The negroes take advantage of the high water to have their everlasting business talks with Bob. Owing to the scarcity of labor every planter is moving heaven and earth, offering every inducement he can put forth to keep the negroes for next year's crop.

The commissary, when I was a child, stood in the yard far away from the house. Bob has converted the old drawing-room into the storehouse where he keeps the plantation supplies. There is an unending stream of negroes at the back door always waiting to get overalls or snuff or pills. A negro will spend his last cent for medicine. The more nauseous the better he likes it.

I tried to reason with Bob about the disorder of it all, tried to find out if he could not dispense with the commissary altogether. He is as patient as ever.

"Sister," he said, "niggers are black pearls of great price these days. I have to keep the supplies they want in order to hold my labor. One more year of good prices for cotton and I'll be out of the woods. Niggers are niggers, just as mules are mules, and so long as cotton is raised here in the delta we can't do without either. Don't skeer my niggers off, honey."

Mandy in the kitchen has reigned here for five years, and she resents me as an intruder. Bob can't see the dust, the dirt, the waste that is going on. She cooks atrociously. Her god is grease. Everything is grease-soaked and loggy. Her breakfast menu is fried onions and grits, greasy biscuit, and atrocious coffee. Dinner is but another variation of food steeped in grease; also supper. Yet she in Bob's eyes is better than nobody. She has a peg-legged kitchen boy to assist her. His name is Isaiah. Bob calls him Isaiah, Hosea, Jeremiah, or Jonah, and he answers to them all. He should be doing all the housework, but Bob implored me not to meddle when I started to suggest training the boy. Mandy has asked me several times "how long I'm gwine stay." At first she thought I was rich, coming from New York. Now I think she suspects the truth, which is more than Bob does.

The front gallery is twenty feet long. Bob's buggy is stored on one end of it for the winter and until danger of high water is over; his various saddles and riding equipment occupy the other end. I walk up and down this a million times a day, for after Mandy's cooking I must have exercise, to stay awake. It is most important to stay awake in the afternoon. The nights are too hideous to take any chances that might keep one awake. The person who wrote that his idea of hell was always three o'clock in the afternoon must have spent a winter on a cotton plantation.

There is nothing to read but Bob's old standbys, the Bible, or Virgil, Horace, Homer in the original (which is beyond me), and a moderately modern translation of Marcus Aurelius. Bob does not know where the books from the library were stored. Somewhere in the attic, he thinks, above the water-line!

I have been writing some business letters for Bob. Without knowing it he has answered any request I might have made to him about money, but that means he still owes many thousands; he is staving his last few creditors off until the end of the year. He has barely enough money in the bank to pay his negroes the wages they demand. All he asks of Heaven this year is, no boll weevil, and for his creditors to be patient a little longer with him.

Poor old Bob! Harassed as he has always been about money, no wonder he has grown blind to everything but cotton, since it alone represents freedom to him; deaf to every voice but that of a nigger and a mule, the magicians that can produce it for him. Bob does not know that his gout is largely the result of Mandy's cooking: Neither does he realize that rust and decay have spread all over the place. Just so the ditches are draining the cotton-fields, just so the niggers are ploughing and planting, fertilizing or cozening the cotton-land, nothing else matters. "Cotton will bring a high price this fall" is the eternal will-o'-the-wisp of the South. It is this illusion that blinds Bob to everything else.

But how can I blame Bob for his lack of progress when I have returned with my foot in the same place from which I started, or Mandy in the kitchen for her inefficiency when I have made no progress myself? I have just petered out, a failure. More than a failure, for I am not needed any more here on the plantation than I was in New York. Bob would be unconsciously relieved to-morrow if I left, and Mandy, too, could then retire from the defensive and probably be more energetic with the little mind she has, diverted from speculating on what arguments she can use next to thwart my suggestions about her housekeeping.

The river is all over the garden now and crawling up to the steps.

We have had no mail since I came, nor any connection at all with the outside world.

Only grease, grease, grease, three times a day, and negroes asking for "two-bits wuth of snuff" or pills—and a wind that whines all day and night—and the river creeping nearer every night.

CHAPTER IV

Palmetto Grove Plantation February

THE river has risen steadily. A cold drizzle set in ten days ago and has kept up; the wind whines night and day like a suck-egg hound. The house is open as the barn, and even Bob's fireplace now smokes.

This is the kind of cold that penetrates to one's very bones. There is no getting away from it Mandy's cooking is worse than ever. With the river overflowing yard and garden and everywhere, with no possible place to take exercise, she persists in frying her grease-soaked fritters, for supper. I have to eat her heavily spiced, too-sweet molasses pudding for dinner, or go hungry. The days are long enough in all truth, but the nights are Esquimaux!

My room is too cold to sit in. No such thing as an oil-stove has ever been heard of here. Bob's gout is very bad. The hen sitting in the hall is trying to leave her barrel nest. Mandy is determined that she shall not until the eggs are hatched. The first sitting was eaten by a hound.

The clouds have hung heavier and lower than ever to-day. Bob could not stand on his foot. The negroes, grown restless and tired of their cabins, make every possible excuse to come here to see Bob, to get supplies. I offered to give the first negro what he wanted out of the commissary this morning. I kept it up all day. Pills and snuff were the commodities for which they came. Toward night I suggested to Bob that I would cook something for his supper. The idea annoyed him.

"Mandy's in there to cook," he said. "She's old and cranky, but she's somebody in the kitchen. Keep out of her way, sister." I think he saw the tears in my eyes. "You won't be here long, honey," he continued. "You don't realize how easy it is to lose a cook, nor how hard it is to get another one. Niggers are all alike these days."

He sighed. "If cotton brings a good price this year—"

He lighted his pipe and lay back, smoking, his eyes closed. He had already forgotten Mandy and me. It was very quiet in the twilight. The rats in the ceiling had already begun their night's revels. As soon as the candle was lighted the bats would be coming in for the night. Every night I get the horrors over the bats. They dart in out of the darkness toward my candle as I start upstairs. Sometimes their wings brush my face.

Night, itself, is a black bat on Palmetto Grove!

One of the negroes came in with a sack of mail just before supper. He had paddled down to the Deer Lick store in a dug-out, and they had sent three weeks' accumulation of mail by him. There were several copies of the **Cottonport Bulletin,** for Bob, and the **Southern Farmer,** a few circulars. Everything else was for me, forwarded from New York. The little clerk at the hotel wrote a friendly note to say that many telephone calls came for my address, but that she had not given it. She forwarded these telegrams and the letters. She hoped I was well again and would soon be coming back.

One of the telegrams was from Timothy from Seattle. He has been up in Manitoba making a road over a mountain that has defied every engineer so far.

Job done. Arrive New York Friday night. Dine with me at the Turk's. I deserve it.

Timothy must have gone straight from the train expecting me to meet him in a quiet little Turkish place where there is good food and no music, and I was not there or anywhere that he could find me.

And nobody to tell him how fine a thing it is to build a road where no road has been, to swing a bridge where there was no crossing!

And there were wires and' phone calls from Crœsus. Christmas letters and cards from far and near, among these a card from little Aline, Jinny Foster's cripple child. And the rest are all bills.

Bills from Palozzi for half a dozen lessons, bills from the accompanist, and a bill that frightens me from the specialist who treated my throat and who infected it. I did not dream the serum he used was so expensive. There is another, a separate bill for the serum—and two letters from Rollins, my dressmaker, imploring me to pay her what I owe her, that her need of money is desperate. Another special delivery from her, dated a week later. Can I not let her have the money before the first? It is dated nearly a month ago. I tried to add up what I owe them all. It is eight hundred dollars. All the money I have in the world is eight dollars and seventy-five cents.

"Calling you to come back to New York, kitten?" Bob was studying my face with tender pride. "I was afraid they wouldn't let me keep you long."

"Whin is you gwine back?" Mandy asked familiarly from the door, which she had just opened to tell us to come to supper. "You is gwine back soon, ain't yer?"

"Nice to hear from so many of your friends." Bob put his arm around my shoulder. We went down the dark, open hall together to the cold dining-room. I could not eat.

"Homesick for New York," Bob rallied me. "I couldn't expect you to put up with me and Mandy long."

I pretended I had to go back to get my handkerchief, and then I crept on up to my little room under the eaves. Better the rain and the wind and the bats than that Bob should suspect the truth!

CHAPTER V

THERE was no spirit left in me as I climbed the stairs blue and chattering with the cold. The sullen, soggy day had turned into a snarling, black night. The chilly drizzle of the past month was now an icy downpour, The river growled and roared and threatened. The whole house was heavy with the fog from it, everything damp and mildewed. My room seemed much colder than downstairs. A fire would have been a comfort, but a fire was out of the question. The wind howled down the chimney and hunted a broken window-pane, like a restless dog, to get out again, The guttering candle only made the gloom outside its radius blacker.

I unplaited and started to brush my hair. It fell like a bronze shower rippling and eddying to my knees. The mirror was blotted out by the fog. I rubbed it off with a handkerchief and leaned closer to survey my face. It is no longer white and thin, but glowing with health. The high tide of life surges through my veins, even as, in place of my old spirit, despair stalks.

My trunks have not been brought from Cotton-port, because of the high water.

I have no warm clothes to offset the lack of a fire. To-night I was not sleepy, and yet I could not sit up in the cold. Even if I had anything to read, the candle blowing in the wind was not light enough to read by. My teeth were chattering, my lips blue. I dreaded the night before me. My heart was like a lump of ice. I was hungry and cold and lonely. I slipped on a silk dressing-gown over my thin lace nightdress and crept between the damp, cold sheets, muttering some sort of pagan prayer for oblivion.

Instead of oblivion, the wind blew me a steady stream of guests. They started to arrive when I began to think of people who could help me get away from Palmetto Grove, away from the slovenliness, the inanity, the futility it represents. Back to the tide of life where there is at least a fighting chance to make a living.

From any one of half a dozen women who consider themselves my friend I could borrow enough to get back to New York. I have loaned money to most of them between the dates of their allowance checks, but borrowing from them, with no security, on the lucky chance of being able to pay back, was another matter. I could not do it.

A terrific gust of wind blew open the blind and Crœsus himself stepped into the room. Crœsus had come to talk common sense. I must listen to him. Not only for myself.

Crœsus began with Bob. Poor old Bob's financial difficulties of so many years' standing would be wiped out, his debts paid. Crœsus could make it possible for Bob to succeed to-morrow. Bob would not have to wait until next fall, nor be dependent on the certain fluctuations of an always uncertain, nervous, or irregular cotton market. Bob could take his gout on to Hot Springs and have all the poison of Mandy's atrocious cooking boiled out of him, and return rejuvenated, to go on with the crop. The trip would give him new ideas about farming, show him that the old order is changing for a new and better one, in which a planter is not necessarily dependent on the vagaries of mules and niggers to get his cotton produced. Bob in an automobile, with tractors and cotton-pickers and all the new aids to agriculture, was the first miracle Crœsus showed me his money could perform.

Crœsus swung open a great grilled iron gate for me. I saw the estate that was mine if I would take it from him. It was set in the beauty of velvet lawns and walks winding among flowers, with a lake in the distance, a swan floating from lily-pad to lily-pad. There stood my own dream orchard of ancient apple-trees in bloom, and a house peaceful and still with well-ordered servants. Beauty enfolded me, tranquillity, and the leisure to cultivate my voice, untroubled by the necessity of hacking it out for daily bread.

The golden dream opened slowly, like a lotos-flower. I left my great estate for a tiny chintz-hung cottage, opening into a lovesome garden. The grand servants were left behind; now only one simple maid attended to everything, but she too was a specialist in peace. The house was still and quiet I could sing to my heart's content And I was unbedevilled by the thoughts of money and bills that I was unable to pay. Nothing menacing or unlovely in life could ever come near me again behind the defense of Crœsus' money.

My bare feet touched the cold cotton sheets, my chin was brushed by the harsh patchwork quilt, the rain blew in through the broken window-panes. The wind whirled a shower of soot down the chimney, over my bed.

Crœsus and all he offered stood waiting for my answer. I asked five minutes to consider the proposition. And in these I asked myself once more what was the use of my chasing will-o'-the-wisps any longer.

I faced the truth, the sheer idiocy of my ambitions. The grand-opera objective is forever out of the question. And if I go back to my old work, singing anywhere and everywhere, there is the possibility of making a living a little while longer, but will it not in the end come to the same *impasse* in which I find myself now? Any time my voice may go, any time a dearth of work means what I face now. And the end—

Crœsus clicked his ponderous gold watch to remind me the time was up. Reason counselled there was only one answer to give him: the answer every failure sooner or later has to give to the practical person who has got on in the world. I was spent and tired of the struggle. Crœsus knew what my answer must be, as all men of his type know. I looked up to tell him.

There he stood, Crœsus the multi-millionaire, with his long, yellow teeth showing in his dull, long face that looked somehow more wolfish than ever, even as he smiled encouragement for my wisdom at last. Quick as a flash every inducement that his money had offered rolled back, like a panorama of a battle scene, reversed on a screen.

Poor old Bob got everything just as I saw he did, but always Crœsus' trademark was stamped on it, "Made by Crœsus." And the sight was as if I saw Bob in the stripes of servitude. No longer could he boast of keeping things under his feet. He was under the foot of Crœsus.

Instead of freedom, Crœsus would fasten real chains on Bob's spirit. Now, even ridden as Bob is by debt, he still has his high hopes of paying out. Mandy may be a cross in the kitchen, but in Bob's mind she has no more reality than the hen sitting in the barrel in the hall. Niggers and mules are but difficulties in the day's work. The game Bob plays is keeping them in their place.

Bob turned his back on Crœsus and petted his gouty toe. Not one of his troubles was for sale to such a bidder. Freedom from such a giver would be no freedom to him.

The screen rolled back. My country estate came on again, with everything as it was before, but this time I saw myself walking along the quiet paths by the pellucid lake, sitting in the dream orchard, steeping my soul in indolence while some great artiste sang—but I was never alone. Crœsus went with me, as he did with Bob, and again he spoiled the picture.

When I would escape, I was followed by his ghost that leered at me for my dishonesty. I was taking all and giving nothing. The quiet little chintz-hung cottage had no charm with Crœsus there. Deep down within me I saw myself ashamed of the man I had married for his money. I was sick to the soul with the feeling that I had married beneath myself, and there was no worldly pride in the assessment.

No! No!! No!!!

Not for all the kingdoms of this world could I consent either to give up my troubles to Crœsus!

The soot whirred down the chimney before the mighty gust of wind that picked old Crœsus up by the nape of the neck and disappeared with him, carrying the window-sash with it.

Oh, how the wind blew! A tree crashed down somewhere in the garden. Hound-dogs howled dismally sheltered on the front gallery. I had to hold tightly to the covers, for the wind's path was directly across the bed as it came in the window and flew up the chimney or blew backward down the chimney on its way to the window.

The real storm began with the lightning and thunder. My room was little better than being out of doors, for the sashless windows, with the open blinds, let all the tempest in. Through the window the lightning came hurtling, to play pranks with the mirror. I could see the zigzag characters reflected in the glass, then, splintering, the lightning ran its deadly fingers over the floor and around the wall, like some uncanny witch feeling to see if the place had been well dusted. The lightning seemed to take a catlike joy in tormenting its victim; it played like a kitten around my room before signalling the thunder to come on with its barrage. Peal after peal it came, shaking the house to its very foundations. It was as if Titans were fighting over an eggshell structure.

I could hear the river booming against its banks, and now and then distinguish the sound of a willow-tree swished up by its roots and sucked into the current.

The flashes of lightning grew more frequent, but less terrifying, and the thunder subsided to a low, persistent rumble. Now it was as if the lightning had spent its anger, and was trying to restore its victim. For the electricity came as a shower; a current turned on from some super-machine that was scattering a restorative instead of a destroyer. The very air was charged and vibrant with a new quality.

The storm was not gone; it still raged, but with a fresh objective. To my disordered fancy the heavens seemed trying to waken the sleeping earth—and I alone had been quickened out of all possible rest.

It was on this current of lightning that Timothy came to bear me company. Timothy, blond as a young sun-god with his warm youth and pulsing strength and laughing, cheerful heart, now that Crœsus was banished, come to offer me life with him. Timothy's very presence, his companionship, just then seemed all I should ever need. I closed my eyes. There he stood strong and big in his corduroys, dusty and sunburned from his day's survey over the hills. All the arguments that Timothy has ever used came back to plead his cause now. All the arguments I have been using to offset his wooing retired before my aching, physical longing to lie close and protected in Timothy's strong arms; to place my cold, aching heart against his throbbing heart for its warmth and comfort Timothy is like fire in a cheerless room, like a candle in the darkness, like the sun new risen over a damp and mildewed world.

He stood demanding once again why I could not come with him, why I could not give up my silly dream of a career as not worth the struggle—and instead have the stars and the moon, and the great out-of-doors; the day's homely work, and the night's sweet sleep with him.

And I stretched out my arms to draw him down to kiss him for the first time and to whisper yes:—to confess at last that the physical need of him was too great for me to fight it any longer.

This is what I saw. A light very blurred set far away in the heavens. It hung in the sky above the oak-tree top. I stared, wide-eyed, at the mysterious, shrouded glow. Then I got up and went to the window.

The rain had ceased—and the wind was still. The lightning and thunder storm had passed. The air was soft and fresh. I knelt on the floor, my elbows on the window-sill, leaning out to see what the strange light might be. Was it a solitary star, trying to shine from behind clouds, that gave the illusion of smoke trying to blot it out, or was it—was it—?

Then I saw (and not only with my physical eyes) that the light came from a lantern.

Set where a star might have been in the velvet blackness of the heavens a lantern's faint flame was fighting not to be blown out. The odds all seemed against it; there was apparently little oil to feed it; unfriendly gusts blew at it from all sides—and its crystal panes were smirched with smoke and soot.

Awake or asleep I caught the significance of the vision. Even as I knelt the light showed me two rivers: neither was confused in my mind with the river rushing in reality beyond the garden below.

I saw two rivers. One flowed through a land lush in the sunlight, with peaceful cows along its bank and all the earth's sensuous beauty, every appeal to the senses embodied in the activities that went with it. It was an idyl of animal content; a sweet picture of peace, as primitive in its appeal as the progress of the seasons through the calendar of the year. It was "dust thou art to dust returneth" epitomized.

The other river, curiously enough, flowed uphill. And its banks were not lush with flowers, nor did I see animals steeped in content in its meadows. Its path was a lonely one, and cruel rocks obstructed the way, and the pilgrims who straggled up the path often stumbled; there was every sort of discouragement to turn back the timid. It was only for those born with the spirit of high adventure who would attempt the passage. To the valley-river travellers, this route would remain forever a joke or a mystery, The ones in the valley could not see the vision that heartened the mountain-climbers to struggle on. One journey ended as it began on a physical plane, the other on a spiritual. One rested content with the beauty of earth; the other acclaimed the tablelands of heaven.

Was it a dream—a mirage? I do not know, though I knelt for the rest of the night, my head bowed on the window-ledge, fighting Jacob's battle of old, the flesh and the spirit. The far-off star lantern flickered and went nearly out; then the smoke would clear a little and the flame burn brighter, only to be caught in another gust of wind and nearly extinguished. In the stillness and blackness of the night I battled for some reason I did not know, to keep the flame burning, and the odds were all against me.

Out of my blackness and despair I knew the light was waning. One more blast and the lantern would be extinguished forever.

The devil's last, best, and unanswerable argument, his hymn of hate toward heaven—"What's the use, anyway?"—was undermining my strength. Why should a moth argue with the night? Destruction it may be to follow the warmth and light, but what matters one moth more or less?

I do not know how to pray. I am not religious. But across my memory flashed "the one adventure in life is the soul's search for God"—where had I read it? I thought of Lura and her last words—"If ever you face a blank wall, remember 'Love never faileth'!" Two lines of a solo I used to sing in Lura's church flooded my consciousness:

"Arise, my soul, and stretch thy wings, Thy better portion trace."

I do not know how it happened, but the battle was over and I was not the defeated army. Maybe I dreamed all that went before, but now I was awake. The first faint streaks of dawn were coming. Now I could see clearly the brilliant morning star over the live-oak's top. It was not a murky, smoky lantern at all, but a star beautiful as the chief diamond in the high priest's breastplate.

CHAPTER VI

THE sun was shining on a new world when a knocking at my door wakened me a few hours later. I was asleep with my head still pillowed on the window-sill. I opened my eyes first in the direction of the garden.

A great commotion was going on down there in the tree-tops. Birds seemed to be discussing an issue of paramount importance. Swelling buds met my astonished gaze; starry white blossoms were scattered border-wise where I remembered walks used to be; a patch of blowing, glowing yellow—could it be jonquils signalled from the far end of the garden. My eyes wandered beyond to the tender green veil laid over the willows along the river's bank. The river was gliding peacefully by, back between its own banks.

The world was clean-swept, new-washed, brushed, dusted, and polished. Spring had come with the storm during the night.

Some one was knocking timidly at my door.

It was Isaiah, the peg-legged kitchen boy. He came to bring me a message from Bob. Mandy was and there were no prospects for breakfast unless I would come get it. Isaiah said the fire was made and the water boiling. He said he could make the coffee if I would let him. We were not going to have coffee à la Mandy this morning, but mine! Bob passed his cup a second time.

"You always could cook, sister," he said. "I'll go down and see what's the matter with Mandy. Every spring she gets the crop-fever."

"You mean Mandy wants to make a crop," I asked, "and you force her to cook instead?" It came to that, Bob admitted.

"Then you don't deserve any better cooking than you get," I told him. "I'm going with you to see Mandy."

The situation was altogether changed when I heard even that much of Mandy's side. Bob and I started for her cabin in the back yard.

The rain had beat the ground hard. The wind had dried it. The lightning and thunder had brought the grass up; everywhere baby green leaves danced in the bright sunlight. The sky was heavenly blue, not a cloud in sight. Far off we could hear the negroes singing as they sorted trace chains and dragged out ploughs getting ready to go to the fields.

Mandy was in bed, surly and "full of misery" in her back. She also had a pain in her head. This she attributed to cooking over a hot stove.

There were also alarming symptoms, as she related them, about pains in her chest, and a strong distaste for food.

"I ain't able to cook,' fo Gawd, Marse Bob," she declared. "De heat frum dat stove always has gave me fever."

Bob hunted for arguments to bring her back to the kitchen.

"You need the fresh air outdoors, Mandy," I prescribed. "Why don't you try working in the field awhile, make a crop?"

For the first time she turned friendly eyes to me, appealing eyes that asked me to help her.

"Miss Diana," she said, "if I could only be gwine to de field to knock cotton-stalks wid de rest ur de niggers to-day, if I could only plough and chop cotton and know I wuz gwine git ter pick it nex' fall, I'd be well in five minutes."

"Then get up," I said; "I'll see that Marse Bob lets you make a crop."

"Nonsense!" Bob snorted. "I've got to have a cook."

"You have a cook," I told him. "Isaiah begins to-day under my direction to do all of Mandy's work. Mandy, get your hat and start to the field."

"Isaiah, Jeremiah, Hezekiah's no-count," Bob said as we started back to the house, now freed from the incubus of Mandy's presence. "You don't know what you've done, sister."

"Isaiah was no-count," I replied, "with Mandy in command. But in charge himself you're going to see what he can do."

Even the first day has proved what I said. Isaiah had only to be showed once. He has scoured the kitchen and scrubbed every pot and pan in it.

The hen in the hall hatched during the storm. The barrel nest is burned.

CHAPTER VII

***Palmetto Grove, March* 1**

THE house-cleaning leaves me little time for anything else. Isaiah found an assistant in a yellow girl who has been teaching the little darkies until the day came for them to start knocking cotton-stalks. Her name is Chattie May. She does not care for the fresh air in the fields, she explained to me.

One by one we are taking the rooms, tearing off the tattered, swaying, rotting paper and canvas, and scrubbing, scouring, purifying them with carbolic and lye soap and scalding water. Mandy has kept house just as a born field hand might have been expected to keep it.

Bob departed to Cottonport the day we got to his room. When he returned it was to find white curtains, that I had found beautifully laundered and carefully put away in a cedar chest upstairs, at all the downstairs windows, the hearths reddened, lamps unearthed from a closet and chimneys found in the commissary to fit them, polished chimneys that one can see to read by.

"By Jove, kitten," Bob said, "the place is beginning to look as it used to look."

"This is but a beginning," I told him. "I found the curtains put away. Where are the other things, the linen and the furniture?"

"Everything is up in the attic," he said, "above the water-line. I had everything sent up out of the reach of Mandy."

Chattie May is to stay. She and Isaiah are to divide the work between them.

"You're what I call an organizer," Bob told me the day I had the three fine cows he had farmed out to negro families, because Mandy was too lazy to milk them, brought back to the house. The old dairy is swept and garnished and whitewashed inside and out. "I never had any idea that that peglegged Hezekiah could do anything but tote wood and draw water."

"Whatever led you to think Mandy could cook?" I was beginning.

Bob chuckled.

"You can't go fried onions and grits for breakfast, can you, honey?"

"I could if there were any necessity," I replied, "but I hate waste and I never could bear a sloven. And as for you allowing that nigger to set a hen in the hall—"

"I meant to change it all, sister, once cotton got high enough and I could get on my feet" Bob looked apologetic. "I have let things go to pot I needed you to jack me up. How about a little game of chess now there's room on the table for the board?"

So we played chess an hour and I went to sleep while Bob puzzled a move. I just do remember him patting me on the shoulder and kissing me goodnight. "If you'll only stay awhile with me, honey," I heard him say wistfully, "we'll have lots of other games."

March 8

Too busy to think of myself these days. Five years of Mandy's housekeeping cannot be brushed away in a day.

The new servants have to be trained, but they are eager to learn. Bob admits that a greaseless, noiseless meal is a miracle he never thought would be achieved again on Palmetto Grove.

Fragrant cedar tubs and old-fashioned water-jugs in one's dressing-room are picturesque enough, but this house has got to have a modern bathroom. All my spare time is spent on the problem—how to get it. Bob reads his Virgil and Horace and Homer on one side of the shining kerosene lamp. I sit on the other poring over the mysteries of a large illustrated catalogue from a mail-order house in Chicago. Here is the page that fascinates me most. It is headed in large letters: "You Can Afford One of These Bathrooms." Then follows a minute description of the Perfection Bathroom Outfit priced at $76.75. When I first suggested the possibility of a bathroom to Bob, he grew restive.

"Honey," he pleaded, "just wait until fall. I can't spare a penny for anything. I'll need it all to pay for having the crop picked. But if cotton is a good price you shall have a mother-of-pearl tub with golden faucets."

All the spiritual issues in life have given place temporarily to how to get the Perfection Bathroom Outfit Once upon a time I would have retired before the hopelessness of the situation, but not now.

Bob forgot until to-night to tell me he heard in Cottonport the other day that the Fosters have come to spend a while on Roseneath.

Dear little Aline, it is four years since I have seen her. I am wondering if her poor lifeless spine has yet been quickened. Bob says he sent them word that I am here. But in the years since they have been away, the bridge over the bayou that separates Palmetto Grove from Roseneath plantation has been washed away. The road is twenty miles around and still pretty muddy.

CHAPTER VIII

Palmetto Grove, March 10

BOB had the buggy rolled off the gallery yesterday and the harness greased. The roads are passable once more. He asked me to drive to church with him.

Deer-Lick church is five miles down the river beyond the store. It is exactly as I remember it, with the paint gone and pickets off the fences that enclose the grave-plots. Mules and horses hitched to all kinds of vehicles surrounded the church. This was the first service of the season, as the roads during January and February are impassable. I did not recognize any old acquaintances in the crowd.

The old plantation families have long since moved away, and managers and overseers are a flitting population. They all seemed to know Bob and we had many invitations for dinner, for most of them had brought the midday meal in a basket, to spread picnic fashion on the ground.

Bob deferred all invitations to me, and I promptly declared it would be impossible for us to accept any hospitality, as it was most important that we get home early. This made them rather timid of approaching me. I cannot say that the crowd appealed to me. I had come solely to please Bob and for the ride. Bob went off with several men to meet the minister, who was in this case a "holy-roller," whatever that faith may be, and to sound him on his doctrine before he got the opportunity to scatter any possible firebrands. When he came back he told me that the young lady who usually played the organ was ill. He had suggested that I would take her place as organist. I said of course I would—to please him. The organ squeaked and groaned, wheezed and sneezed, like Mandy's accordion. I threw the whole volume of my voice into the hymns, only making a pretence of playing the accompaniment. Suddenly I realized that I was singing alone to a house that held its breath in awed attention.

I asked the congregation to join me. The minister spoke for them: "They wish to hear you." The tribute was so spontaneous, as from all parts of the church came the echo: "You sing to us," I turned away from the asthmatic organ and stood facing the congregation.

I saw their faces lighted up with new hope as they hungrily drank in the comforting words of the old hymns and the tears welling up in their eyes; my own heart melted and I had a new sense of neighborliness. I felt as the two small lads with the loaves and fishes that fed the five thousand by the Galilean Sea must have felt when they saw their little converted into bread of life, enough to feed the multitude!

The preacher rose at last and took a text and preached a very unilluminating sermon on it, but he had the saving grace to make his discourse brief.

"In view of the fact that we have with us to-day," he said after his "Finally, my brethern," "a singer of such gifts, I make bold to offer the suggestion that we conclude our service by asking her to favor us with our favorite hymns, if she is willing."

I replied that I would be glad to sing what they might request. They asked for "Nearer, my God, to Thee," "Rock of Ages," and "Jesus, Lover of My Soul."

Instead of leaving after services I asked Bob to stay; we ate dinner out of everybody's baskets, and afterwards I offered to sing again for them before they started home.

I found myself trying to recall stray passages from the textbook of the church where I sang in New York. There they came to be healed; here they came to worship and praise the God whom they thought sent the afflictions.

"That little preacher's brain-bin was pretty empty, kitten," Bob observed as we drove homeward late in the afternoon, "but your singing sent them home filled up and happy on the way."

I said I hoped so.

CHAPTER IX

Palmetto Grove, March 12

MY trunks have come, and we have had another mail made up almost entirely of bills for me. My dressmaker writes that unless I send the amount due her, she will be forced to put my bill in the hands of a collector. The specialist has already turned his over to a lawyer. The lawyer sends a notice that unless I settle up immediately he will begin suit. Palozzi and the accompanist bring up the rear. A prompt remittance is all any of them ask, but they must have that at once.

And I have eight dollars and seventy-five cents in the world!

Before, I have always been able to pay my debts, but now I have no money. No prospect of anything until fall, and even then there is always the uncertainty of cotton prices to reckon with.

I tried all night to think what to do—how to get the money. Something happened to me the night of the storm, something mental. I find myself thinking in a new way. I owe the money. I want to pay it. But how can I do it?

Bob is not involved in the matter. He has no money that he can spare. I knelt by the window, putting my head down on the cool sill. One thought persisted. It seemed vocal; shouting in my ears: ***There is a way out. For every problem there is a solution.***

I thought of Lura, recalling what she had told me of the time when her back was to the last wall.

Of myself I could do nothing. I found myself turning away from my own thoughts, from my own direction.

Suddenly the feeling that had swept over me the night of the storm came back. The feeling that I was as cut off from human aid as a shipwrecked person in mid-ocean. Any help that reached me would have to come from a higher power. If I prayed it was not with words, nor in any form familiar from the prayer-book or memory. But quick as the first appeal had been answered during the storm came a realization that my S.O.S. call had registered and aid been dispatched that quick. I was enfolded in peace. It was as if some divine antidote had been administered that removed me far above and beyond all possible anxieties. I had let go and some new tide had lifted me into an ocean of living waters, electrical currents directly connected with the spiritual part of me; a new law was functioning, and I had only to be still and know it was God. This may or may not be prayer, but it came as an answer to my silent appeal for wisdom, to be shown what to do next. The amount of money I owe, put into my hand, would have been no more reassuring than this new peace and joy that flooded my heart. Where the money was coming from, I did not know, but that no longer troubled me. I knew the bills were going to be paid. This peace and joy was the answer to my prayer, to be shown how to pay them. I wrote to my dressmaker and to the specialist. Then I went quietly to bed and to sleep. I had a vague idea that a revelation of wisdom would be poured into my consciousness. Instead I drifted off into a sweet, dreamless sleep.

The last thought that came to me was that the attic must be tackled to-morrow. In a house as clean as this one, that old junk-room must be aired and fumigated and the dust of years disturbed at last.

March 15

THE hardest day's work I ever attempted is done. It has been a day of discovery, adventure. The attic is treasure-trove with lovely old furniture. There are four-posters enough even for every room in this great house, four-posters with testers lined with crumbling satin and cords that go to dust at a touch, but the carving is perfect, pomegranates and grapes, pineapple and flower design. Year by year all the really good furniture, it seems, has been sent upstairs to safeguard it against the spring overflows and the shiftless servants. Bob recalls that Mammy Linda packed all the curtains and best damask in cedar chests the year before she died. I have found most of this in perfect preservation. One set of lovely old glazed pale-green chintz goes in my little bedroom under the eaves. It is now newly kalsomined. I also found a lot of old Chinese things packed away in sandalwood boxes, bales of matting, fresh and fragrant as if it had just come from the Orient.

Bob does not want me to bring any of the good furniture down until we get the house done over.

"Wait until fall, sister," he said when I told him of my day's work. "If you'd wait, honey," he handed me the New Orleans paper he was reading. "Just see this editorial on the world's visible supply of cotton, the need of it."

I took the paper.

"I meant to tell you," Bob said, "I'm on a trade for a saddle-horse. I went to see the man to-day. Thought maybe you'd enjoy riding like you used to—with me."

The thought flashed into my mind: If it were for my pleasure he was getting the horse and paying real money for it—

"It's a trade," he answered my thought. "I've got two more registered Jersey heifers than I need and Wilkes offers me the saddle-horse in exchange for them. He's got a Ford."

The horse is named Jenny Ribbons and she will be here to-morrow. It has been so long since I have seen a newspaper that I pored over this one, long after Bob's gentle dozing drifted off into stormier waters and he began to snore in his easy-chair.

"Wanted—Old furniture. Best prices paid for genuine antiques.

"Dupré's Antique Shop, Royal Street, New Orleans."

It was as if a door had opened before me in a stone wall. "Best prices paid."

"Wake up, Bob." I kissed him rapturously. "I've got important letters to write upstairs!"

"All right, honey. And so you think you'll like Jenny Ribbons?" He sat up blinking and filled his everlasting pipe, "She'll give you less time to put in around the house."

His blue eyes twinkled. I hugged him again.

"If you think you'll stop me from house-cleaning," I warned him, "it can't be done. I've decided to paper and paint and restore the West Wing."

"Honey, I tell you—"

"If you'll just wait," I jeered back at him halfway upstairs, "until I sell my cotton next fall."

"You little boll weevil!" Bob shouted after me.

CHAPTER X

Palmetto Grove, April

APRIL is here again. For the past ten days that is all that has mattered. I am drunk on the spring's new wine and not responsible. I know just how a heady bumble-bee feels, when the whole garden is spilling honey-scent and he has only his limited capacity to get his booty home.

The apple-trees are in bloom; the peach orchard is a veil of rose-tulle. The whole place is a bouquet of wood-smoke—we are burning as we clear away the deadwood and trash in flower garden and yard—ploughed ground, flowers, and whitewash! Birds are singing and billing and cooing in their honeymoon nests in the oak-trees just outside my windows. The brilliant blue sky seen through the vivid new green leaves is like some wonderful awning, specially placed to reflect the tender green of my glazed chintz draperies.

Somehow now this little whitewashed room set high up under the eaves seems like a sanctuary. My trunks are unpacked. The book Lura gave me, the textbook of her church, lies on my desk beside the Wisdom of Confucius. But I do not have time to glance into either often. I am full of a whipped-cream, lined-with-pink-roses, satiny satisfaction of spirit All's right with my world.

Everything seems to be different somehow, to have changed; even Mandy has grown mild-tempered and humble and devoted to me. She comes several times a week from her cabin on the bayou riding an absurd calico pony, to bring me vegetables from her garden. Perhaps after all nothing has changed except myself. Undoubtedly I have a new focus to my mind. Whatever it is that has happened, I have never been so quietly happy. Something has happened, but what and when? I am not enough interested in myself these days to follow this effect back to its cause. I am too busy trying to make up to Bob for all these years I have left him alone with debts and niggers and mules for his only companions.

Jenny Ribbons is a great success. I ride over the place twice a day with Bob, and on mail-days to the Deer-Lick store. No reply yet to any of my letters. I at least expected an inquiry from the antique dealer in New Orleans about the furniture. Still not the prospect of a dollar in sight.

April 11

THE wistaria arrived overnight. We went out after breakfast to-day to find two old dead trees dripping with lavender bouquets and vibrant with bees.

The garden calls for a row of straw-thatched beehives. I have set my heart on having them, and on a maltese kitten. Bob says we'll get everything we want after cotton is picked this fall.

Three more hens have hatched, and the vegetable garden is planted, under my direction; not that I know anything more about planting a garden than I gleaned from the directions on the packets of seed.

April 13

I WENT back to the attic to-day, hoping to find in some old trunk or chest something which I might use to paper the best rooms in the West Wing. I did not find what I sought—but my heart stopped beating when I pulled out a great roll of bills—money! I could hardly meet both my hands around it. I did not examine it. I just sat there and cried and cried and cried for joy. This money would solve everything. Bob's debts could be paid and he could go to Hot Springs, and the West Wing could be done over—and my own personal mountain be laid low, the dressmaker and the doctor and everybody I owe could be paid and that would be the last of them forever. I must have stayed up there for hours, while my astral body floated away, busy settling up Bob's debts and my own.

Bob's voice called me back to earth. The last rays of the setting sun came through the attic window. I ran downstairs. Bob was on the steps. His horse and

Jenny Ribbons were waiting for us.

"Oh, Bob!" I cried, throwing my arms about his neck; "you don't have to wait for next fall and the cotton crop!"

His arms were about me, patting me, for I was crying for joy again. Then I dragged him back behind the honeysuckle vines, for I did not want any negro that might be passing to see all that money, and I pressed it in his hands—new crisp money, for all I knew thousands and thousands of dollars, to judge by the size of the roll.

"Bob," I cried, "we can pay all our debts!" " Debts, damn' em!" he said, still patting me. "Where'd you get this, honey?"

"In the attic, in a tin box, in an old horsehair trunk. There may be thousands more up there."

Bob was hunting for his glasses. I think maybe his own old blue eyes were misty. Then he gave a whoop such as I haven't heard him give since I was a little girl, and he hugged me tighter and laughed and laughed so I could hardly hear the point of his joke:

"It's Confederate money, sister!" he sputtered out at last. "It ain't worth the paper it's printed on!"

We went to ride, but Bob's horse couldn't keep up with Jenny Ribbons and me. Her middle name and mine were dark blue. A white-lace parasol set at an angle of sixty degrees gleamed up a ravine. We left Bob and finally reached the white plum-bush in blossom, hanging over a crystal spring. "Root and all, branch and all," I gathered it, and left Bob to ride on to Deer-lick alone. I came home to make a Japanese flower arrangement to compose my spirits. Confucius on his grass-green cushion sits under it now, splendid as an emperor. Confucius counselled philosophy as I made a special toilette for dinner.

Bob and I talked more than usual at the table; at least I chattered away. It was a case of I-laugh-that-I-may-not-weep with me. Then we played chess until ten o'clock.

"Sit down here a minute, kittens." Bob drew me to the arm of his chair when I stooped to kiss him good-night. There had been a quizzical cast in his eye all the evening. "What did you mean out there on the gallery by 'our debts'?"

"Just that," I hedged. "Haven't we always as a family been alive with debts? We have ever since I could remember." Bob breathed easier.

"Our debts don't trouble me," he said, "but what I want to know is—have you got any debts, eh?"

"You old goose, Bob"—I kissed the back of his neck to avoid his X-ray eyes—"the biggest thing I owe is my debt of love to you."

"If you really owe anything, child," filling up his pipe, "and it's troubling you, it must be paid. Palmetto Grove belongs half to you, your father's share, and we'll just sell part of the old place off and get your mind easy."

"Then why don't you sell part of it and pay your own debts?" I asked. "You can't hide it from me that you need money, for I know you are just living looking forward to next fall's crop, bringing enough to pay everybody off. Sell all this old land so far as I am concerned and be free."

Bob sighed and took a long pull at his pipe.

"This delta land is bringing twice as much as we could get for it last year," he said, "and if cotton stays up I'll be out of debt this fall, and land will be worth four times what it is now. I don't want to sell, sister. Palmetto Grove is your inheritance, and the thousand acres we have in cultivation and the cypress-brakes will bring a million dollars in five more years. I don't want to borrow any more money. I'll live on parched corn and smoke china-berries before I'll get in the clutches of another bank or commission merchant. But if you need money, honey—"

"Bob"—I lied with a clear conscience—"what have I to spend money for here with you? I haven't even a purse to put it in if I had it."

Bob patted my hand.

"There's no devil in hell, child," he said. "He's right here on earth and his name is Debt. Don't ever get in his clutches."

And I promised solemnly, while I lighted my candle, not to ever—!

The April moon is flooding my room. I blew the candle out. The garden below breathes spring. From the plum-blossoms over Confucius fragrance rises like incense. In five years Palmetto Grove will be worth a million, ten times a hundred thousand dollars! And to-night, if it were not for poor old Bob, who has toiled so long, and without reward, who has, little by little, paid off this debt and that one, with all the accumulated and usurious interest, I would sell what he calls my birthright for a mess of pottage. For the million that may be ours five years hence, I would take eight hundred snake-cold, icy silver dollars now—to feel that I was out of debt and free!

CHAPTER XI

Roseneath Plantation, April 15

TOM FOSTER hailed us this morning from the other side of the bayou. He was on horseback as we were. He had ridden down to see if he could not ford the bayou where the bridge used to be, connecting the road from Roseneath to Palmetto Grove. It could not be done.

There is a cypress log that the negroes use as a foot bridge, but one has to be in better training than Tom Foster is these days to venture on its narrow width. The bayou is very deep and the water everywhere is up to the top of the banks. There are alligators in the bayou and the path getting to the log is through a tangle of blackberry-vines.

"Thought you were in Washington representing us," Bob called back after the first greeting.

Tom said he was chairman of a committee that had been sent South to prepare a report on the cotton acreage. It was to discuss this that he was trying to get across now to Palmetto Grove.

"No way to get here except by the road, twenty miles around," Bob said. "Since you-all have been away there was no one to use the bridge, so after it washed away I never put it back. Now we can't spare hands from the fields to build a bridge."

Then, Tom said, he would come in the car later today. He said he had been commissioned by Aline to capture and bring me back with him to her. Why could n't Bob come, too, and spend a few days?

"You must be making a picnic out of life these days, Tom," Bob laughed. "When did you ever hear of a man from down here going off junketing during cotton-planting time?"

Tom looks as if he might have forgotten everything about a Mississippi plantation. Certainly no one would ever take him for a native in his smart sporting togs. Well, then wouldn't I come, he persisted. Aline was better, but could not stand so long a ride—Cousin Clara, still the housekeeper at Roseneath, was expecting me—and Jinny was arriving from Washington to-day. Just a family party.

Bob said of course I would go, and that he'd have me packed and ready against Tom's arrival. So we rode off, back to the house, while Tom disappeared to get his car and come around the road.

He arrived early in the afternoon in a runabout. He brought Bob a bottle of Scotch whiskey and drank about a third of it himself.

"You mean to tell me," Tom asked, "that you really are cutting the cotton acreage down one third?"

Bob explained that all the planters were raising corn and sugar and feedstuffs because they could afford to do it, since cotton was a good price last year.

"Heretofore, as you know," Bob said, "we could borrow money only on cotton, and it took every acre in cotton to pay even our interest. Now we are cutting cotton acreage because we are getting out of debt and can afford to do so."

They were hot on prohibition when I came down with my bags packed. Bob thinks prohibition the salvation of the country, in spite of the fact that a bottle of Scotch whiskey is about the most acceptable present any one can make him. Tom Foster isn't thinking of the elimination of the drink-crazed negro, the menace of the South, but of his own personal need of a stimulant every time the clock strikes.

We were well on our way when Tom gave me a note from Jinny.

"But I did not know that Jinny had arrived," I said. Yes, Tom said, he found Jinny and a private car full of guests when he reached home after leaving us this morning. It slipped his memory, quite, he assured me, as I opened the frivolous envelope. It was the latest word in stationery. "Roseneath Plantation," duly embossed on the letter-head, with post-office, express, and telegraph address.

"This looks as if you were moving back," I said.

"Maybe for six weeks or a month," Tom replied. "Got a bunch down who are used to that sort of thing, so Jinny got ready for' em."

Jinny's note said she had been hurt with me for deserting her as I had done for so long, but that I was already forgiven if I would come prepared to stay indefinitely.

"Bring your smartest things," she wrote, "and your music. We have a dozen guests, four women besides yourself—eight men—four of them Congressmen—and susceptible. I need you."

"Why didn't you tell me it is a smart house party?" I asked Tom "I expected to see only the family."

Tom speeded up. His face was flushed, he evaded my reproaching glance.

"Tell you the truth," he said, "I had an idea you wouldn't come if you knew about the crowd."

I would not and told him so. I even asked him to take me back home, promising I would come later. He said he would not disappoint Aline; that she had her heart set on seeing me. Also, he added, there was some one else who wanted to see me, Peter Wentworth.

Peter, he explained, had come in his official capacity to write a series of editorials on the cotton situation and other matters involving the progress of the South.

"What's the idea?" Tom asked—"the way you've dropped us all; nobody seems to have seen you in over a year."

I said I had been working and that I had discovered I could not work and play.

"You mean play with our crowd," he corrected. "They are bores, I grant you."

I denied being bored. "I never had one real interest in common with them, and they are even less interested in what interests me."

"Idlers are never interested in anything," he said. "Killing time is no sport."

I almost felt sorry for him.

"If it weren't for Jinny," he said, "I wouldn't put up with a houseful of fools, try to entertain them. But they are her style."

I knew what he said was true, but I defended Jinny and reminded him what a social power she had become in Washington.

"What are you doing down here?" he asked, with the license of an old friend. "Given up the career?"

"I don't know," I told him. "Perhaps so."

"Decided to marry Crœsus?"

"No." We drove on in silence until we came in sight of the big house on Rose-neath Plantation. It is a very handsome old Colonial house with great fluted pillars and long French windows. The house on Palmetto Grove looks like a wren's nest beside this stately green-and-white edifice. The grounds are always perfectly kept.

Gay awnings were up, and flower-boxes in the upper windows and on the balconies. Everything along the broad shell driveway was in bloom. On the lawn I could see a tea-table and a lot of people. They were waving me a welcome. I was not near enough to distinguish one from another. But even at that distance I saw that Jinny had not relied on the traditional old family servants. She had brought her trained foreign servants. The whole place looked stagey to me, and the white servants in livery were the last touch of artificiality. Tom remarked that he wished he had made Bob come along for tea, even if he would not stay longer.

I laughed at the picture of Bob drinking tea. He would as soon be caught with gloves on! Traditions die hard in the South.

"D' you think Bob has changed much?" I asked. Tom, half drunk though he was, laughed good-humoredly.

"Changed!" he exclaimed; "I'd take an oath that the old sun-helmet he had on this morning is the same he wore the first time I ever saw him! Why, I'd recognize those old riding-boots of his by their wrinkles if I'd meet the Japanese Mikado dressed up in them in Timbuctoo! Everything changes down this way; even the river gets a hump on and changes its bed every twelve years or so; but Bob is moulded and stays put like a granite mountain. Changed! I say, does he still read Virgil in the original—"

"Yes," I returned, "and the Iliad and Marcus Aurelius and the Bible, every day of his life."

"Old mossback!" Tom slowed up at the front steps; "he needs you to get him out of his rut."

Aline in her rolling chair was being wheeled down the steps to meet me. Little old Cousin Clara, leaning on her cane stick, was behind her.

"Come on upstairs with us," Aline said, "before the others get you."

We had tea on the balcony giving on Aline's room, and Cousin Clara, every time she got the chance to put a word in, explained how much she had wanted to see me, and how she had planned to send for me when the roads got better; then Jinny's letter came telling her to get ready for the house party, and decorators and gardeners and chauffeurs and whatnot began arriving to prepare the place for the guests and she had been too busy to even write me a letter.

Aline has grown. She is almost a woman, and seems perfectly developed if it were not for her spine. It is as if she had no backbone at all. Black Tilly, who has been her nurse since she was born, is still her devoted shadow, and Jupiter, the old bull-dog, her constant companion. Freda, a powerful Swedish masseuse, is now supposed to be Aline's trained nurse.

"Peter is here, Diana," Aline told me when Cousin Clara's monologue had run its course. "But I sent word to them all that you belong to me until dinner."

That reminded Cousin Clara of something that had to be attended to in the dining-room, so she tapped off on her cane, saying she would see me later to-night.

Aline turned eagerly to me, with "Do you remember, Diana," when Jinny's high-pitched voice floated in. "S-sh!" Aline's slim fingers went to her lips. "S-sh— later," she whispered as her mother joined us.

Jinny welcomed me exuberantly. Freda, the big Swede, was at her heels. Aline anticipated her designs: "If you have come to massage me," she said, "you may go, Freda."

Freda turned watery, pale-blue eyes to Jinny, who shrugged her shoulders. "If she won't, she won't," she said.

"But, Madame, she steadily refuses, day after day, week after week, her treatment."

"Oh, well," Jinny said, "you can give me the massage she refuses, ungrateful child."

"Thank you, mother," Aline said sweetly. "I've told you I'm not going to have my back rubbed—"

"Don't start all that over again!" Jinny raised her hands in protest. "Come on, Di; I'll show you your room."

She took off my hat herself, babbling on at a great rate, how she had tried to find me, how she thought I must be in Bermuda or in Burmah or in some remote corner of the earth. If any one had told her I was at Palmetto Grove! Crœsus had' phoned her half a dozen times to know when I would be back in town, and to ask if she knew where I was. Only the week before she left New York she had run into Timothy as she came out of Delmonico's. Timothy could give her no help. He said he had' phoned, wired, written, with no success. If he did happen to locate me, he promised, he'd be sure to let her know. Now that she had found me, she was going to wire both Crœsus and Timothy to come on South and join her house party. I pleaded with her not to do this. She replied by telling me Peter was to take me in to dinner, and asked what I was going to wear.

She was annoyed to find how few things I had brought and that these were old. My choice had to be between a black gauze and a shaded yellow chiffon, for I had brought only the two evening gowns.

"You've surely got something newer than these!" she reproached. "I'll lend you one of my new French frocks."

But I refused to wear her fine feathers. "Rollins told me," Jinny said," that she had made you a lot of new things. She spoke particularly of a peacock-colored evening gown. Where is it?"

I had to admit the truth, that it was at Palmetto Grove.

Jinny said she would send for my things the first thing in the morning.

I did not wish her to do this and told her so.

"But why not?" she persisted; "there are eight or nine men here worth dressing for, and five women who have trunks packed with stunning new things." Why didn't I want my new clothes?

I fenced by saying I could only stay a day or so.

"Nonsense!" she dismissed that argument; "and even if it were so you need that new evening gown."

Again I hedged declaring Bob could not find it, even if I sent back for it.

"Céleste will go with the boy I send," she said, "and she can bring all the clothes she thinks you need. You know Céleste's judgment of old."

Céleste is Jinny's French maid. No, I would not hear of Céleste going after my clothes. Every possible reason I advanced for not sending for them, Jinny met and overcome.

At last I grew impatient.

"I have a few new things Rollins made me," I said, "but I do not like them, and I should have no pleasure in wearing them, Jinny."

"Nonsense!" she replied. "Rollins says you are a dream in the bronze and blue frock, that it is the most satisfactory thing she has turned out this season. She raved over you in it. If I could wear blues and greens with my black hair and eyes, I'd offer to buy it from you on her recommendation. I've got to see it, no matter what you say!"

Jinny sat on the side of the bed, her slippered feet drawn up under her. Céleste came, drew my bath, and when I told her I did not need her to help me dress, as noiselessly departed. Jinny's sharp black eyes still studied me.

"Rollins told me she had also made you—" She was beginning all over again.

"Do hush, Jinny," I begged. "If you must know why I can't bear the sight of those things, it's because I still owe Rollins for them and I'm worried to death because I haven't been able to pay her."

Jinny laughed as if it were a good joke. "I always owe old Rollins," she said. "I never pay all I owe her from one year's end to another—"

"But Rollins has always relied on me to pay her," I replied. "She made my clothes cheaper because I always pay promptly."

"You can now," Jinny said. "I'll write you a check this minute to give her."

I refused to accept it. Jinny argued until the first dressing-bell rang, then she rose to go to her room. At the door she turned again.

"I don't know the adjective to describe you, Di," she said, "but I think feeble-minded comes pretty near what I want to say."

CHAPTER XII

Roseneath Plantation

I WORE the black gauze and went in to dinner with Peter. He seemed overjoyed to see me after so many years. Alice Grant also welcomed me warmly.

"Hello, Mariana," she greeted me; "Jinny tells me you are living in a real moated grange now."

"Not even a telephone," I laughed.

These two are the only ones I knew in the crowd. There are Tom's four Senators, Harris, Downs, West, and Calhoun; a Colonel Sinclair, who seems to be a capitalist, as he only talks in terms of a million; Jimmy Wilson, Fred Dunstan, a nice boy named Miller, and a swarthy South American with a name as long as he is. More men are expected. The women besides Alice Grant are a Mrs. Prescott, a widow; Rose Dunraven, a cousin of Tom's; Viola Fortescue, and Barbara Anderson, all friends of Jinny's, and in her set in Washington. Alice Grant's latest flirtation is Colonel Sinclair. They are openly engaged to be married, as soon as she gets her divorce. She goes to Reno from here.

Jinny spoke truly when she said these women had come equipped with clothes. Aline had sent me a round bouquet of old-fashioned cinnamon roses with one of her characteristic notes:

"Wear these at dinner," it ran, "to remind you to come back to see me before you go to bed. Bring Peter with you to the balcony."

I wore the roses tucked in the low bodice of my black gauze gown. The spicy clean fragrance from them was very pleasant. At dinner the women drank as heavily as the men, and everybody smoked cigarettes between courses. Jinny called attention to the fact that I was not smoking. Peter apologized and lighted a match for me, but I did not feel the need of a cigarette. Alice Grant ragged me about being conspicuous, but Jinny softened up and explained I was saving my voice so I could sing to them after dinner.

We had coffee out on the lawn under the soft light from Chinese lanterns. Peter threw a scarf around my shoulders.

"See that seat down yonder near the river under that oak-tree?" he asked. "What do you say to a cigarette there, while we watch the moon rise?"

Peter lighted his cigarette and smoked in silence. He put his hand to his forehead wearily, and bent over to inhale the breath from my roses.

"Diana," he said at last, "you are like a clean cold drink of water from a mountain spring after one has been drinking pink lemonade all day at a circus."

I laughed, but the compliment pleased me.

"It's these cinnamon roses," I told him. "Aline sent them. She wants us to come to see her on her balcony."

Peter sighed.

"Poor lamb," he said, with more tenderness and pity than I have ever heard in any voice. "Life hasn't much for her, I'm afraid." It was very peaceful and quiet; the river lapped against the low banks below us.

Then: "How is life treating you, Diana?"

"If contentment could be banked as money, Peter," I told him, "I'd be the richest woman in the world."

He threw his cigarette away.

"Who is the lucky man?" he asked after a moment. "I suppose you are confiding to me—that you are in love, engaged."

"The only man in my life," I told him truthfully, "is Bob, my gouty old uncle."

"Then things must be booming for you in business," he persisted. "Is it to be symphony work or grand opera next season?"

"Neither, I haven't the ghost of any sort of prospect."

The mask of weariness dropped from his face. His eyes were eager and young in the starlight. He reached for my hand.

"You almost cared for me once, Diana," he said. "You almost cared, didn't you?"

"Yes," I confessed, "***almost,*** Peter, but not quite."

"We could find the way back to that crossroad," he pleaded, "and go on together. Love to me will never mean any one but you, Diana."

"Oh, but, Peter," I heard myself arguing, "really—we—never—felt—"I halted. "Our valuations of things, people—"

Peter stopped me.

"Diana," he said, "don't judge me. I am sick in my soul of the world I have had to live in to do my work. These people are no more my people than they are yours. For years I have been writing editorials against a political party that I believe to be the salvation of the country....But, thank God, I see a way out at last. The chance has come to write what I want to write; the opportunity to travel. Come with me around the world, Diana. It is the first of my new duties—to see the different countries that make up our great globe, and to study each nation's need in relation to the others."

Peter's voice was impassioned. He seemed to have stepped into an ideal self that showed him amazingly different, a Titan in mental stature as in physical. His eloquence swept me along; his magnetism silenced every argument I tried to put forth.

"You do love me!" he declared. "Say 'yes' now," he begged "I am the loneliest man in the world."

Colonel Sinclair's voice almost at us saved me the necessity of a reply.

"Oh, here you are, Wentworth!" he boomed. "I see now why you forgot your appointment with me, this red-headed girl beguiled you!"

Peter apologized rather more than I thought necessary for forgetting the appointment, and suggested that he was entirely at the Colonel's service now.

"No," Colonel Sinclair said, "I was sent to fetch Miss Cameron in. She promised some one to sing for us."

"Will you ride, with me in the morning?" Peter asked, as the Colonel offered me his arm.

"I am visiting Aline," I told him. "We'll have to consult her before I make any plans."

I sang two songs, then begged off. Peter and Colonel Sinclair had disappeared when I looked around to remind him Aline was expecting us. Tom looked in the billiard-room, out on the verandahs, and in the drawing-room for him. Gibbs, the butler, conveyed the information that Mr. Wentworth and Colonel Sinclair were in the library and had asked not to be disturbed. Gibbs had carried Peter's regrets to Aline. Tom tried to detain me for a talk, the others were dancing or playing bridge, but I pleaded fatigue and went upstairs.

I found Aline on her sleeping-porch, ready for bed. She sent Tilly away and indicated a chair near her cot. I could see even in the shadows where she lay how bright her eyes were and the eagerness in her face, as she satisfied herself we were alone. Jupiter, the old bull-dog, rose solemnly and stationed himself sentry-wise at the door.

"Diana," Aline began, "I want you to promise me not to tell what I am going to tell you." I promised; even as I gave my word there flashed through my mind the quaintness of it. What secret could Aline have, Aline stricken from birth, all of whose brief life has been spent in either a rolling chair or in bed. Aline, whose spine is fluid nerve, with not one normal vertebra.

She was raising herself with infinite caution; then she sat up alone, slipped nearer the edge of the bed, placed her feet timidly on the floor, and stood erect, with no support whatever. I was too amazed to speak; I was frightened. Jupiter barked a guarded assurance for me to go on and say something, that Aline was quite all right.

"Aline," I begged, "get back in bed, child."

"But see," she persisted, turning, "I can stand, Diana. Don't you ever tell!"

Finally I persuaded the child to lie down and tell me who had wrought the miracle and why it must be such a secret.

"You remember"—Aline was telling her story breathlessly—"how I love to be taken to the park to watch the children play?" I nodded. "One day a young man came by my rolling chair and stopped. It was not long before he knew that I had never walked. But never to have walked, he said, was not so sad as to be blind. Then he told me he had been blind until two years ago. Hopelessly blind, and all the famous specialists and eye-men said he could never see because all the nerves in his eyes were quite dead. And here he was seeing! I asked him who finally cured him and he replied: 'The Great Physician, and he can also heal you.'

"I have heard the specialists give their opinions so often about my spine that I know quite well why they know I can never walk. I told him. It was the same verdict they had pronounced on him, and here he was seeing! Black Tilly seemed to understand what he said better than I did. It was she who asked him to tell me if he knew how I could be healed. I don't know what happened, but before he finished telling me about the church through which he was healed, I knew that the same Truth that restored his sight could strengthen my spine and show me how to walk. And it has. Now I can stand. I am growing stronger every day. As soon as I master all my fear, I shall walk."

"That is the church where I sang," I told her, "I never thought once that it could do for you what it has done." And yet for over a year I had seen the miracles that Christ wrought done over and over again there. Cripples in rolling chairs came to church, pushed by attendants, and then one day they would walk in, without the chairs! The paralyzed and the blind, the deaf and the dumb. I had heard them week after week bear witness to the truth, and yet never once had I thought of Aline being restored through it.

"So far no one knows but you and Tilly. I study the books, and I am having treatment even at this distance from my friend. Shall I tell Peter?"

"Wait until he sees you walk," I advised. "Shall I sing you one of the hymns I used to sing at the church?"

She tucked her warm little face down in my hand, and I sang softly so they could not hear downstairs.

"O Love, that will not let me go, I rest my weary soul in Thee, I give Thee back the life I owe That in Thy ocean depths its flow May richer, fuller be.

"O Light, that follow'st all my way, I yield my flickering torch to Thee. My heart restores its borrowed ray That in Thy sunshine blaze its day May brighter, fairer be."

Lura's church had done this.

CHAPTER XIII

Roseneath Plantation, April 16

WHEN Tilly brought my breakfast this morning, there was a note from Bob on the tray, and a letter from Terence Woode in Bermuda. When I asked how the letters came, Tilly replied that the boy who went after my other clothes brought them back from Palmetto Grove.

This was by way of breaking it to me that Jinny had ridden rough-shod over my wishes, and sent for my things whether I wished them or not. Tilly's white teeth shone.

"I heerd Miss Jinny tellin' Miss Grant," she said, "dat she gwine steal a march on you, and fix it so you hadder stay whedder you want to or no."

Bob's note was characteristically brief:

Honey, Jinny has her heart set on your staying. I don't need you. Enjoy yourself with your friends.

The bees you expressed a wish for, some weeks ago, arrived yesterday. About a million emigrants swarmed on a tree in the garden. Obadiah and Chattie May have got them in an improvised hive.

Hope these duds are the ones you want.

BOB

Tilly informed me that Miss Jinny had my clothes, and that Mistah Gibbs had a note for me. He would deliver it himself, he had told her.

When I opened Terence's letter, a troop of pressed "little red soldiers" fell out. The letter was six weeks old. He had been under the weather and lonely for Tink and the Commodore who are off on a cruise among the Southern Islands. He was sending me under separate cover in manuscript the Bamboula music, and an old book full of stories about its history. Also he gave me news of the American branch of his family. The niece he had never seen, so he had been formally notified, had died in Louisiana, leaving a baby daughter. Her husband had been buried two weeks before she passed on. Her brother, Stephen Abercrombie, had sent him a brief letter from New York, on his return from France, after the signing of the armistice. The nephew is a hydrographic engineer, Terence writes, and one of a commission that will be sent South or West to report on a new system of waterways to be utilized in reaching the Gulf with a view of connecting up the Middle West and South with the South American trade.

Terence's heart is plainly with this nephew he has never seen, the American son of an English mother.

Jinny arrived before I was dressed. She was triumphant. She was followed by Céleste carrying the box of Rollins's clothes. "Now there's no excuse," she said, "for any more foolishness, for here is a check. Fill it out for all you need, and smile, smile, smile!"

I tore the check in tiny pieces and threw it into the waste-paper basket.

"I asked you not to send for these things," I reminded her when Céleste had gone. "I told you I would not borrow any money from you."

"See here, Di," she said. "We are going to have a Governor here to-night to dinner and some big cotton men from New Orleans and Memphis. I want you to look your loveliest and I'm counting on you to do the entertaining. The check is in payment for your singing to-night" (the idea came to her, I knew as she talked); "don't be a goose. You have the opportunity to cancel your debt to Rollins—and certainly you must be a dream in this."

She had taken the blue gown out of the box and held it up.

"What a gorgeous peacock you'll be," she said, "with your bronze hair and blue eyes over all this color!"

I felt myself growing furiously angry and tried to control the tide.

"And as for your going back to Palmetto Grove," she continued, "I'm not going to hear of it. I have taken a house at Newport and announced to everybody that you are going to spend the summer with me. Crœsus is going to take us all for a cruise on his yacht to South America. He's giving the party to you."

"You are entirely mistaken," I said; "I am going to spend the summer at Palmetto Grove with Bob."

"Bob is n't going to let you," she said. "I'll attend to that part of it. By the way, how about all of us driving down for a day with him? There's no place to take these people except Cottonport, and they hate that."

Jinny met all my objections coolly. That Bob was n't prepared for guests at Palmetto Grove she dismissed by saying that she would have luncheon prepared and taken over for us to eat picnic fashion—and she'd take her own servants.

"It would give him a shaking-up he needs," she laughed, "and I want to have a talk with him about you."

"You know perfectly well, Jinny," I said, "that these people are not Bob's kind. They could never be his friends."

"What's the matter with them that they can't be your friends!" she demanded. "They are mine."

"Because you and I are the antipodes," I flashed. "I detest, and you know it, these idle, bridge-playing, cocktail-drinking wasters. Palmetto Grove would only bore them, and I won't have them taken there."

Jinny's black eyes narrowed. "Oh, well"—she shrugged her shoulders—"if you refuse to have them, that's the end of it. Don't be mad with me, Di. We are cousins, after all, and I am awfully fond of you, old girl."

She put her arms around me and begged me to forgive her again. We patched it up, and I asked her if I could drive back to Palmetto Grove after lunch. She said there wasn't a car on the place, that most of the men had gone to a cotton convention at Vicksburg, and would not return until late in the afternoon, and the rest of the party was going fishing.

"Anyway," she warned, "I am not going to let you go home until this party is over. You can do anything else you like, but the Palmetto Grove road is prohibited." I knew Jinny well enough to know she meant it.

Gibbs delivered the note Peter had entrusted to him for me.

Sorry not to see you [it ran] and the ride must be postponed. Cotton convention at Vicksburg. Think it out, and tell me to-night. I love you.

PETER

Alice Grant and the other women, and the men who didn't go to Vicksburg, were getting ready to go to Reed Lake for a day's fishing. Jinny did not urge me to go after I had proved that Aline expected me to stay with her. Jinny was anxious to be friends, and they drove off and left Aline and me for a quiet afternoon in the garden. We had our luncheon under a tree, and, between visits from Cousin Clara, Aline rapturously told me of her progress, and read me passages from the book that had been instrumental in her healing. I must confess that my attention to her was for the most part a mere pretence.

I was deep in my own problems. I dreaded the weeks to come with Jinny arrayed against me. Jinny with her will to have her own way usually gets it, by hook or crook. She is quite capable of passing all her own plans up for the summer, to see that I do not carry out mine. Jinny has neither principle nor conscience when either stands in her way to an objective. I must keep her away from Bob. The unguarded confession I gave her about my debts would be her first point of attack with Bob. His peace of mind would be entirely gone when she had finished with him. If I do not take the money from her to pay what I owe, I see no prospect of getting it. My confidence that somehow, some way, my need will be met, is weakened. If I do take it, I deliberately sell myself in bondage to her for the summer.

Then there is Peter. Peter who loves me, and whom, after a fashion, I almost love. Peter has solved his problem at last. He no longer has any dependents to look after, and with his new freedom to write what he wants to write, his hard-won independence at last, is not Peter the solution of it all?

Peter is the one reality in my world of unrealities. Peter and I running away around the world. It appealed to me very much. I felt ready to start this minute.

"Diana," Aline's voice brought me back, "when you and Peter marry, I want to come live with you."

"But, Aline," I said, "Peter and I may never marry."

She sighed. "I wish you could. I am always planning my visit to you."

"Come to see me at Palmetto Grove," I said, "when I go home." Then I told her all about the place, even the bees that arrived yesterday and how we were going to build straw hives for them in the old flower garden.

"It sounds very peaceful as you tell it, Diana," she said.

"It is," I replied. "Did you ever hear that bees won't stay on a place where people quarrel?"

"We could never keep bees, then," she said. "Daddy and Mother quarrel more than ever. Their words are like wasps, each with a burning sting, hate."

When time came for her nap, I sang Aline to sleep, and arranged a net canopy from a low-hanging bough to keep off a chance mosquito or gnat Then I lay down on the warm, pulsing ground to take a nap. But there was no sleep for me. Peter had to have his answer. Since yesterday my new-found peace had left me. I found myself thrashing over the same ground I reviewed five years ago when I told Peter I could never care for him. Perhaps that was a mistake, after all.

After all, Peter and I could probably be very happy. Certainly there are more ties that bind us than the average married couple have. Bob is getting old, and he has lived too long alone to really be dependent on me. Negroes and mules and cotton are his world. And when he has gone, and my youth has entirely finished passing, I shall find myself old and lonelier than ever, and even if I have a home it will be no home unless there is some one with whom I share it, some one to whom I am necessary, whose need demands my bit of service to my kind. I was back in the old slough of despond.

I decided what my answer to Peter to-night would be. It will be very pleasant seeing new lands, and old countries, the salt sea in our faces, going around the world together, Peter and I.

Several telegrams came for Colonel Sinclair. The calls became so urgent that Gibbs appealed to me. The Colonel had left no instructions; he and Mr. Wentworth had gone in a runabout to Vicksburg, that was his impression. Could I suggest, being more familiar with this part of the country, where he might be reached there, or on the road? I could not.

"Long-distance from Washington is now trying to locate him, Miss."

The fishing party returned sunburned and mosquito-bitten. Alice Grant was demanding some magical beautifier for her nose. It was red as a beet The day had been a failure, the fish would not bite, but everything else had, Jinny declared, and her women guests were all more or less spectacles with freckled necks and blistered faces. They were in a conspiracy to have their dinners upstairs. Jinny's temper was at the boiling point.

It was late before the men got in from Vicksburg. The day had been very hot and dusty, and for the most part they sounded in no better humor than the women, as they trooped upstairs.

Tilly drew my tub and made it deliriously soft and fragrant, with Jinny's choicest verbena salts. Jinny fetched them herself as an excuse to beg me to wear my peacock frock, and outdo myself.

"Everybody else is cross as two sticks," she said. "May the Lord forgive me for undertaking a house party in this canebrake."

I dressed and went down early. Climbing pink roses in pots were placed to screen the piano at the far end of the long open drawing-room. I had come down to look over some music that I had seen there the night before. Just beyond was a balcony. The breeze swept through the long windows, and, absorbed in going over the words of certain old ballads to refresh my memory, I did not notice when Gibbs turned on the shaded lights. I heard some one enter the room, but supposed it to be a servant, until I heard Colonel Sinclair speaking. It did not occur to me that his conversation was confidential.

"I find these wires calling me back to Washington at once," he was saying. "But before I leave I want to turn over this check to you in return for using your influence as we arranged, editorially."

Peter's agreeable voice assured him that there was no hurry.

"This certified check is for a hundred thousand dollars," the Colonel continued. "As I explained to you I shall clean up half a million if the market goes as I expect after the editorials embodying your opinion that there will be no reduction in cotton acreage are published—When will they be published?"

"I put them on the wires at Vicksburg," Peter replied. "The first should appear to-morrow morning as leader in our four papers."

"I made the check out to cash, in the event anything ever should come up—But I promise you it won't." Colonel Sinclair spoke rapidly. "I feel that the check is only a small payment on what you have done. In addition to making you editor-in-chief of the four newspapers, I shall see that you are also one of our chief stockholders."

Peter gasped and grasped Colonel Sinclair's hand. "And I can rely on you," he asked, "to hold to your word as to our confidential relations?"

"Absolutely," the Colonel assured him; "and don't let your conscience cause you any regrets in the matter. Your editorials only express your opinion. The South says it is going to reduce its cotton acreage. Nobody really knows how many acres the other fellow is putting in, even if he has signed the pledge. Anyway, you have done no lasting harm. Your opinion will help me bear the market at the time it suits me. If it is true that cotton acreage has been reduced, the Government reports later will show just how much and the 'poor down-trodden Southern planter' will get all that's coming to him, by the time his crop is ginned and marketed."

Gibbs announced the car; Colonel Sinclair met Tom in the hall, and in the hasty good-byes, and with the swirl of skirts and laughter coming down the stairs, I heard no more until the guests came into the drawing-room. I slipped out by the balcony and on to the shadows of the lawn.

I had overheard an incredible thing. I refused to believe what I had seen, what I had heard; that Peter could realize what he had done. I told myself over and over that it was not true, that it could not be true. And yet every word of the simple transaction, by which one man had sold his birthright to another, was etched on my memory.

And these were the terms by which Peter was to win his freedom, his independence, his escape from the bondage he hated. He had sold himself for a price, a price high enough, he felt, to buy me.

"There she is!" Peter's voice called back from the balcony to the ones in the drawing-room, and he came down the steps toward me, a cocktail glass in his hand. Alice Grant, Tom, and Senator Harris stepped through the window out on the balcony. Gibbs, making his round with the cocktails, appeared at my elbow with his tray. I felt the need of a stimulant. Peter had not tasted his, and he held out his glass to touch mine. I pretended not to see. I spilled half of the cocktail, then drained the glass.

"You are pale as a lily"—Peter was all solicitude; he took my hand—"and cold as ice, child. And you are trembling."

"Haven't got a chill, have you, Miss Cameron?" Senator Harris came down the steps to take one of my arms while Peter supported the other. "We should have taken better care of our song-bird."

The cocktail braced me. Something within helped me to rise above my momentary weakness. I suddenly felt myself hysterically gay, instead of depressed, and so we went in to dinner. I sat between Senator Harris and the Governor, though Peter had planned otherwise. It was a stupid dinner. In spite of their high-sounding titles, the Governor, the Senators, and the Congressmen were for the most part ordinary to a degree. Perhaps in the servants' quarters, with Jinny's foreign-born white servants, they might have shone. They gave no distinction to the dinner at which they found themselves the featured guests. The wines were what appealed to them most, and most of the men drank heavily. After the champagne they had mellowed to the point that the only topic that interested them was national prohibition. Very little was said about cotton. At last Jinny gave the signal and the women passed out. I would have tried to escape upstairs, but Jinny anticipated my design.

"Political pigs"—she nodded in the direction of the dining-room—"but don't desert me. If you don't sing they'll all go to sleep, and we can't get them off on the midnight train."

She went her rounds to the other women, appealing to them to brace up and help her. The local men did not appeal to her guests, that was apparent. Each of the women guests had a flirtation, or several, going with the men who were house guests, and everybody was too beat out with the day to make much effort to prolong the festivities of the evening. There was some dancing, and a table or two played bridge. Barbara Anderson did a few monologues which were applauded feebly. Tom had taken the political crowd out on the lawn, where they smoked cigars and drank black coffee intermittently. Peter tried every way possible to get a word with me, but I aided Jinny's endeavors to divert a loggy individual from New Orleans. At last even she gave him up.

"Go on and sing," she begged me.

"What's the use?" I asked her. "They wouldn't listen to Caruso."

"But they can look at you," she said. "That may wake them up."

So I went to the piano behind the pink roses. I had hardly started to sing before Peter dropped quietly into a chair behind me. I hunted desperately through the music and found a hideous jazz number, and in the din of this conversation was impossible. This type of music appealed to my audience, and I kept it up. They came in from outside to hear me.

"By Jove, it's homelike," one of the politicians said. "It's like a million guineas singing at once—and a different tune." Pretty soon everybody was joining in. The jazz music was not my own, but Viola Fortescue's, and when I pleaded my inability to play a certain accompaniment, she took her seat at the piano, and, unnoticed, I slipped out on the balcony and down the steps. I could not hope for much of a respite, but I felt the desperate need of getting hold of myself.

Peter was seated on the bottom step smoking. He laughed softly at my surprise and faced me, holding out his hand. "I knew what you were planning to do," he said. "I am waiting for you."

I did not take his hand. He did not notice this, but caught my arm and guided me to the lower walk.

"Now," he said when we were beyond earshot of the others, "tell me! Is it to be love and peace and you, Diana?"

CHAPTER XIV

THE river glided purringly by a few feet away. The scent of flowers from the garden was overpoweringly sweet. We sat on the seat where last night I had promised to give Peter his answer to-day. I could see him perfectly in the starlight. Peter had never looked so big, so handsome—nor more honest. I never felt so spineless, so helpless, so utterly in his power.

His strong hands held both my wrists. He drew me toward him.

"Peter," I stammered, "I was behind the roses in the drawing-room. I heard every word of your conversation with Colonel Sinclair."

I felt his heart suddenly stop throbbing in his hands—then the next moment I heard the bones in my wrist snap. The sharp pain brought back my senses.

"You've hurt me," I said, wrenching my hands free. I rose to go.

"Sit down here," Peter commanded, "and listen to me."

"Why should I listen—what need?" I heard myself ask wearily.

"Because I love you and you love me; because our lives lie together."

"Oh, no, Peter Wentworth!"

"I have told you my miserable story," he said; "there is no reason why I should try to conceal from you the transaction you witnessed to-day. For twenty years I have been writing editorials against principles, the party, and men I believe in. There has never been a question of personal responsibility in those articles; I was hired to follow the policy of the paper, not to air my personal opinions of right and wrong.

"I was sent South to write a series of editorials on the cotton situation. I was given no instructions, further than that I was to go over the ground, meet representative men, talk to those in authority, attend cotton conventions, form my own opinions and write them. I have done this."

"I saw you paid by Colonel Sinclair for writing the editorials as he wants them written."

"Sinclair has gone to Washington to meet the syndicate who owns the string of papers in which my editorials appear, to sign the contracts that will make him sole owner of these papers. The hundred-thousand-dollar check he gave me was an advance, a bonus on my services. I also am to be given part interest in the papers and to be editor-in-chief. It is true I wrote the cotton editorials as he wishes them written, but it is also true, as I have told you, I have been writing editorials at the dictation of the owners of the papers I serve ever since I started to do newspaper work."

"But what you wrote is not true. Neither of you pretended it was. Cotton acreage has been cut one third and you know it."

"You heard those men at dinner," he said. "Would you place reliance on anything a crowd like that would say? They say the cotton acreage is a fact, Just as they say, for an audience outside the State, that prohibition is a fact here. Drunkards and liars, talking about their State being dry—"

"The men here to-night are not representative," I replied. "They are politicians who fatten on the labor of the ones who really work. If your editorials are substantiated by the signed statements of such men, you know as well as I do what their word is worth. And if you deliberately write such lies you are no better yourself."

Angry as I was, Peter did not lose his temper.

"Child," he said sadly, "I make no brief for myself, I have tried to keep my ideals; but only one remains, that is yourself. I do not doubt that your uncle is an honorable and a high-toned gentleman. I am sure he is incapable of double-dealing or deceit. Tom has mentioned him several times as a survival of the past, the old-time Southern gentleman, now up to his neck in debt, and faced with the most difficult proposition of all, the certainty of losing his labor in a few years. But perhaps things are not so bad with him." He studied my face.

I could not deny that Bob is in debt; neither could I pretend that he has any delusions about negroes.

"Colonel Sinclair does not own one acre of cotton land," I said, "and yet before this week is out he will have made half a million dollars. I heard him say so, if your editorials and probably other pressure he is able to bring 'bears' the market—depresses the price of cotton. Year after year men like him make fortunes out of cotton, for which the planter who raised it has to take less than it cost him to produce!"

"Getting yourself worked up into a reformer isn't going to change Wall Street, Diana. Be a philosopher. Sinclair's business acumen nets him half a million or more. The Southern farmer isn't really injured if he does not sell the day cotton is down. The market recovers its tone quickly. You and I can say good-bye to them all and start out on our honeymoon—"

"Peter"—I felt strangely calm and collected now—"I may be a freak in my ideas of love, as I undoubtedly am in my principles of business, but love to me is founded on respect And I—despise you!"

"Beg pardon, sir"—Gibbs's oily tones preceded him as he picked his ponderous way across the wet grass—"but you are wanted on the long-distance' phone, and Mrs. Foster, Miss, asked me to say to you the crowd will soon be leaving if you care to say good-night to them."

"Will you wait for me?" Peter asked anxiously as we rose. "You do not understand what I tried to say to you."

"What could we ever have to say to each other after this, Peter?"

My voice must have carried farther than I meant, for Tom, coming down the walk with Senator Harris, exclaimed, "Hoity-toity! but they are parting in anger!"

Senator Harris held out his hand.

"It's the red-headed girl again!" he exclaimed; "as a prima donna I must say you are a fraud."

"She's a finished flirt," Tom corrected, familiarly taking my arm; "the high-brow, spiritual type whose victims never recover."

Jinny was hurrying everybody to get wraps. Half a dozen automobiles were throbbing around the front door.

"We can all crowd in somehow," she said, "and there'll be plenty of room coming home. The moon will be up then."

I never felt less like taking a moonlight ride to Cottonport In the excitement of placing people in cars Jinny assumed everybody was going. She was giving final instructions to Gibbs about supper on our return.

"Aren't you going, Diana?" Alice Grant called out from a big touring-car. "There's room for one more in here." She was packed in with Senator Harris, Barbara, and two of the men from Memphis.

"What's that?" Jinny turned to Gibbs. "Mr. Wentworth is waiting for a long-distance message, and can't go with us?"

"Wait a minute, Alice," I begged. "Of course I want to go!" I had no intention of staying behind if it meant another tête-à-tête with Peter.

We reached Cottonport a little before eleven, and said good-bye to the departing guests. Three of the cars were from the local garage and returning to it. A rearrangement was necessary in the cars going back to Roseneath.

"Diana," Jinny said, "please go home with Tom in the roadster. The other women have arranged themselves with the men they want to be with, Senator Harris wants me to go with him. You don't care anything about moving pictures, do you?"

The town clock was striking eleven. Jinny was all excitement; she hung on my reply, and when I said, "No, why?" she explained that the other men and all the women had their hearts set on the lark—to get the man at the motion-picture place, which was just closing, to run the picture off again, just for them.

"Tom hates' em," she explained. "He's cross as a bear, anyway. If you'll take him on home, I'll never forget it, Di."

So Tom and I started back to Roseneath in the roadster. Jinny had told him the truth when she said I had a headache and wanted to get home in a hurry; she did not know it was the truth, however. My head throbbed and ached. I was glad enough to feel the wind against it, and for the quiet, as we turned back down the river road. Tom seemed to be deep in thought.

"Not much chance for a reconciliation between you and Wentworth, eh, Diana?" he asked at last.

"None whatever."

"And you say you are not going to marry Crœsus?"

"That is even more remote."

"Jinny always has stood out that you'll end up marrying that young chap—

what's his name?—who builds bridges."

"Timothy is younger than I am. Besides, I don't love him, Tom."

"And you've given up your work?"

"I had to. I was ill and had to come South."

"Aren't you going back?"

"I don't know."

"Look here, Diana. Excuse my frankness, but tell me honestly, are you down and out?"

There was a ring of genuine affection, concern, in Tom's voice. After Bob, Jinny, distant cousin though she is, is the nearest relative I have. And Tom seems more a blood relation than she. For he has many of the traits I love most in Aline. If Jinny were a finer woman, Tom would be a better man. Tom took the reply I did not make for granted.

Only last night I had boasted that if contentment could be banked I would be the richest woman in the world. At this moment I felt myself the poorest. The last worldly hope I had set my heart upon had vanished.

"When a man's business gets in the state your affairs seem to be in," Tom said, "he hires an expert to point out where he has made his mistakes. Shall I tell you where you've failed to take advantage of your opportunities?"

"If you like."

"I recall no young girl who has started out to achieve what is known as a career," he said, "who has succeeded without the help of some man, powerful enough to fight her battles with money or influence. Your mistake is that you were childish enough to think your contralto voice would win its own way. Not that the voice in itself was n't as good as many that are now where you thought to be by this time.

"You are pretty nearly thirty years old aren't you?" Tom asked. I replied wearily in the affirmative. "You've had several good chances to marry, and you don't seem interested. The situation resolves itself into this: If you go on with your work, and have intelligent help and no financial worries, there is every chance that you can still make your objective. You have personality, magnetism, charm, in the most extraordinary degree. Why don't you ^buck up and take what you want from life, Diana?"

"Why don't I?" I laughed mirthlessly.

Tom studied my face as he slowed the car.

"Don't think I am advising you from any success I have achieved myself," he said. "I am the most pitiable failure that lives to-day. The money I inherited has multiplied and I am rich, but in all except money I am a pauper. Jinny has no heart—she never had—but I have not always known it. I no longer expect love or affection or even a semblance of a home from a woman of her type. Our relations as husband and wife are a farce. She has what women in her circle consider—her love affairs as they have theirs. Heaven help such love! I know what is going on between her and Harris, and I am indifferent."

"Perhaps if you were not—"I began—

"We are dealing with facts," he replied, "not fancies. I have no illusions.... Diana, I love you—as Aline loves you."

He hurriedly added "as Aline loves you," when he felt the effect of his words.

"Thank you, Tom." I was determined not to misunderstand him. "Aline is an angel. Her affection alone makes me rich in friends."

"I love you," he repeated, "and if you would accept help from me you could go on with your career. I could guarantee it."

"If you mean that you will lend me money," I said, "on the chance of my earning enough to repay it at some future time—"

"I shall not expect any repayment," he interrupted, "except—"

"Except what?"

"I love you," he said; "I shall make no public claim on you; our relations could be absolutely dignified and secret. In every way I should protect your good name, and you shall be provided with an income more than sufficient to relieve your mind of every worry."

I heard his words, yet the meaning did not register, and he talked on and on.

"What have I ever done," I asked him finally when I could speak, "to make you—imagine—you—could—say—these—things—to—me, that you could insult me—"

"Don't be a mid-Victorian fool," Tom interrupted roughly. "You know perfectly well that I have no thought of insulting you. There is a new order of respectability going around. You know it. Jinny and her friends practise it. Its code is: 'Do as you please, only conduct your affairs with dignity.' " He laughed harshly. "My proposition to you did not include an offer of marriage—"

"Don't," I begged.

"Because," he continued, "I am not fool enough to think that marriage allures you. Jinny will get rid of me, sooner or later, when it suits her convenience. If my name would justify you in accepting my assistance, I make you a formal proposal of marriage as soon as Jinny gives me my freedom."

He had taken his hat off. I looked at him, half bald, with his fine eyes buried in the sensuous flesh of his face. I knew that this Tom Foster was not offering me what he considered an insult. The Tom Foster of fifteen years ago would have been the first to challenge the man who had said such things as he had said to me, no matter who the woman might have been. Now he waited for my answer. We were halfway up the drive. I was suddenly overcome by the grotesqueness of the situation and I heard myself laugh, and I kept on laughing, though it hurt me hideously. Peal after peal, while the man beside me grew furious.

"Stop that!" he commanded; but I could not He caught my hands, and shook me; still I laughed, like a loon. I seemed to be detached from myself. My head ached as if it would split, and if the laughter jarred him, it caused me excruciating pain.

Cousin Clara hurried down the steps. "Oh, Tommy," she said, "don't tell me Diana is intoxicated. I feared the consequences with all that wine for dinner!"

I laughed louder at this, even while I heard Gibbs, hovering solicitously near to help if needed, say: "Madame, Miss Cameron did not touch the wines at dinner. She drank only half a cocktail."

"Then it's that," bewailed Cousin Clara.

"Hysterics!" Tom caught and lifted me out, shaking me roughly. "Control your-self, or I shall send for a physician."

"O-oh, hysterics," Cousin Clara was in her territory again. "Then let her alone. Come along with me, child." She led me to my room. I begged her to leave me. She hobbled off murmuring something about ammonia. I locked the door, and fell across the bed in the dark.

Far off a light that came nearer. A lantern on the prow of a boat I recognized—a sampan. I was on the banks of a familiar stream, and the two boatmen in blue blous-es were waiting for me. I stepped aboard, and they pushed off again.

The landing on the far side. . . . The path up the hill. . . . The red lacquer bridge....And coming through the gate with both hands outstretched for mine— You.

You turned the leaves of an old Chinese book I recognized. I read:

The Master said: "Her thoughts were not with Him, or how could he be far away?"

CHAPTER XV

I WAKED with a feeling of buoyancy, lightness, freshly energized as one feels after a morning dip in the sea. The house was dark and still. Outside the blackness had faded to grey. A cotton-batting moon was fast melting in the heavens. A few stars shone here and there.

My plan of escape was clear in my mind. There was not a moment to lose if I meant to carry it out I hurriedly braced myself under the cold shower and dressed for walking, putting on my high tan boots and the brown tweed suit I wore when I came to Roseneath. All of my other clothes I packed in my bag and a box, excepting a dress I left out as a parting gift for Tilly. I labelled the box and bag to myself, by parcel post to Deer-lick, and wrote instructions to Gibbs to send both to Cottonport by the boy who leaves every morning before seven for the mail. I pinned my last five-dollar bill over the final directions to him:

Gibbs: A messenger from Palmetto Grove came for me. You *saw him.* I left at once with him, not wishing to disturb anybody.

I knew Gibbs, bribe-taker that he is, could convince himself that he had seen me depart with the messenger, and that I could count on his discretion. Gibbs has his price, but he stays bought. I carried the bag and the box downstairs cautiously, placing them with the mail to be posted on a table in the hall. I wrote Aline a few lines; my note to Jinny was even briefer: "Called home. Don't worry and don't bring any of these people down there. Thank you for all you ever wanted to do for me. Can't come back."

A clock was striking five as I cautiously slipped out the front door. There were a few faint streaks of dawn in the east, enough light to show me the way to go. It had been years since I went over the road connecting Roseneath with Palmetto

Grove. It was five miles down following the river.

I stepped softly, following the drive to the entrance gate, then taking a short cut through the pasture. I came out on the old road. It was little more than a cow-path now. Tall, wet grass bordered it closely. I had to hold my skirts high. The path ran near the new garage, and I held my breath, fearful lest some early rising chauffeur might see me. But apparently the whole world was still asleep.

Half a mile away I knew all danger of being discovered was past, and my adventure assumed a new aspect. I was enjoying the crystal clear bubble of the new day. The east was pink and golden, and as suddenly the birds had taken their places and were timing up for their overture to the morning. The green willows swaying against the grey mist from the river beyond gave the impression of a drop curtain about to be lifted. Blackberry-vines, white with blossoms, dripped from every stump and fence corner. The scent of wild honeysuckle and Cherokee roses from the river-banks scented the sharp cool air. The world seemed freshly created, new from the hands of its maker, uncontaminated. Its air was ethereal wine; its beauty and freshness marvels that I seemed to appreciate for the first time. I had a feeling that I, too, was expected to contribute my mite to the outpouring of adoration all around and about me. I sank down on a fallen tree and bowed my head. That it was prayer I do not know, but my heart proclaimed its peace and thankfulness.

Everything viewed in the light of the sunrise looked different. The two days at Roseneath were as unreal as a theatrical performance seen in retrospect. Peter, conjured up to be reviewed, was no longer a villain, bought with a price, but a man whose sense of real values was hideously warped and twisted. A man who did evil in the vain hope that good might come of it; a worshipper of Mammon from whom he only asked enough to enable him to live at peace with the true God. Poor worldly Peter! And Tom, examined under the searchlight of Truth, was revealed no more or less than a sensualist, groping, too, in his blind way, for something higher than he knew, still thinking that the things of the spirit can be bought.

Millions of gnats whirling before me in a shaft of sunlight seemed to symbolize the people I had left. They were as purposeless, driven by the chance winds of this world, and, as I saw them now, as helpless.

I resumed my walk, hurrying in order to reach the bayou by the time Bob should pass on the other side on his morning rounds. Blue smoke curled from the cabins dotted here and there in the fields of Roseneath. I knew the negroes were getting ready to go to work, and I kept in the protection of the undergrowth following the rail fence. I knew the dangers I ran in undertaking a five-mile walk along an un-travelled road through a plantation. Hideous tragedies have come by a white woman taking less chances. And I was unarmed, and too far away for any help to reach me should the need arise. And yet I felt no fear, only a sweet sense of deliverance, of freedom. I was thinking of Aline and the things she had told me. And a "realization" such as I had often heard grateful invalids speak of at Lura's church, a "realization" of the protection of Truth and Love seemed to flood my consciousness and bear me along as if I had wings. I was not afraid of anything that might cross my path, now or ever. I seemed to have stepped into a new world, out of a period of mesmerism and unreality, The sun was well up when I came in sight of the bayou. I must have been quite two hours on the road: my shoes were sopping wet with dew and my skirts bedraggled.

I made my way through a tangle of dew-berries, and reached the log stretched across the yellow waters of the bayou. The sun dazzled me as I came out of the shadows. I put my hand up to shield my eyes, to examine the narrow foot-bridge, and I saw stretched out luxuriously upon it, enjoying a sun-bath, an enormous grey snake, whose jewel eyes darted around in all directions, probably speculating on what he could pick up for breakfast.

I had not reckoned on this, though I knew the bayou was full of alligators. From some recess of memory flashed Cecil's story of the two goats who met on a narrow foot-bridge, and his tribute to the one who laid himself down that the other might walk over him—that he was as fine a gentleman as Lord Chesterfield. The situation amused me. Here I was on the last lap of the journey, and my path obstructed. I laughed aloud in sheer happiness—across the sluggish yellow stream lay my home, and I was in a hurry to get there. Never before had I known this homesick feeling for Palmetto Grove and Bob. The snake was now observing me attentively. There was no expression of facing a foe in his behavior, only a lazy interest in a strange new creature, a type he had not seen before.

"Would you"—I heard my foolish speech directed to him—"be kind enough to let me have the log to cross on? I fear I am already late for breakfast." The snake raised his head, seemed to listen, and then instantly hastened to comply with my request. He glided off into the water, and leisurely swam downstream without one backward glance. If half a dozen alligators had appeared just then, no more would I have feared them. Some magic spell lay on this morning. I walked in a strange new world, and yet in the same old one where all God's ideas dwell together in peace and harmony.

The smell of a strong pipe floated from behind a clump of willows. I sniffed its familiar, and once disgusting, fumes. Mandy! She was passing on her way to the field, with breakfast for her family in a shining tin lard bucket. She looked at me, as if I were a ghost.

"Law, Miss Diana!" she exclaimed, when I hailed her. "Dat sholy ain't you yoh-self!"

Assured that I was not a ghost, she was entirely at my service. It was two miles to the house and I was tired. Had Marse Bob passed this way yet?

"Naw'm, dey ain't had brekkus at de big house," she said; " 't ain't seven o'clock yet. Marse Bob doan never get down heah tel nine or past." Was there any one I could send to the house to get my horse? Mandy set down her bucket.

"My squad's workin' over in de new ground," she said. "It's about a mile over dere. I could send one de li'l' boys atter Jenny Ribbons, but you'd hadder wait." A sudden idea occurred to her. "I'll go git him fer you, Miss Diana," she said; "I'm too fat to walk very fast, but I'll git you home."

"Wait, Mandy," I said, for I had caught sight of her queer calico pony grazing near the cabin; "can't you saddle your horse and let me ride him?"

"Law, Miss Diana, I never thought you'd ride dat calico pony," she said. "He's gentle as a lamb an' bline as a bat, but he'll git you dar."

I went back with her to the cabin. She put a rope bridle on the calico pony, and some sort of a makeshift side-saddle, and proudly led him to the steps for me to mount.

And this was the woman, only a few short weeks ago, that I disliked and mis-judged.

"Mandy," I said, "I didn't know that I'd ever come to a place where your pipe would smell sweet—or that you would look as beautiful as you were coming from behind those willows."

Mandy's fat sides shook. "Me an' you," she said, "didn't understan' each other at fust. Seem lak ter me you ain't de same young leddy you wuz when you rid up so gran' an' Marse Bob warn't ever expectin' you ter come home no more."

"I'm not the same person, Mandy," I told her.

"I sho' laks you now," she said.

"I laks myself better now," I laughed as we parted, she to hurry on with breakfast to her squad waiting for it in the new ground, I to the big house before Bob should get away. The calico pony fox-trotted along the soft field roads, and sure enough I could see, as soon as we were in sight of the house, that Bob's horse was hitched in its usual place. I must have presented a picture rivalling Mandy on that blind calico pony. The hounds set up a welcome baying. Chattie May spied me through the kitchen window. Isaiah was taking hot biscuit into the dining-room. And by the time I reached the steps the entire household was waiting to help me dismount. Bob, the napkin still in his hand, waved directions to Isaiah.

"Get around at his head, Elijah. That pony's blind," he said.

"What's the meaning of this, sister?" He looked in all directions as if expecting the rest of the Mardi-Gras parade to come into sight.

It seemed years since I had seen him, and the welcome he gave me, and the joy of the peg-legged boy and Chattie May over my return, went to my head.

"Oh, Bob," I told him, making it up as I went along, "I slipped away. I had a hideous dream and I had to come home to see if you were safe."

"You had a nightmare about me!" he roared; "but where have you been?—not visiting Mandy, have you?—that you had to come home on that calico quilt frame? I thought you were at Roseneath."

"I ran away before daybreak this morning. I had to see you, to get home to-day. And I am starving."

CHAPTER XVI

Palmetto drove, April 20

CHATTIE MAY scurried off to the kitchen, followed by Isaiah, to bring my breakfast.

"I thought you'd left me, kitten." Bob waited for me to light his pipe. "Jinny said in her note, when she sent for your clothes yesterday, that she was going to take you on back North with her. She said she wanted to come down here to see me and bring her guests, but that you wouldn't hear to it. Ashamed for your friends to see me, sister?"

I kissed him again.

"I was ashamed for you to see that crowd," I said. "And they were **not** my friends, Bob."

He lifted my chin and looked at me quizzically. "You've given up all your friends for me, honey?" This question was too absurd for me to answer seriously.

"Aren't you worth it?" I teased.

But Bob's face did not clear.

"I'm sorry you came back before your visit was finished," he said. "The fact is, I'm thinking a change would do us both good."

"You mean—? But you said the place was a graveyard without me."

"How about giving it up and making a new start somewhere else, sister?"

"You mean you want to go off somewhere, Bob?"

"I think it would do us both good," he hedged. "I've been in a rut so long that it has worn deep as a well. I haven't had any idea about the world except on Palmetto Grove." His eyes avoided mine. "I—I never realized, never dreamed the difficulties that—er—some people had to face, trying to make a living—up North."

"Bob!" I demanded, "I don't understand one word you are saying. It isn't like you to hem and haw like this."

"Palmetto Grove will bring several hundred thousand dollars, I think," he continued. "I'm tired of niggers and mules and nervous cotton—"

"There's not a word of truth in anything you are saying," I accused. "Who has been here talking to you since I've been gone, that everything you've planned and worked for all these years is to be thrown away—and at this season of the year? You're planting cotton, Bob Cameron; not picking it!"

"I know it," he said. "But now that the peace treaty is ready to sign, cotton-land values are probably better than they will ever be again. And I have a fine opportunity to let Palmetto Grove go just as it is."

"Who made you the offer?"

"I went to Cottonport yesterday," he said, "to send a wire in reply to an ad.

that appeared in a New Orleans paper of the day before. I wired to Pinckney, my old friend on the Cotton Exchange, to see the party advertising for a plantation on the river, one thousand acres or over of cotton land, and especially specifying the desirability of cypress timber on it. The Palmetto Grove cypress brake is one of the finest in the State."

"Go on."

"A reply came back immediately that the man would come up to see me personally. Pinckney vouches for his reliability, but did not give his name."

"But if I do not want to sell my part of the plantation?"

"It will mean money for you to live as you like, honey. You won't have to work. You won't have to worry as you have had to do all these years you've been away." Bob was deeply moved. "I never dreamed, child, what you were going through in New York. I did not know you were singing for what they would give you, anywhere they needed a song…I couldn't have stood it if I had known you sang in a theatre."

Quick as a flash I knew Jinny had written him more than a brief note, asking him to send my clothes.

"Where is that letter Jinny sent you?" I demanded. "That's the reason I refuse to visit her. She is a hypocrite and a liar and a meddler. She can find time to manage everybody's affairs but those of her own household. Was it her plan for you to sell Palmetto Grove?"

"Oh, no," he said. "Jinny said she felt it only fair that I should know the truth about your work. She says that you overtaxed your strength, and worried until your voice was gone, and that now you are in debt and very unhappy over it, and that that's the reason she wants to take you in hand. That there is no reason for you not going with her this summer to Newport, and that, with delta land as valuable as it is now, there is no reason why I shouldn't arrange for you to have an income from Palmetto Grove that would place you beyond the necessity of competing with cabaret singers and the professional riff-raff that lives by its wits in New York."

Bob had evidently memorized the note.

"Jinny is quite right," he concluded. "Palmetto Grove should be sold. Then both of us could enjoy life with our debts paid, honey."

There was a muffled blowing up the river. I immediately concluded it was Jinny in an automobile after me, and restrained what I had to say until she arrived.

"De Annabel Lee's comin'' roun' de bend, suh!" Isaiah announced breathlessly. "She's de bigges' steamboat evah is been past heah!"

Bob rose hastily. "I am halfway expecting the man from New Orleans to come on this boat," he said. "He could have caught her at Vicksburg yesterday. That's why I am late in starting over the fields this morning."

"My mind is made up," I told him as he hobbled off toward the landing; "the stranger may offer what he likes, but I am not going to sell my part of Palmetto Grove."

Chattie May had the house clean as a new pin. Prim bouquets of woodbine were the flowers she had chosen for its decoration out of the riot of bloom in the garden. Vases and crystal bowls of it overflowed every available table, stand, or mantelpiece. The effect was unpretentiously charming against the whitewashed walls.

"How clean and honest it all looks, Chattie May," I said; "how clean and honest you look—and—and how homelike and—kind."

"Ma'am?" My words bewildered the little yellow school-teacher. She followed me upstairs to help me change. In all truth I needed to be tubbed and scrubbed and rubbed, and fresh raiment. My bare feet were browner than her own, from the dust and the dew.

Chattie May brushed my tangled hair and polished it with a silk handkerchief and spread it out like a bronze shower in the sunshine and stood off to admire its sheen. She discovered the powder of fresh freckles across my nose and bewailed them, and all the while she was babbling away about what had happened in my two days' absence.

Isaiah had hived the bees in the garden—she had churned twice—she had reddened all the hearths—she had engaged herself to be married to Isaiah. This all by way of paving the way to the favor she wanted to ask: Couldn't I order off and get her a real bridal outfit, "chulle veil and all," not "furgittin' the artificials."

"Artificials! Oh, g'wan now, Miss Diana, you does know what artificials is! Don't you? Artificial orange-blossoms and a chulle veil lak brides in picture-books wears."

Isaiah's peg-leg telegraphed his approach up the stairs. Chattie May met him at the door to see what he wanted. The message he brought was that the gentleman who came on the boat wished to see me, and not Marse Bob.

Chattie May whispered something to Isaiah, then told me he also wanted to ask a favor. Wouldn't I order off and get him a black coat, a second-hand spiked-tail one, and a new leg.

"Er artificial laig," Chattie May interpreted.

I promised to see what could be done. Promised—remembering I had only $3.75 in the world. It struck me as being a very droll situation.

My caller had sent no card, gave no name, further than that he wished to see me on business. He was waiting for me in the hall and rose as I came downstairs, the quaintest little figurine of a man I have ever seen. His face belonged to another century, and his clothes might have come down from Noah in the Ark.

He had been directed by my uncle at the boat, he said, to the house where he would find me prepared to talk business. I interrupted before he presented his credentials. He was searching his coat-tail pockets for them.

"It is quite unnecessary for us to speak of the matter," I anticipated. "Palmetto Grove Plantation belongs half to me, and under no considerations could I be induced to sell an acre."

He had found what he sought, a letter, and held it out to me.

"As to that, Mees Cameron, I am not interested," he said; "it is the antiques, the old furniture, my good friend Dupré, in New Orleans, has sent me to examine for him." The paper he held out was worn and soiled. It was the letter I had written weeks ago to the old antique dealer on Royal Street, and which I had quite forgotten. "My name is Jacques Fontaine. May I be permitted to represent my firm and view your treasures?"

We spent the remainder of the day in the attic. The little antiquarian could not be persuaded to come down to have our noonday meal. Chattie May carried him a tray. He stopped only long enough for a glass of milk and a biscuit. I left him darting like a delighted spider in and out and all around in the attic, appraising, appreciating, what he found.

Bob's face was not so easy to read. I could not tell whether he was or was not disappointed because his man had not come on the boat.

"Y' see that little French dancing-master who was looking for you?" Bob asked.

"Buying up junk, eh?"

"He's in the attic now," I replied. "Do you mind if I sell some of the old furniture stored away up there?"

"Go ahead. It's all Confederate money when it comes to realizing on it, I warn you. But we'll probably be able to get rid of some of the rats, with the attic cleaned out."

I was for hurrying back to join M. Fontaine, but Bob detained me. He was still troubled about what Jinny had told him. I had dismissed the incident from my thoughts.

"The reason I did not send you money after the first year you were in New York, honey," Bob said, "was because I did not have it. The boll weevil cleaned us all out. It was all I could do to hold to Palmetto Grove. If cotton plantations had not been a drug on the market during those years, the place would have gone up the spout."

"That is the reason I went to work," I told him. "I knew things were difficult with you. Part of what Jinny told you is true, but she misrepresented most of it. The idle society world that she lives in is the vicious set. The working world is, so far as I know, made up of people trying to make a living, not air ways in ways they would choose, perhaps, but by honest work, just the same. It is true that I sang at entertainments, at club meetings, bazaars, even for one season behind the scenes on a theatrical stage, but none of the experiences hurt me. If I have been deluded, it is in thinking I could live in Jinny's false world and compete with worth-while artists. Hat's the mistake I made. And every insult that has ever been offered me has come from Jinny's society crowd, and not from my associate entertainers."

I chose my words unfortunately. At the word "insult" Bob's face burned red. "Don't misunderstand, Bob," I hastened to add. "I only meant in a general way that the geese Jinny has around her are an insult to any one who has ever associated with a real man—like you."

Bob brightened up a little. "lake to ride with me to Deer-Lick this afternoon?" he asked. "There may be some mail."

I had no intention of leaving the attic When I went back I found the little Frenchman on his knees in a far corner. Neatly arranged on one side of the room was a great heap of disjointed furniture. Most of the parts he had assembled were from the lot in an unlighted gable. He had not yet started to putting them together. I thought he would faint when he discovered a new vein of Chinese things, a lovely old red lacquer cabinet, a gold-lacquered sofa, and a chest done in marvellous drag-ons and peonies, hidden under the dust of seventy-five years. My own pulses ran away at the sight of these. Here was furniture worthy of Confucius. I knew it was not for sale, no matter how much I needed the money it would bring. M. Fontaine was for putting these aside with the other things, but I laid a detaining hand on his arm and shook my head.

"You are entitled to some reward for finding them," I said, "for I didn't know they were there, But I could not sell them."

"No amount of money would tempt you?" he asked wistfully.

"No amount." Like the little gentleman he was, the Frenchman turned regret-fully back to the rosewood and mahogany.

He put the pieces together and explained the process by which they might be restored to their original beauty. He told me the price Dupré would probably ask for each, and when he had indicated all that he wanted, he asked what I would take for the lot. I had no idea what price to put on them. But I felt the little man's honesty, so I put it up to him.

"What do you consider a fair price?"

"I will give you fifteen hundred dollars cash," he said. "And if you will sell the Chinese things—No?—Then fifteen hundred for the others."

I accepted his offer. He dived into his extraordinary coat to find his still more extraordinary pockets. He drew out a great roll of green money, and peeled off fif-teen one-hundred-dollar bills, and counting them again, he handed the money to me, with the air of one who has been done a great favor.

The boat would be returning the next afternoon. In the meantime could I sug-gest where he might lodge himself in the night? I had gone to the window to hide my emotion, and as I turned he saw the tears in my eyes. No doubt he knew, with an antiquarian's divination, the cause of them.

"If there is any reason why it is necessary for you to sell more," he said, "later I could make you an offer for other things here."

I thanked him and invited him to spend the night as our guest. He played crib-bage with Bob until all hours. I crept upstairs the minute dinner was over, dead tired. I had not rested all day, and my muscles, from the long walk, were stiff and sore.

I did not tell Bob about the money, for it was late before he returned from Deer-Lick, again without his expected letter.

I left Bob and the little old Frenchman, sympathetic allies, over the cribbage-board. My eyes were so heavy I could hardly keep them open to find my candle. But my heart—my heart rested in swan's-down peace and quiet. I could neither remember nor think. Under my pillow lay fifteen hundred dollars. My problem was solved, I slept.

CHAPTER XVII

On board the Annabel Lee April 21

I LEFT Palmetto Grove at dusk on the boat returning to New Orleans. "Diana for getting things done!" Bob exclaimed when I told him my plans.

M. Fontaine nosed around the garden before breakfast this morning. I tried to sing the doxology, but the piano refused to accompany one step. The little Frenchman joined me. He thinks the manufacturers of the piano, which is of a famous old make, will give me a new one in exchange because of the beauty of this case. Maybe there will be a small difference to pay. He offered to see the company manager in New Orleans for me. I decided at once to go to New Orleans to-day. The idea of a new piano thrills me. Besides, I am full of commissions that can be executed properly only in a city.

Chattie May's impatience to get her bridal gown and the necessity of getting the money due to my creditors off from a regular post-office decided me on New Orleans, Then there is the bathroom outfit. With the money in hand I could not possibly wait to send for it from a mail-order house. Isaiah also wants a white vest with pearl buttons, and nowhere nearer than New Orleans could I get him the desired spiked-tail coat, second-hand. And he is very particular about getting just the right kind of an artificial leg.

"I made dis heah one myse'f," he confided, when he showed me how he had hived the bees in the flower garden; "ef you cud git me one dat jines at de waist and operates natchul, an' I wants it rubber-soled so it won't sound lak a peg."

I have promised to be home in less than a week. And Bob, in turn, has promised to do nothing further about selling the place until I return.

M. Fontaine is below somewhere with his esteemed purchases. The night is clear and the river full of trembling stars. I sat on deck, talking to Captain Parrot until he pointed out Roseneath a mile ahead by a flaming bonfire on the river-bank.

I could see shadowy figures silhouetted against the blaze as we came nearer.

"We take on some passengers here," he said. "Perhaps you know them—"

I had risen hurriedly, and pleaded the truth that I was very tired and asked him not to tell any one who might get on that I was on board.

"I'll see that you are not disturbed to-night," he said. "We won't make another landing until six in the morning, when we reach Vicksburg."

Jinny and her guests came aboard. They are going to New Orleans just on a lark, and from there, I heard her tell Captain Parrot, they may go to South America or may go to New York. Jinny's high-pitched voice sounded tired and irritable. Providing entertainment for a houseful of bored people on a cotton plantation has been too much for her. She was entreating Captain Parrot to help her out now.

"These Northern people want to hear the roustabouts sing," she said.

The boat churned her placid way down the river. The soft, throaty voices of the negroes were very soothing, as they rose and fell in a plaintive old darky ballad:

"Dig my grabe wid a silver spoon, Dig my grabe wid a silver spoon, Dig my grabe wid a silver spoon, And let me down wid a golding chain."

To-morrow morning at six o'clock the boat reaches Vicksburg. That's where I change my plans and take a train for New Orleans.

CHAPTER XVIII

***New Orleans, April* 26**
CONFUCIUS and I reached New Orleans several days ago. We drove straight to the post-office, and when we left it I didn't owe a penny in the world, to dress-maker, throat specialist, Palozzi, or the accompanist. The amount due each went by

money order, registered, and special delivery.

Confucius and I continued our drive. I got out at a Chinese shop to buy a jade-green silk for a new cushion for him and a teakwood stand, tiny enough to put in the side pocket of my purse.

Where to stop was the next question, and we had several hours to make up our mind, for the sun was still high over the levees. None of the big hotels were to be thought of. Jinny and her crowd could not be side-stepped if I registered at a hotel. The ancient horse attached to a still more ancient victoria ambled leisurely out magnolia-flanked Prytania Street, and came back down palm-shaded St. Charles Avenue. Dear New Orleans streets whose scents and sounds never change! It was so easy to tell to-day, as it was fifteen years ago, what the people in this tall, long-windowed house, and in that one with its fluted pillars and iron galleries would have for dinner.

Gumbo! What bouquet ever lingered in memory so vividly as the savory smell of gumbo in the making in New Orleans! I, too, knew what I was going to have for my dinner, even while I had not the faintest idea where I would eat my dinner, or where I could find a place to stop.

I remembered the Woman's Exchange down on Camp Street, and drove there. They had no rooms unoccupied, but I was directed to a place near by, where the pretty little cashier at the desk thought I might be accommodated. The quarters proved to be all she said, so I engaged them for a few days. Confucius accompanies me to the Woman's Exchange restaurant where I am taking most of my meals. We are stepping softly, or jogging along in victoria or hansom down streets unfrequented by tourists.

I bought a glowing peony for Confucius to sit under on his jade cushion while I read aloud to him what he had said so many thousands of years ago:

The Master said: "What has this to do with love? . . . In seeking a foothold for self, love finds a foothold for others; seeking light for itself, it enlightens others also. To learn from the near at hand may be called the key to love."

Excellent philosopher as he is, Confucius does not quite satisfy my idea of a companion. I miss Bob, and am hurrying to get my shopping done and home to him.

I stopped by the Cotton Exchange to see Bob's friend, Mr. Pinckney, to see what he would tell me about the man who wants to buy Palmetto Grove. I can't help being nervous for fear he will arrive while I am away and convince Bob of the wisdom of selling. Mr. Pinckney reassured me.

"By Jove, now," he put his hand up to his handsome head. "I've forgotten his name. Knew it perfectly well, too. He's a fine fellow, some kind of a hydrographic engineer, whatever that is, just back from France. He's on a Committee to make this old Mississippi River behave. They're gone down to the jetties to-day. I'll tell you his name in a minute."

But the name was gone for the time being.

"Fact is we had a lively time in the Exchange today," he said. "Four Northern newspapers are using Yankee editorials, purporting to be written by well-known men who have made personal investigations and canvasses in the Southern States, to 'bear' the price of cotton. There is no reason except this for it to have shot down as it did to-day....But the name of that chap will come back to me....Where you stopping?"

He sent me some roses to-day and invited me to have luncheon with him, but I pleaded a previous engagement and too much shopping to accept the hospitality of his wife for dinner when she came to call for me. Mr. Pinckney forgot to tell me if he remembered the name of the hydrographic engineer.

The bathroom fixtures are purchased, also grass paper and tissue curtains for my Chinese room. Also the wall covering needed so sorely for the other rooms, and much varnish and oil and paint and various new kalsomine washes with which to experiment.

May 3

M. FONTAINE went with me to see about the piano this afternoon. His opinion on my piano counted for a good deal. The piano company has agreed to give me a baby grand (oh, the beautiful tender tones of the creature) in exchange for mine, I to pay a difference. But it is a bargain at any price, and they are not going to take my last penny in payment, not until the autumn, anyway.

M. Fontaine jubilantly assured me that the old things in the attic will bring many times the amount I shall need by that time. So the baby grand goes to Palmetto Grove, and the old piano there comes back to New Orleans.

"May I assist you with other errands?" the little Frenchman asked as we came out.

"If you can direct me to a spiked-tail coat, secondhand, and a white waistcoat with pearl buttons, suitable for a wedding garment for Isaiah," I told him, "I shall be very grateful. Also where I might find a maltese kitten, young enough to lie on its back and play with its feet, but old enough to purr."

He conducted me first to Madame Ravenel's second-hand establishment on Bourbon Street, where Isaiah's desired wedding finery was waiting for me to call for it! Then in a bird store on Royal Street we found a kitten even more bewitching than I had specified it must be.

The bird man agreed to have the kitten properly done up for travel to-morrow morning. I am to come for it on my way to the train. It was too late to finish my commissions for the affianced lovers. The shops were now closing. M. Fontaine chuckled quietly over the artificial leg, and wrote out the shop where I could look over an assortment in the morning.

"You have friends in New Orleans?" the little Frenchman asked.

I explained that it had been many years since I was in the city, that my only relative, a cousin, had died several years ago, and that my old friends had probably forgotten me or had moved away.

"Where are you dining, then, may I ask?"

"At the Woman's Exchange. Won't you join me, Monsieur?"

No, but if I would do him the honor—

I was delighted, but specified it must be at some restaurant where there was no chance of my running into the people I was trying to avoid.

So we went past Antoine's and the Louisiane, on down near the French Market, to a little restaurant with sanded floors and thick dishes and coarse napery, but where Madame cooks like the angels sing. We had gumbo, an omelette, a salad, a bottle of red wine, a sweet, and café bruleau. I felt as if I were dining with a Marquis of France, Lafayette himself.

M. Jacques Fontaine is a very great gentleman. When he bade me farewell at my door at ten o'clock, he gave his promise to pay us a visit to Palmetto Grove. He is sending Bob, with his most distinguished compliments, a set of ivory chessmen that belonged to Paul Morphy.

May 4

THESE things—Chattie May's bridal outfit, Isaiah's artificial leg, a box of pralines to be sent to Aline, vetivert root to be sent to Tink—have to be attended to, and the kitten called for before the eleven o'clock train this morning. Jinny pervades New Orleans. Twice I have been in sound of her voice, and I have seen Alice Grant half a dozen times from a distance on Canal Street. Delay is dangerous. I must get away to-day.

I left my bag in the cab and went into the Woman's Exchange to get breakfast. Displayed in the window of the needlework department I saw a white organdie dress, a diaphanous tulle veil, and a delectable large and showy bridal wreath of artificial orange-blossoms. Here, then, was where I could save time, by purchasing Chattie May's trousseau. It was quite early. Only the girl who had charge of the jellies and preserves had come in. The other young lady who managed the fancy-work department would be in shortly, and she could give me the price on the bridal consignment. I asked her to send me word across the hall, to the restaurant, when the fancy-work girl came in.

I set Confucius on his thoughtful green cushion beside the coffee-pot to remind me of things I must remember while the little waitress went back into the kitchen to get my bacon and hot rolls. Here I was about to go home without a present for Mandy! I took out the list, and added a present for her to the things that must be attended to before train-time.

Some one entered as Collette set my breakfast before me. I heard the pretty cashier explaining they had so few calls for breakfast that only one waitress came this early in the morning.

A man's voice begged her not to trouble, but that if the baby's milk could be prepared by the directions on the bottle he would be very grateful.

"Your speech itself is quietness" flashed through my consciousness, maybe because I am most sensitive to voices. Subconsciously I heard the conversation, while I tried to decide on something to carry Mandy.

"Collette understands perfectly how to prepare it," the little cashier assured the man behind me. The gift that would appeal to Mandy above all others, some demon whispered, would be a large tin of lard.

"What a little love she is!" the cashier evidently appraised the child whose breakfast was being prepared. The cashier was apologizing because only two tables were set. The small one at which I sat, and another the same size beside it.

"There are only two of us," the man replied. "And I am expecting a lady." Collette set a high chair at the next table. A tall man in grey clothes passed, a baby in his arms. He bent over the small person until she was secure in the high chair, then he took his own seat at the table. I looked up and into his eyes.

It was you.

CHAPTER XIX

I WAS too agitated to bow to you; too shy to smile when you recovered from your confusion; you thought you knew me. Then you remembered you did not. It was the old mistaken resemblance. But why were we, both at least surface creatures of convention, so awkward, so self-conscious? I felt the Red Sea surging up into my face.

You bent over the small person. She, in turn, extended both her arms in my direction, and out of a clear sky began to cry.

You untied her cap and took it off. You rattled the knives and forks and spoons and patted her waving pink hands helplessly. She bawled, adorable baby as she was, and she was no less enchanting with the teardrops chasing each other down her pink cheeks.

You looked appealingly at me, and I tried to pretend that I thought you could get her quiet. The little cashier stepped down from her pedestal and went to the baby.

"Why," she said, as if she had solved the whole mystery, turning to me, "she's crying for you!" I knew all the time she was crying for me, but I was too weak-kneed in spirit or in body to go to her.

"Come here and see if she isn't!"

"I think that would quiet her," you said.

I rose and the baby's cry turned to a coo. Two steps to where she sat, and her little arms reached up to welcome me. I bent over to hide the thrilling things that might proclaim themselves should you chance to see my eyes. Nearer the tiny pink hands drew my face, until my cheek rested against her rose-leaf cheek. She was purring like a kitten, cooing like a wood-dove. The little cashier accepted all the credit for quieting the baby as her own admirable stage-management. The baby with one ecstatic gurgle lifted both hands and buried them in my hair, then swung back with her trophy, a long sorrel lock.

"She thinks you are her mother," you said. That remark saved the situation. That and a voice at my elbow.

"Beg pardon, but aren't you the young lady who wants to buy the Wedding-dress and veil?" It was one of the waitresses who had just come in. "They asked me to tell you the fancy-work lady has come now, if you want to know the price."

I bought the wedding outfit in about two minutes. The little cashier was waiting for me at the screen door of the restaurant as I came out of the Exchange across the hall.

"You'll have to come back and quiet the baby," she said. "I think she is the kind that holds her breath."

"The father is expecting a lady." I hunted frantically in my purse. I had not paid my breakfast check. "Her mother will quiet her."

"Perhaps—Will you wait for the change?"

"Give it to Collette, please; I am rushing to catch a train."

"Where, young lady?" the cabman asked when I got in and told him to hurry.

"I don't know. Go to Canal Street first" Anywhere to get away from that baby crying for me.

Suddenly I was filled with compassion and understanding for gipsies who steal babies. Perhaps the babies themselves are largely to blame. Surely no one with the provocation I had just had could blame me for listening to the voice of such a charmer "charming never so wisely," begging me, if I *had* to go, to please take her with me!

"Pinky Wood-Dove," I christened and mentally addressed the baby, trying to disentangle her from my heart even as I had firmly disentangled her from my hands and face and hair. "You have a father of your own, and a mother who has probably finished telephoning and come back to you by this time. Leave me in peace. We are ab-so-lute-ly nothing to each other, Pinky Wood-Dove—*Precious!*"

I bought Isaiah's artificial leg and the salesman insisted on showing me how to run it, dilating on its qualities of human intelligence until I begged him to put it in a box and let me go.

On down my list I attended to the various gifts that I must have dispatched. Then I called for the kitten and we just did get through the gate in time to catch the train.

We were nearly in Cottonport when I remembered I had after all not brought anything to Mandy. It was then I missed Confucius.

I had forgotten him again! I left him on the breakfast-table at the Woman's Exchange.

CHAPTER XX

Palmetto Grove, May 15

ALINE was waiting for me when I reached home ten days ago. She can walk. Her movements are those of an angel or a mermaid. Her walking is somehow winged. Her feet do not give the impression that they touch the ground. Her happiness is uplifting. Like Lura, she seems to me to be "joy made manifest." Black Tilly is with her.

Tom Foster and his political guests have returned to Washington. Jinny and her crowd are not going back to the plantation. The arrangement was for Aline to spend the summer at Roseneath with Cousin Clara. Freda, the Swedish trained nurse, was left there, nominally in charge of Aline.

The day after her mother left, Aline bade Tilly pack their belongings and she and Tilly set forth to pay a visit to us at Palmetto Grove.

I sent a wire from Cottonport to the Woman's Exchange asking that the small Chinese image I left on the table be sent registered mail to me.

The little cashier replied promptly by letter, regretting that they have been unable to find it. She does not think it could have been taken by either of the two waitresses who served breakfast that morning, as both are honest girls, who have never been known to take anything.

Chattie May and Isaiah are duly married. They went to Cottonport for a day and night on a honeymoon bout. Both came home exhausted, and glad to get back to the monotony of work. Isaiah has decided to keep the artificial leg for Sundays and state occasions, honeymoons, and the like. The old peg is more comfortable for every day. He says that home-made "laig" is shaped to fit his "jints." He bought a rubber tip for it in Cottonport. He spends his time bewailing the expense of the artificial member.

Aline has christened the kitten Arabella, which amuses Bob very much. The hound-dogs all over the plantation also take her as a joke. Apparently they do not know she is a cat. She picks her way daintily around the garden, always ending up before the beehives. The bees belong to the industrial world, Bob tells her, while Arabella at this stage is purely ornamental. Aline says she thinks Arabella wants to be their queen.

I am up these mornings with the sun. We are papering and painting and kalsomining, and a regular plumber came down from Cottonport to put in the bathroom fixtures.

"I say, sister," Bob told me the first day of my return, "the commissary couldn't be comfortable in the house with all these changes going on, so I moved it out. The old drawing-room is now at your disposal."

As we have only the two servants to do everything, it is up to me to do most of the paper-hanging and painting myself. Aline and Black Tilly are my assistant decorators.

Our hardest job was restoring the drawing-room. But now it is fresh and shining, smelling of beeswax and paint that isn't dry. The old portraits are re-hung in their places; and the tarnished old gilt mirror is put back. Even the big potpourri jar has been unearthed, its bouquet only mellowed by being in bond so long, and restored to active circulation.

May 18

THE Annabel Lee brought the new piano to-day. Aline and Bob conducted me jubilantly to it when I returned from a long ride over the fields this afternoon. I worked in the garden all the morning. I told the truth when I said I was too tired for any music to-night.

But when my fingers touched the cool ivory keys I forgot I was weary.

"I had all that old music brought back," Bob said, indicating a great pile of music and among it some of the yellowed old Italian portfolios. "See if you can find 'When You and I were young, Maggie.'" Then he must have "Molly Darling." Aline claimed it was her turn to choose next and she wanted "The Land of the Sky-Blue Water."

Aline was tucked up on a sofa, Bob in an easy-chair. Soon they left the choice of what next to me. Arabella minced in and arranged herself for a nap in the crook of Aline's elbow. It was very peaceful. The old drawing-room I remember as a child seemed to have come back, with its intangible presences; the smell of dried rose-leaves and verbena from the blue Chinese jar, the vague scent of beeswax from the polished floor, the flickering soft candlelights combined to re-create the atmosphere of the room as I knew it first. I reached for the oldest portfolio, the one that held the operas which my great-grandmother sang, when the gallant young Virginian, destined for the diplomatic service, saw her—and ended her career and his—here on Palmetto Grove.

Amber and coral and jade, fuse in the old current of crystal light! The current swept around me and through me, and my consciousness was the reservoir that caught this rainbow of color and melody.

The old miracle of my childhood was repeating itself! I could sing with perfect familiarity operas that I had never read a note or heard a word of before, and in a language that ordinarily I translated with greatest difficulty.

After all these years, when I thought I had lost it forever, for this power to come back to me! The entity, the personality, the ego that calls itself Diana Cameron had faded away, dissolved in a feeling of Light, Intelligence, *Spirit,* that was in no way related to material sensation or a tangible mortal body. The thought: "Oh, to be able to hold this forever mine" came like a cloud, obscuring the sun.

And that second the power, the Presence, vanished.

The yellowed pages before me were unillumined. I knew, before I tried to repeat it, that the power had left me. Try as I might, I could not even translate the Italian words before me. The attempt to sing them was even more of a failure.

Bob and Aline were sound asleep. Arabella, nestled in the crook of Aline's elbow, was wide-awake. Not until the last note of the old operas died away did her bright eyes close.

A great wave of nostalgia swept over my spirit. Of heart longing for *your* baby.

I sang lullaby after lullaby to comfort my own heart, pretending that wherever she may be I was rocking Pinky Wood-Dove to sleep.

CHAPTER XXI

PINKY WOOD-DOVE is crying for me. This is why, I am sure, that I cannot keep my thoughts away from you to-night. I sang those lullabies downstairs to quiet your baby.

What is your child to me? What claim upon me could she possibly have?

Even as I ask myself the question and answer it, ***None whatever***—I am conscious of a kinship, mysterious and remote though it may be, with that baby who turned from you to me for comfort.

Bit by bit I piece the incident together. I must assemble all my arguments to win the freedom I am trying to achieve for myself.

You said the baby thought I was her mother. Then your baby's mother must resemble me. The riddle is solved. "No man is ever faithful to one woman," some one has said, "but he is everlastingly constant to a type."

What I accepted as a personally directed kismet is, after all, only the law of natural selection, working itself out. You married a girl who looks so much like me that your baby and hers cried for me because she thought I was her mother!

What is done is done. You are married. How completely or incompletely the love of the woman you chose fills your life is no concern of mine. She is your wife. My heart shall have no part in a secret treaty. If I cannot be sun, moon, and all the stars to the man I love, I will be nothing at all.

Our romance exists only in my absurd dream of what might have been. I accept as Fate only this much: It was arranged for me to go to New Orleans to see you as you really are, Pinky Wood-Dove's father, waiting for Pinky Wood-Dove's mother who had gone to telephone.

Destiny, seeing my honest efforts to do my duty, let us say, set the machinery in motion to show me I have been following a will-o'-the-wisp; touched the vulnerable spot, my pride, knowing that I, given authentic proofs that another had prior claim to the estate I had considered my own, could be counted to do the decent thing.

Shall I turn down the lantern of my love; blow it out and draw down the shade to that window of my mind?

I find myself temporizing; making excuses. The lantern was lighted for you. Its rays never reached you, but before its flame my own old shadows and despairs have certainly fled. No doubt there are understanding ones who can explain the significance of light in vision and metaphor. It is beyond me. Is there a lantern of love that each of us may light to illumine "the dark cottage of the soul"? By it is one enabled to distinguish the false from the true; duty from restless desire? By the light of that lantern if one looks honestly is one shown the "path of life" into which the psalmist prayed to be directed?

I am searching for words to make clear to my own understanding what spiritual laws I have discovered since I lighted my lantern of love. It began as a selfish experiment. Gradually I have come to see that it is not the love given us, but the love we give, that brings the blessing. In the light of it I have come to see that love's rays, cast even upon venomous serpents, reveal not fangs that poison, but potential friends, ready to serve us. My old personal equation has been lost before the proof that love is universal.

The dawn is coming. It is all very well to write out one's resignation and hand it in to Fate when the clock ticks slow and the lamp flickers long past midnight. I re-read what I have tried to write. It sounds as tin-panny as a nigger sermon, only words strung together, words, verbless, and void of ideas.

I am not tired nor sleepy nor resigned.

The dawn is rosy as Pinky Wood-Dove's fingers. The sky as blue as her eyes. A red-bird two feet away in the oak-tree is singing his love-song.

Try as I will I cannot blot out of my memory your brown eyes begging me to come in, and how they put forward Pinky Wood-Dove as an interpreter.

I won't come in, now or ever. All the magnetic currents that encircle this world may be trying to bring us together, but my pride will keep me in my right place, here, in Palmetto Grove, far away from you.

Oh, how could you—just because she happened to have hair and eyes and skin like mine—how could you have been so blind? None of these things mattered.

Nothing matters—really nothing! Only I'd give this world and a mortgage on Mars if I owned it—to give Pinky Wood-Dove her bath this morning!

CHAPTER XXII

Palmetto Grove

BOB is ill. Isaiah brought word that he did not wish any breakfast, that he would just stay in bed and rest. I found him with a burning fever. He thinks he must have had a chill, and declares the fever is nothing; that quinine will control it.

I made the round of the fields twice to-day to see that the negroes are at work. Every man, woman, and child large enough to handle a hoe is chopping cotton. They have only one idea and that is "to get out of the grass" before another rain. Even Isaiah and Chattie May have been hoeing to help out in the afternoon.

Nothing would do Aline but she must go to Mandy's grandchild, who is very sick. She and Tilly set out for the cabin just after breakfast. If I had not been so busy I would not have let her go. When I rode over the new ground, Mandy was hoeing contentedly away. She told me the child was improving.

"Miss Aline an' Tilly," she said, "done sent Liddy" (the child's mother) "on to de fiel'. Dey gwine nuss son fer her."

I stopped by Mandy's cabin to persuade Aline to leave Tilly, if she was needed to look after the little darky, but for her to come on home with me.

Tilly met me at the gate. Her face was beaming.

"S-sh! Miss Diana," she warned. "Miss Aline done got him to sleep. She's workin' fer him, so 'm I."

I tiptoed to the cabin door. It was clean and dark and quiet within. A small negro boy lay in a pallet on the floor, sleeping peacefully. Aline, with her eyes closed, sat like an angel, perched on a rickety chair, beside him. Her face was transfigured. Her lips moved. I knew without Tilly's explanation what she thought she was doing. Her little face was glorified. As silently as I arrived, I crept away, Tilly following me to the gate.

"She ain't gwine ketch nothin' heah, Miss Diana," she anticipated my objection. "When the young man healed her, he told her to be about her Father's business, just as Jesus wuz. De doctors said she could never be cuohed. Doctors couldn't do nothin' fer her, but de truth Jesus come to teach, when she had it explained and understood it, did make her whole. Dat's why she has to speak de truth to every form of disease she meets. Dat's de way she has of showin' her gratitude to God."

Tilly was glad to see me safely remounted and on my way home. I warned her that I would not give my consent to her and Aline spending more than the day in the cabin.

"She, now, Miss Diana, us doan want to," she said. "Dat li'l' boy gwine be well as eveybody by sundown."

I found Bob much worse. He was delirious; the fever, instead of wearing off, was much higher. There is no physician nearer than Cottonport, twenty miles away, and we have no telephone.

I have sent Isaiah to Deer-lick store, with a note, asking them to telephone to Cottonport to the hospital, for a doctor to be sent down at once. I also wrote a note to the mail-rider, asking him to get a physician wherever there may be one found in this part of the country. I gave Isaiah instructions to stay at the store until they get the message through to the hospital.

I am trying to think, to remember what to do for fever. I am so ignorant I cannot diagnose the case, nor tell how serious it may be. Bob complains of his head. The fever stays up.

I am giving him sponge baths, and keeping cold cloths on his head. Oh, for some ice!

Midnight

ISAIAH has just returned bringing a note from Rice at the Deer-Lick store. After a long delay he was able to get Cottonport on the wire. There is not a doctor to be had in town to-night. There has been a big wreck on the railroad just above, in which many were killed and injured. The Cottonport hospital is overflowing, and they are trying to get medical assistance and nurses from Memphis and New Orleans.

Isaiah says they will try again in the morning in the hope a physician may be spared to come here.

Chattie May gave out at ten o'clock. I sent her off to bed. Faithful little creature that she is, she wanted to stay, but I shall need her more to-morrow.

Aline and Tilly had to get supper. They returned at sunset from Mandy's. Both with the same expression of having spent a day in heaven. The little negro was up playing as well as anybody when they left him. They think it is the "treatment" they have given him to-day. I have seen enough of such darky children complaints to know that a quiet day, with no food and plenty of sleep and no flies, would restore almost any pickaninny stuffed to his capacity with green plums.

Dear Aline! She thinks, and Tilly would swear to it, that her prayers nullified the poison of the green plums and restored Mandy's grandchild.

I have made them leave me to get their rest. Now Isaiah has come and gone on to join Chattie May. I do not want any of them to know how uneasy I am about Bob. He is quiet now. I must think of some way to get help for him.

It is two o'clock. I am not able to tell whether Bob is dreaming or if it is delirium. It breaks my heart to hear him. For he is talking of me. His whole thought is centred about what he has tried to do for me. He is reviewing the years since I left him to go to New York.

Reviewing the years by the calendar of his cotton crops, telling off his failures as if they were beads on a rosary. He is calling himself to account for his failures.

Now it is the first year the boll weevil came and overnight destroyed all possible prospect of a crop. "I did n't make enough cotton that year," he is saying, "to pay for having it picked. And little Diana up there, counting on me to send the check for her singing lessons . . . had to be told I could not send her anything. That was when she had to . . . go to work . . . No bank would lend me money that year." He blamed himself for failing the year of the overflow, when everybody failed because the water was not off the land until the end of June when it was too late to plant cotton. Then came fairer prospects next year and good weather and again the boll weevil swept like a plague out of Egypt and took everything . . . and with each year's review of his work came a summary of mine. A summary that he had pieced from what Jinny had written him. Always it was his failure to send me money that made my hardships, my deprivations, in New York. He was to blame for everything that had happened to me.

Then came the first year of the war, when cotton could not be sold for any price. . . . I put my fingers in my ears to keep from hearing. For his accusation against himself was the most cruel arraignment of myself. What he had failed to do for me was as nothing at all, compared to my sudden realization of how I had neglected him. Not once had he failed me in any way, except the material, while

I, absorbed in my own selfish dreams and ambitions, had virtually forgotten him. Never once did I blame him, he babbled on. No, I was not thinking enough of him in those days to give him a thought either of praise or blame. Whatever was happening to him he carried it himself. It had n't troubled me.

As he raved on, his every word was like a knife not aimed at, but plunged deep within me. I was conscious of pain that went so deep, it seemed to penetrate a dozen superficial hearts of flesh, to unseal a fountain of remorse.

With this brave soul working for me, slaving in sunshine and rain, beaten by all the winds of misfortune and still game to get up and try it again in the hope that next time he would win, not because it meant anything to him, but what it would mean to me. I was in New York, deluding myself (poor fool, poor fool) that I was working toward a goal, honestly striving for an ideal!

Then came the year when cotton went up with war needs, and Bob made a good crop. The year everybody he owed demanded at least part payment on his notes. And so there was nothing for either of us then. Again came the cat-o'-nine-tails down on his own back. He did not know how things were with me then. Jinny had told him of my debts and worries. He did not know! He did not know! he moaned. Oh, he was to blame for it all! But he did not know! If I had only told him! If I had not tried to keep my need from him! What meant anything to him but my happiness?

Why, he thought I wanted to stay in New York. . . . He understood that I could not waste my youth and my great, my beautiful voice, in a Mississippi mud-flat plantation. There was nothing here but niggers and mules and himself. And he, God knew, he knew how lonely, how desolate, it was. He could n't, and he did not, expect me to come home even on visits.

His poor twisted hands wring my heart!

"I couldn't write often, sister," he explained, "these darned old fingers—See!"

And my letters to him were only an occasional postcard at Christmas-time and Easter!

He had only one thought all along, he moaned—to make a big cotton crop and get a fine price—and pay out of debt—and come on to New York and say: "Honey, old Palmetto Grove has justified herself at last. Here's your share. I could n't give you anything before, because we had to pay out of debt."

Bob's eyes are wide and shining. But he does n't seem to recognize me. He talks on to somebody, the person maybe I used to be in New York: "I got you in debt, sister. It was up to me to pay out. . . . Always been in debt since the Civil War, kitten."

I hold Bob's hand and my tears rain down upon it. Oh, if he owed millions in debts on this plantation we own together, these would be paltry beside the debt of love I owe him.

The clock ticks on. I do not know what to do. There is no use to try to talk to him. My throat aches with trying to make him understand. It is his head, I know that, from the way he puts his hands to it. If I could only make him see mentally, **understand,** that there is no truth in the accusations with which he lashes himself, that he has never neglected me! Oh, if I could only make him understand that I am on my knees for the rest of my life trying to make reparation to him!

CHAPTER XXIII

IT is half-past four. The hounds are howling dismally. It has grown very cold and damp. Bob's eyes are closed, his breathing is more even. Thank God, he has passed on to the present. He is dreaming now of selling the plantation. I listen eagerly to hear if he really wants to sell Palmetto Grove. I cannot tell. He is talking about the man he expected weeks ago, telling him about the cypress-brake.

"Whether you buy it or not, sir," he is saying, "I want you to have a look at the finest lot of cypress-trees in this part of the country. I take great pride, sir—"

The lamp is burning low and smelling of kerosene. The heavy mist that rises from the river just before dawn pours through the open window in grey billows. In spirit and in body I ache.

I blew out the lamp, and tried to build a fire from the oak wood and pine knots piled on the hearth. But nothing could keep me from hearing every word:

"My reasons for selling the plantation, sir, are personal. If it were left to my business judgment I would not sell at this time. Cotton will touch new high levels this fall. But I am not one, sir, who believes in human sacrifice.

"Cotton, sir, is a commodity. A contralto voice is a gift from heaven. Unless it is carefully cherished, guarded, jealously taken care of, it goes. The angel's gift, sir, of song lifts its possessor to higher ether. An æolian harp cannot be expected to stand the rough usage of a drum. To expect a song-bird to do drudgery—"

Oh, if I could only say something to divert Bob from this!

"Of course I know there are arguments to the contrary. I know that most great artistes have known privation and want. But I do not believe that any sensitive, high-strung nature ever really benefited by the sordid experiences of making a living, competing on a lower plane for the necessities of life, while struggling for a foothold on the higher. A grand-opera temperament, sir, is hopelessly exiled on a variety—or as they call it now—a vaudeville bill. There are embryo prima donnas, I am told, who sing for a mere pittance, placed maybe between a nigger minstrel act and a performing monkey."

Bob's voice rose as he grew more excited.

"Not so long ago, one who is now acclaimed the sensation of the musical world, a grand-opera star, in the class with Patti or Christine Nilsson, was refused the position she would gladly have taken to sing in a; moving-picture theatre. This, sir, is a state of affairs highly deplorable. It is for this reason I contend that no sacrifice is too great for us to make in order to give an artiste to the world. . . .

"I have only to think of Adelina Patti as I first heard her in New Orleans to renew raptures I expected then to experience only in heaven. . . . 'D you ever hear Christine Nilsson? There was a voice like a waterfall of diamonds with the sun shining upon it. Now this is a prophecy." He stopped for his words to be more impressive. "There is a new star in the horizon—such a voice as has not been heard for fifty years. . . What is a paltry cotton plantation to give that such a voice be not lost to the world!"

Outside the window in the cedar-tree a mockingbird began softly, his flute like a rhapsody to the dawn.

"D' you hear that, sir?" Bob lifted his head from the pillow and listened. "Sweet and clear as a bell, is it not?

"They tell me the nightingale sings with her heart pressed against a thorn, in order to give her best notes to the world. Emotionally she may suffer, sir, but any good physician could tell you that the nightingale, starving for food and without a proper place to rest and shelter, would soon degenerate into as squabbling a worldling as an English sparrow.

"We must see to it, sir, that our few real artistes are conserved. Angels must be fed angel-food; the rest of us don't matter."

I know now what hell is like. Fire and brimstone are but feeble metaphors for remorse. If Bob dies I am his murderer. My selfishness has slain him.

I crept to his bed and knelt beside it. I put my cheek against his hot hand. Before I could pray to God to spare him, I must try to make Bob understand.

If I could only make him hear my confession, to realize it is I who have failed him and not he me! Before God and Bob if I could only pour out my plea for forgiveness! If I could at least reveal myself as I see myself this moment! and make Bob understand. Stripped I see myself at last. I never had the temperament of an artiste, nor the capacity for suffering by which genius is tried out in the fire of circumstances. I have minced along carefully, holding my own skirts out of the mire. Art is self-abnegation. I have demanded silken hangings for my spirit even if I have not had them for my body. I have lived as remote from' life as a spider in his cobweb fortifications in some unused attic. The world has interested me only as a potential audience. I aspired to be the pipe organ aloft, in the balcony; the hand-organ, perhaps my true *mitier,* was too near the crowding rabble to interest me.

I am a failure, not because Bob's cotton crops failed, but because my spirit is not fashioned of the stuff that endures. A true artiste borrows, burrows, begs, robs, steals to make the objective. The world, the flesh, the devil are but incidentals, to be used as such in the struggle to make the goal. The flame of a heavenly voice must be carried forward, protected, fed, no matter by what expedient. An artiste born great enough throws every consideration but the divine gift to the winds. She has but one passion (what if she throws the pearls of her flesh to the swine of the world to feed this!) and that is her art.

I an artiste? I a great singer?. . . I see myself truly at last, a spiritual snob—counterfeit spirituality at that. My one concern has been to keep my own skirts clean.

Fastidious—yes, a fastidious pharisee, and a cheat and a swindler, a liar and a fraud—I—encased in my oyster shell of selfishness! I see myself at last.

Bob sat up in bed, wild-eyed. " 'D you ever hear Christine Nilsson, sir? There was a nightingale."

"Oh, Bob," my tears rained down on his poor twisted hot hands, "listen to met

Forgive me! Forgive me!"

"Eh! Eh!" Bob seemed to hear, turning toward me. "Sing to me, sister."

Aline stood in the doorway. "Sing to him, Diana," she repeated. "Sing that song, 'O Love That Will Not Let Me Go.'"

I could not sing a note. My memory was like a slate sponged clean. I could not recall even one word of any song.

"Sing," Bob muttered "Sing like a nightingale. . . . Now Jenny Lind was a nightingale, too, 'the Swedish nightingale,' they called her."

Aline began to sing a lullaby:

"Rock-a-by, baby, in the tree-top, When the wind blows—"

I tried to join in, but I could not. . . . Black Tilly on the hearth, mending the dying fire, joined in and crooned softly with Aline. Bob stopped turning and twisting—

"Rock-a-by—ba-by— Rock-a-by—ba-by—"

CHAPTER XXIV

I COULD hear Isaiah shaking the ashes out of the stove getting ready to make the fire to cook breakfast. Aline rocked back and forth softly, singing. Tilly on the hearth swayed and sang with her. Bob was asleep at last.

Aline nodded for me to go out in the air. I stumbled blindly, so stiff I could hardly walk, out on the back gallery and to the kitchen. I must get help from somewhere. A physician must be found. I asked Isaiah to tell me again what they had told him at Deer-Lick about 'phoning this morning. He told a different story altogether. He had forgotten, negrolike, once it was told, what message he had brought last night.

"Why don't you ride down to the store, Miss Diana," Chattie May asked, "and telefoam yoh-se'f? You cud get a doctor quicker'n dey'd come for dem men."

I knew she was right. Yet I did not feel that I could leave Bob with these inexperienced negroes and a child like Aline. Perhaps I could get her out of the house in the garden. Frail and nervous as she has always been, I feared to have her realize the gravity of Bob's condition.

Chattie May poured me a cup of strong coffee which I forced myself to drink, while Isaiah saddled Jenny Ribbons. Aline and Tilly's voices, singing over and over again the old lullaby, came to me, with some assurance. Perhaps Bob would sleep until I could get back. I beckoned Aline to come to me in the hall.

"I have to go for the doctor, dear," I told her. I tried to tell her it was nothing to be alarmed over, but the words stuck in my throat. I was afraid to go and leave Bob, and afraid not to go.

Aline lifted her quiet, starry eyes. I could not tell her an untruth. She read my anxiety, my misery.

"I—I must find a physician," I heard my voice tremble. "Bob must have medical help at once." She slipped her cool little hand into mine. Somehow the very touch of it gave me courage. "Of course I can get a physician," I said. "Try to keep him asleep until I get back."

"If you don't get a physician," she said, "don't be worried. Remember the Great Physician."

I stared at her, again trying to remember.

"*My* physician," she whispered; "the one who healed me after the doctors could do nothing."

"Aline"—I caught at a straw—"I can't seem to pray. Pray for me, child."

"I am working," she said, quite simply. "I am about my Father's business. Don't you worry."

I met two of the men from the Deer-Lick store about a mile from the house. Jim Rice had been riding all night trying to get a doctor; the other, John Todd, a clerk in the store, told me he had been trying over the 'phone to get a doctor from Jackson or Vicksburg. All the physicians were tied up with cases they could not leave. Not one could be spared from the wreck victims at Cottonport. There might be a chance after the morning train got in, they had told him, of sending a physician, provided other physicians and nurses came to their relief. Todd and Rice were on their way to offer their services to help me nurse Bob.

A physician was more needed, I told them, and they turned back to the store, in the event I should want one of them to go to Cottonport.

The telephone connection was very poor. I was an hour getting Cottonport, only to be told there was not a physician or nurse that could be spared from the hospital. I called Memphis with no better success. At twelve o'clock I succeeded in getting connection with Vicksburg and the promise of help. A Dr. Clark said he would start at once in his car. If he were delayed it would be on account of the roads. He understood there had been a heavy rain a few miles out

The glare of the sun was blinding. The heat waves quivered before me. Rice was to wait for the mail-rider to get his report. I promised to let him know if I needed him to sit up with Bob to-night.

"Sounds like he might be in for a spell of hematura fever," he said by way of comfort.

Of all the fevers that devastate the swamp lands along the river, hematura is feared as the most deadly. Jenny Ribbons galloped homeward, covered with foam. She felt the need of haste, and seemed to divine my anxiety, sympathetic, sensitive, high-strung creature that she is. I patted her neck. She whinnied.

Isaiah was on the front gallery, kneeling down praying out loud. I knew by that Bob must be dead. My knees knocked together; I was as one stricken with ague as I dismounted, and tried to go up the steps. I saw the old peg-leg first of all, and wondered vaguely why Isaiah did not have on his new leg.

"O God," he prayed, oblivious of my presence, "we thank Thee and bless Thee and mercify Thee—"

Chattie May, wide-eyed and almost hysterical, stood in the shadow of the honeysuckle vine. "It is a miracle," she intoned, "and may Thy Truth ingratiate us—"

"What does this mean?" I asked. "Did n't I tell you to keep quiet?"

"Miss Diana," they turned to me with streaming eyes, "Marse Bob is up and dressed and out in de flower gyarden."

I do not profess to understand, much less to explain Bob's recovery. He was sitting in a cane chair under a tree in the garden; shaved, dressed, and apparently in his right mind. He had called for his breakfast some time ago and eaten it, Chattie May whispered. I stood on the back gallery, too weak and frightened to go to him. Aline was gathering roses at the far end of the brick wall. Arabella, her back daintily arched, was playfully slapping at a bee that buzzed around a lemon-verbena bush.

It was as if in a pitch-black room I had dreamed a hideous nightmare that had been dissipated by the bright sunlight of morning into its native nothingness. Everything started to go around and around. I was giddy and weak and very wobbly.

And I remember Chattie May running toward me, then everything went black.

Dr. Clark arrived late in the afternoon. Bob's voice wakened me.

"They sent for you for me, Doctor," I heard him say, "but I'm all right. My niece who 'phoned for you rode in the sun all the morning after sitting up with me all night, and eating no breakfast. Have a look at her."

I sat up on the cane lounge, rubbing my eyes. I was still drowsy with sleep, but refreshed and hungry. Dr. Clark, an anxious little newly graduated physician, was feeling my pulse.

"There seems to be nothing the matter with her," he said. "But I understood the case to be one of life and death."

"Perhaps it was," said Bob, very quietly. "But help came sooner than was expected."

Little Dr. Clark spent the night. After dinner he repeated from memory the graduating paper he had delivered at Tulane a few weeks ago. It was on Malaria and its many manifestations. I was asleep when he finished it, and I am sure that Bob was not listening in spite of his air of courteous attention.

Bob did not want to listen, but I made him, to all I had to tell him. He looks ten years younger. He says if he were any happier he would know he is in heaven. Aline lifted a finger at him: "You are," she said. ***"Now!"***

" 'A little child shall lead them' "—Bob's eyes rest on Aline with wonder and awe, a dozen times a day.

"Aline," I asked her, when I knew that Bob was really all right, "how did you do it?"

"I did nothing," she said. "All disease is a lie and must go before the searchlight of Truth. It was only a dream from which he had to be awakened, just as I was awakened and found I could walk."

Such wisdom is too high for me. I cannot attain unto it.

May 30

I FEEL like a garden that was full of stones and briers and underbrush must feel, when the clearing is over, the last rock dug up and thrown over the fence. When the ploughing, the harrowing, the raking, is done: the whole planted in heart's-ease and the heart's-ease in bloom.

CHAPTER XXV

Palmetto Grove, June 7

BOB has turned most of the riding over to me. The sun is very hot and it was not difficult to persuade him to take things easy for a while. He rides over the fields with me once a day, late in the afternoon.

June 17

THE fields are green with the new crop. Row on row it stretches as far as the eye can reach. The negroes, "chopping cotton," work together with the uniformity of a troop of soldiers drilling. The sunlight reflected on the shining hoes gives an almost unearthly illumination to the fields. Seen through the heat waves, and the almost visible emanations rising from the hot earth, the effect is hypnotizing to the last degree.

It was noon. The sun is the negroes' clock; their shadows the dial hands that they can read to the minute. Suddenly the whole field of negroes as far as my eye could reach fell on their knees and raised their voices in one accord of wailing. Some one started to pray. From all sides went up moans and terrific pleadings for one more chance before the judgment day.

I called to the ones nearest me, to know what this meant. They were on their faces, praying. I heard a mighty whirring overhead and looked up. An aeroplane circled and darted in the high blue sky, then gradually began to descend.

"O Marse Gabriel!"—Mandy raised her stentorian voice—"jes' let us finish out dis week's work. Jes' let us git de cotton out uv grass 'fo you teks us!"

"It is not judgment day!" I made a trumpet of my hands and shouted. "That's not an angel, but a man, and that's a flying machine. Look at it!"

I laughed and rallied them, riding down the rows to reassure them, explaining that an aeroplane is only an automobile with wings. I gave them permission to stop work and go to see it if it should land on the plantation. They stopped work, but hurried to their cabins for dinner. The call had been too close for them to compose themselves to the point of having any curiosity about the visitor from the sky. I could see the machine circling down and toward the house as I rode home.

Like a kildee flying to earth, it made its descent and landed in the pasture just behind the stables.

Bob and Aline and the servants were grouped around its two passengers as I rode through the pasture gate. My arrival was not observed.

This was Bob's first sight of an airship. He and one of the men seemed to be looking at a map.

"Yes, that's Memphis," Bob was saying following a route on the map. "It is an all-day trip, sir, from here."

The aviator lifted his cap, touched a lever, sprang into his machine lightly, leaving his companion, a bag beside him, talking to Bob. Again the whirring as of a million wings as it soared aloft.

Jenny Ribbons reared, and bolted back through the gate and sped down the plantation road. She was running away with me, trying to find some place of safety for us both far from this terrifying, circling, swooping monster bird. I gave her the reins, soothing her with my voice and hands. The airship was now only a dragon-fly in the sky. Gradually her snorting ceased, her frightened gallop slowed down to a trot, and she obediently turned homeward.

Bob was mixing two toddies in the dining-room. Isaiah was laying an extra plate on the table. I dismounted at the side door, for my hat was gone and my hair flying in all directions, the hairpins scattered all over the plantation. Whoever the visitor was, I was not dressed to receive him. Bob looked up as I entered. He was evidently in a state of great excitement.

"You missed the aeroplane, sister," he said. "That's too bad, a most remarkable invention. Lieutenant Keating has gone on to Memphis. He dropped by here to bring his friend." Bob's hand went up to his forehead—"Abbott, I think his name is. By Jove, did he say Allen? Anyway, he is the gentleman with whom I had the correspondence about selling the place. He's a fine chap, I judge, and he brought letters from my old friend, Pinckney."

I had sunk down in a chair while Bob went on with his monologue, stirring the toddies all the while.

"Abbott—that's his name—or is it?—will be our guest until to-morrow. Hadn't you better change, honey?"

My linen riding-habit was dusty and crumpled and damp; flecks of foam from

Jenny Ribbons made it look as if I had been rained on. I must have looked pretty seedy for Bob to suggest a fresh toilette before I met his guest.

"Don't wait on me," I said. "I'll slip upstairs and come down later."

"This way," I heard Aline say outside the door. And the next moment she entered the room with you.

"By Jove, honey," Bob caught me. "I forgot to tell you. I told Obadiah to announce lunch. Blame me! Mr. Abbersly, your aeroplane, as you see, wrought death and destruction to this young lady's toilette—"

Bob's twisted hand held my hand tightly. "Mr. Abbersly, I present you to my niece and partner, Miss Diana Cameron, joint owner and manager of Palmetto Grove Plantation."

Again the Red Sea engulfed me from head to foot. I was self-conscious and miserable, knowing the spectacle I presented. I managed a refrigerated bow, and escaped, pleading a sun headache.

Whatever your name is, Allen, Abbott, Abbersly, you were as amazed, as astonished, as startled, as shaken out of your self-possession as I!

Oh, Sisyphus, I know! I know what it is to get within an inch of the top of the hill with my stone, then to slip all the way back to the bottommost bottom!

CHAPTER XXVI

BOB knocked on my door cautiously. I pretended to be asleep. He opened the door and came in, fanning with his old sun-helmet. He sat on the edge of my bed; I could feel his tenderness, his solicitude. Who could pretend with him? I opened my eyes.

"Sister," he said, "we have some more company." Hesitatingly: "This lot is a little more rough than usual. It's the mail-rider's brother and his wife. They live on Alligator Bayou. They'll only be here for the night."

"And that strange man?" I asked.

"Oh, Allison?" he asked, brightening up. "I'm going to hold on to him as long as he'll stay. Don't you like him, honey?"

"If we were regularly in the hotel business," I teased, "perhaps I'd welcome them all."

"Come on downstairs," Bob pleaded. "You know it has always been our custom to welcome our neighbors."

It developed that the mail-rider's relatives had ridden twenty-five miles on muleback to take the boat which is expected to-morrow. My heart went out to them. They were so poor, so pathetically sure of a welcome.

Cousin Clara arrived, also unheralded, just before dusk. Aline was dismayed at the sight of her with the bristling masseuse, Freda. Cousin Clara had heard of Bob's illness and made the trip, expecting the worst. Aline's bright spirits evaporated before Freda. She did not stand or even walk. It was plain she dreaded to break the news to them. Even Black Tilly hovered in the background, troubled. Tilly found the old rolling chair and wheeled it in. I could see the struggle in the child's face whether she would or she would not announce her recovery.

"Heah's yoh chair, Miss Aline." Tilly's voice counselled prudence.

Aline rose and walked to the door. Cousin Clara's horror-stricken eyes upon her, Freda rushed to support her. Aline pushed her back.

"I have been walking ever since I came here," Aline said, "and for months before then I had been standing and taking steps."

"My treatment, it have restore the vertebræ to their place—"Freda began.

"You have n't touched my spine in eight months and you know it, Freda," Aline said.

Further discussion was interrupted by the entrance of the mail-rider's brother and his wife.

On a cotton plantation there are no class distinctions, only white and black, Freda, the Swedish masseuse, sat with us, because she was white, ill at ease and as uncomfortable as the snuff-dipping wife of the mail-rider's brother. Conversation was strained after the weather and the roads had been well thrashed over. I went to the kitchen to tell Chattie May to prepare more dinner. Isaiah was picking two more chickens.

"Dem two white men from Deer-Lick sto' sent word dey'd be heah for supper," Isaiah announced. "Dey all wanter come heah 'bout dat airship."

Bob was off with you riding over the fields. The two men from Deer-Lick store, uncouth and embarrassed, arrived and joined the self-invited assembly, waiting for the evening meal. The table was set with our best old damask and silver, lighted with candles and gay with a great bowl of nasturtiums. Once I would have been ashamed of these people, but I was not now. Bob came in genial and whole-souled. He was glad to see everybody. He presented them to you as if each were his special friend and intimate associate. And your breeding was perfect. You did not hear them eating their soup, nor see them almost swallowing their knives. Bob was like a person intoxicated on new wine. You had gone to his head utterly. Airships and tractors, electrical ice-making machines, power-plants to supply energy and light: he had heard for the first time at first hand of these modern miracles. After an airship alighted in his pasture, he was prepared to believe anything. He hung on your words, and the other men sat with mouths agape, while Bob plied the questions that they wanted.

"If these things can be done, sir"—Bob hit the table—"the river controlled, land worked by machinery, nitrogen taken as fertilizer from the air, we are living, as I have always believed, in the site of the original Garden of Eden."

You were sitting next to Bob at the opposite end of the table from me. If you had been disposed to talk to any one else, Bob would not have let you. In you he saw the salvation of this country that is part and parcel of himself. He must hold on to you until he heard about the blessing. His strongest conviction was that it was in your hands to bestow it.

Freda was talking to the wife of the mail-rider about the alligators in the bayou in which she lived. Aline and Cousin Clara and I were making feeble attempts to camouflage a conversation. Cousin Clara's attention wandered to the other end of the table. When we rose at last, she and the other two women went out on the gallery where Bob had marshalled the men to get your views on the present levee system. Aline and I went into the drawing-room.

"I have told Cousin Clara," Aline said, "that she must go back to Roseneath to-morrow morning and take Freda. They have come for me. I am not going."

There was no defiance in her voice, only a ringing courage. Aline has just started to fight for her rights. She passed to the far end of the long room and settled herself quietly on a sofa, her hands over her eyes. I knew she was working her problem out.

I sat down in the long window. The garden below was steeped in the peace of twilight. The scent of phlox and stocks and verbenas, of roses and lemon-verbena and jasmine, mingled to make June's heady bouquet. Fireflies held high carnival in the gloom, a soft wind swished through the willows on the river's bank.

Bob's deep voice boomed from the gallery:

"I've never been an advocate of automobiles on these dirt roads, sir. They are impassable in winter, but our skies are as fine as can be found anywhere. I shall not be satisfied until I can get an airship, built after my own plan as a passenger-car. By Jove, Allerton, I've been buried here! I've got to get out and see what's going on in the world!"

Bob doesn't really need me. To-day has showed that he only needs fresh interests—to be connected up with the world's progress. In the fascinations of this stranger he had forgotten my very existence. Something rose within me. Not regret because of this revelation that I am a non-essential in Bob's life, nor yet bitterness because you turned out to be the biggest practical joke Fate has yet played on me.

Bob was not involved in this new emotion, and neither were you, and strangest of all no more was I in it.

Suddenly I found myself able to step aside and view things impersonally. No longer being in the picture I could get the true perspective on it. I found myself rather liking this detachment that enabled me to regard so calmly, so indifferently, the Providence that one by one has taken away everything it promised me in the beginning.

I felt myself grow spiritually, as I have seen cotton shoot up an inch before one's very eyes. It was even more like the growth of a mango under an East Indian fakir's magic. In this new stature I moved up far enough to look down on the personality I had been; that was left as a shell outgrown. I no longer felt the desperate need, the aching loneliness, for any person, place, or thing.

"Life might keep on being an endurance test, but I felt that nothing that might happen could really touch me now. I knew once and forever that I could endure, perhaps even enjoy, catching any stone, or side-stepping it, that Fate might hurl at me in the future.

"Throw me a harder one," I could challenge in my new-found courage, "I'm not afraid!"

Cousin Clara hobbled in to ask me to sing. The mail-rider's brother and his wife, the two men from the Deer-Lick store, and Freda followed when I touched the piano. Bob and you remained outside. The scent of your cigar mingled with the garden's fragrance and with the old potpourri's incense, and the smell of beeswax seemed the base of it all.

You and Bob were discussing your buying Palmetto Grove. It made no difference to me. I was free at last.

My voice had a new crystalline quality. I seemed to be singing in a clearer ether. I forgot my listeners in the joy of my new range and timbre. I sang as a mockingbird sings when he pours out his heart in the forest in the moonlight, singing that he may attune himself to the music of the spheres. Not that the celestial orchestra needs his note, but because he must make the connection if his own harmony is to be preserved.

Amber and coral and jade! The old feeling of crystal light enveloped me.

My miracle had come back! I had no fear now that I would lose it. This time I knew it had come to stay; to enfold me forever.

Seemingly from no volition of my own, my fingers found the old Lantern of Love theme. The last time I sang it was at Terence's party in Bermuda:

"In the desert of life, when the sands blow high, Oh, love, light a lantern for me; In the dust and the dark and the lowering sky, Oh, love, light a lantern for me— A lantern of love!"

The words seemed to sing themselves:

"In the mist and the fog and the blinding rain, Oh, love, light a lantern for me; When I stumble and slip and rise up again, Oh, love, light a lantern for me— A lantern of love!"

You were listening just outside. But you no longer mattered. My heart's adventure had passed beyond the personal stage.

"In the sea of the senses are treacherous tides; Oh, love, light a lantern for me. The channel is deep and false are my guides— Oh, love, light a lantern for me— A lantern of love!"

I heard you get up and start to come in. Then you turned and went down the steps into the garden. Bob knocked out his pipe and relighted it.

I never felt so buoyant, so free, so like a lark at heaven's gate. I knew now that I could sing the end of the song:

"In the high riding waves and the wild tempest's roar, Oh, love, make a lantern of me. A searchlight to guide the ship-wrecked ashore— Oh, love, make a lantern of me— A lantern of love!"

I heard your returning step and fled. The concert was over.

There was a letter from Terence on my dressing-table. It was brief. Only a few lines to say that "Cedarwoode," the house he has been living in so long, has been let. He must move out. He will write again, he says, as soon as he is settled.

"The caves on the coral beach," he adds in a whimsical postscript, "are really quite habitable. I may spend the summer in one of them."

A troop of pressed "little red soldiers" saluted me, pasted on the last page.

I fell asleep and dreamed that life was a big checkerboard and that Terence, Bob, and I were pawns. I could see the hand above moving us, an Abraham Lincoln hand, your hand.

CHAPTER XXVII

THE Annabel Lee was blowing. It Was early dawn. The grey chiffon mist still hung heavy over the river.

The mail-rider's brother and his wife were down on the river-bank waiting for the boat to land.

Jenny Ribbons was saddled and bridled and neighing impatiently. I was in my crispest riding-habit, eager to get off on my rounds before any one came down to breakfast. Chattie May brought my coffee o the back gallery, so Jenny Ribbons could see I was eager as she to be on our way.

I wanted to side-step Cousin Clara and Freda's departure, and if you were going to-day, to let you go, knowing no more about you than I did when you came. Even now I realized that discretion had its part in my valor. I wanted to stay free.

Just then around the corner down the brick walk from the garden you came walking and talking with Bob.

"I was just getting ready to send Hezekiah up for you, sister," Bob kissed me good-morning, brushing my face with a spray of wet roses. "I've got to go down to the boat this morning to see about getting that last lot of cotton seed aboard. Allison here"—he indicated you—"wants to have a look at our famous cypress-brake. Take him along to ride over the place with you. I've explained to him my disabilities in walking." Then back to you. "Diana's as sure-footed as a deer. There's over a mile you two will have to go on foot."

I couldn't slip away by promising to come back for you after breakfast You and Bob had already breakfasted.

The sky was a clear soft blue, the day throbbing with heat even this early in the morning. I had no intention of personally conducting you over a thousand acres planted in cotton and corn and sugar-cane. We swung off in a lively gallop toward the back of the plantation where the cypress-trees loomed, a pensive background for the smiling fields.

It was easy enough to eliminate conversation. Jenny Ribbons pranced and shied and danced, and I pretended I had to give all my attention to her.

"How beautifully you ride," you said, and I caught myself warming up toward you in spite of the determination not to. I caught myself trying to remember where I have seen eyes like your eyes.

Again I encased myself in ice; self-preservation demanded it, I felt, even while a tropical sun shone over the cotton-fields, pulsing with heat about us. You thought my veiled unfriendliness was because I did not want to sell Palmetto Grove.

I slipped from my horse before telling you the rest of the way must be on foot. Then we plunged into a tangled undergrowth, where briers and thorns barricaded the path. The air was heavy with the dank scent of swamp lilies and water flowers. Underfoot the grass was deep and wet. You went ahead, beating the path for me. Occasionally a brier caught my riding-skirt or a thorn-tree reached after my hat. And each time you disentangled me. A foot-log was stretched across a bog. You held out your hands for mine and guided me across, ignoring my protests that I was used to walking such places alone. We had long ceased trying to keep up even a pretence at conversation. Now we were crossing a level place, carpeted with the soft leaves of last year's cypress-trees. It was like a springy brown carpet. Just before us lay the brake. As far as the eye could reach in all directions it stretched out like a vaulted cathedral. The tawny water beneath might have been a curiously patterned tiled floor. The cypress "knees" looked not unlike seats for a worshipping congregation.

I sat on a log and watched a turtle sunning himself on a stump in the water.

You walked on alone to examine the trees from a new angle farther down. You were making estimates, entries in a small notebook; then you passed out of sight.

From the fields behind us came the voices of negroes singing as they rhythmically chopped grass from the cotton. Happy souls, they! No regret for yesterday, no dread of to-morrow. To-day is the day they elect to live and love. In the face of what all my planning had come to, the negro philosophy seemed the best wisdom, after all.

My mind was made up, to let Bob do as he liked about the plantation. A stronger will than either of ours was somehow shaping events. A new tide was rising, and I would not row against it. Perhaps it would carry me to the haven my own futile navigation had missed. Would it be Japan with its gardens, India with its Taj Mahal, Italy with its poetry, or Greece with her memories? The whole world beckoned. I could trust the adventure to unfold itself. . . . And yet—and yet—the only place that really allured me, after all was said and done, was Palmetto Grove Plantation! A drop of rain splashed on my glove. You hurried back to say we had better return. There was only a scrap of cloud in the sky, but it was growing larger and blacker. We started to retrace our steps. A few more drops fell.

"We can make that shelter." You indicated a group of small trees, off the path, and we started to run for it, reaching shelter just as the shower descended. Not one drop came in on us.

Honeysuckle-vines made a natural arbor; above us was a roof that shed the rain like a waterproof. Inside was a bower of blossoming honeysuckles. The place was hardly larger and very much the shape of a telephone booth.

A baby rabbit crept in shyly and hunched himself up at my feet. I stooped and lifted the small, quivering bunch of fur. Its foot was bleeding. We bent over it together to see the extent of its injuries. You tore your handkerchief in strips, and we caught raindrops to wet these, to wash the wound, and then you bound it up, skilful as a surgeon. The rabbit, terrified, was comforted only when I lifted and held it close. You looked at me, and my heart felt as if Jenny Ribbons were running away with me without a bridle on. A thrush flew in, no more disconcerted by our being there than the rabbit had been.

"The thrush is just the color of your hair," you said. "Exactly!"

"This is a public telephone booth" (the honey suckle had gone to my head).

"The thrush has come to call up his family to ask them to send him an umbrella!"

You laughed gaily—then both of us remembered New Orleans at the same moment. I began my old argument with myself. If your wife had not gone to telephone, then Pinky Wood-Dove would not have mistaken me for her mother.

"This is your property, I believe." You drew a small parcel from an inner pocket of your coat and handed it to me.

It was Confucius. "I thought you were coming back," you explained awkwardly. "The baby was inconsolable when you did not."

"I was catching a train"—I avoided your eyes—"and my impression was that her mother was telephoning."

"The baby's mother is dead."

"A-ah—"

I was terribly sorry for you.

"She has neither father nor mother—poor little kiddy," you said. "And she hates trained nurses—like poison."

"O-oh!" I repeated.

"It was her trained nurse who was telephoning to the hospital," you went on, "to see if she could keep the baby there until I could make some other arrangement. I'm her nearest living relative."

The little rabbit cuddled closer to my shoulder. The thrush piped a silvery rain-song, for the shower began all over again. "I would have come back to Pinky Wood-Dove if I had known she was crying for me," I heard myself say. "Why didn't you tell me?"

"You left in such haste," you reminded me with a poor imitation of a smile, "to buy a wedding gown, and an orange-blossom wreath and a veil—"

(The little rabbit's teeth were going like fairy castanets, my heart was beating so.)

"—That it seemed an unwarranted impertinence for a strange baby to demand your attendance." You hesitated again. I could not trust myself to speak. "I wish you great happiness," you said, as if it were nothing to you.

"Thank you," I replied. "The bridal outfit was for our cook and the peg-leg boy who waits on the table."

"I don't know why"—you suddenly unbent and made the confession—"I picked up your property from the table, nor why I did not turn it in at the desk—except—except—" You took another tiny Chinese figure out of your pocket. You were the confused one now. I was quite composed. Confucius and the little Chinese lady rested on the palm of your hand.

"Confucius was given me by a dear old friend in Bermuda," I said. "Terence Woode."

"Terence Woode is my uncle," you said quietly.

Terence's eyes are your eyes and your eyes are Terence's! It came back to me in a flash what Terence had told me: that the little mate of Confucius went with his sister to her new home when she married. The two tiny Chinese figures were reunited after all these years.

"Then your mother was Terence's sister who married the rich American?"

"My father lost all his money," you explained. "My mother would never let her family know."

"And you are the hydrographic engineer lately returned from France, one of the engineers appointed by the Government to report on the Mississippi River?"

"That is what I was doing in New Orleans," you said.

"But Bob said your name—"

Again you laughed.

"My name is Stephen Abercrombie," you said. "Your uncle found it difficult to remember."

"And Pinky Wood-Dove is the baby left by your sister in Louisiana who died just after her husband was killed?"

You nodded.

"There was no one to take the baby but me," you said. "I don't know what I'm going to do with her. She hates trained nurses." You looked straight into my eyes. "The only human being who has interested her in the least is yourself."

I could think of nothing to say.

"Now that you know who I am," you continued very quietly, "I will tell you who you are—the girl in the fog. You can't deny it any longer."

"Have I ever tried to deny it?" I fenced.

"Have you?" Your accusing eyes held mine with the old grave tenderness. "That morning at the Holland House—the minute I saw you I knew you—then the next second you convinced me I had made a mistake. I looked at you again. You only vaguely suggested the little girl I thought you were."

"If I had known—"I began, and ended.

"And the next time I saw you in that shop," you went on, "hanging over a little landscape garden, I was positive. Then you denied me again, and I called myself a greater fool than ever for thinking it was you. And I felt I ought to send an apology for annoying you. Instead I sent you the Japanese garden."

"I pretended it came from you," I confessed, "even when I knew it did not."

"And I pretended it went to you even when I knew the one to whom I sent it was not the girl I had mistaken her to be.

"And again in New Orleans!" You reproached and studied my face. "Why?"

The honeysuckle booth melted into thin air. I was in a cave under the jutting rocks. The wind blew the smoke into my eyes; the salt smell of the sea mingled with the wood smoke from the driftwood fire and tobacco smoke from your pipe. Happiness and peace enfolded me; the feeling of home. The feeling that you, a stranger I had never seen before, across the fire reading aloud the Wisdom of Confucius, were less a stranger to me than any one I had ever known in all my life.

"Just outside the door—" I tried to recall the words you read. "Perhaps I felt that the great guest you read about had—had—come."

"What was the point in slamming the door in his face?" you asked softly.

"How could I know," I faltered humbly," that you wanted to come in?"

"Since that night when you held the lantern for me in the fog," you said simply, "I have had but one beacon light."

We were tremulous on the brink of the divine miracle.

Amber and coral and jade! And the crystal bubble was enlarged to enclose you. Our hands found each other at last.

"I have been an orphan all my life," you whispered, "waiting for you."

"Take me," I said.

CHAPTER XXVIII

I love you for your splendid silences, your soul's fine reticence. Your speech itself is quietness; your deep heart Is like a wayside well That bubbles coolness for the pilgrim's smart, But of its sanctities, withheld, apart, I, only I, can tell.

C. K. B. in *Pall Mall Gazette*

Palmetto Grove, June

CAN this peaceful peachblow river, full of silver stars and a melting sickle of a new moon, be the same stream, that stretched its tawny mane over these banks a few months ago?

Then it was disposed like a jungle thing, growling like a famished beast after its prey. Now it slips by singing in the soft June twilight.

You and I sat in an embrasure of the roots of the old oak-tree where I, as a child, made my first playhouse, and where Pinky Wood-Dove in a few years will be making a playhouse for her dolls.

We watched the antics of Arabella. She was devilling a frog, enamored of a firefly at the water's edge.

The asthmatic breathing of a far-off accordion floated from the direction of the bayou, and a rickety voice wailed:

"Jesus, feed us on bread and wine— Jesus, feed us on bread and wine— Jesus, feed us on bread and wine—"

"What is that?" you asked, bewildered. "Mandy singing," I replied. "Has she not a sweet voice?" Even the old accordion seemed music to me now, as Mandy played the one line of the only hymn she knows over and over and over again. "It's improved since she moved out of the yard. Sometimes she sings all night long."

"Jesus, feed us bread and wine— Jesus, feed us bread and wine— Bread—and— wine; bread—and—w-ine."

This was the first quiet hour we had had alone since we left the honeysuckle telephone booth yesterday with the affairs of our life settled.

"Diana for sudden!" Bob could only repeat when we told him our plans.

"I'm going to marry Stephen Abercrombie because you are so in love with him," I teased Bob.

We had a strenuous Saturday afternoon in Cotton-port. (You insisted on having deeds properly drawn up and checks deposited. They were your checks in payment for one-third interest in Palmetto Grove Plantation.) With all that money on hand Bob and I realized at the same moment that the last note, mortgage, indebtedness, against our home could be cancelled without waiting for fall and the certain fluctuations of an always uncertain cotton market.

We opened safe-deposit boxes that haven't been opened since long before my father died, in order to find certain deeds and papers needed in the new division of the plantation.

One of these boxes held a sealed package. It was my mother's diamonds. Enough to have paid the place out of debt years ago!

"I had forgotten they were there," Bob said. "They are yours, kitten."

But diamonds have nothing to do with me! Even my mother's diamonds leave me cold. There was another, older parcel, carefully done up in Chinese parchment paper, secured with green sealing wax.

A mysterious excitement swept over me as I touched it. We opened the box. The scent of sandalwood came from it.

Amber and coral and jade! I caught my breath as I poured out the beautiful old things.

"These were her jewels"—Bob read the faded writing on the box—"the Florentine opera singer's. I remember now to have heard she cared only for amber and coral and jade—"

"They are mine," I said, slipping a jade bracelet on my wrist, a string of amber about my throat. In the box were two old Etruscan wedding rings. In each was engraved the one word: "Eternity."

One of these rings is on my third finger, and you wear the other.

We were married at the little old Deer-Lick church this morning. The ceremony was very brief. Probably it is the only wedding on record where the bride song her own Epithalamium.

The firefly flew away and the frog said good-night in guttural tones and plunged into the river. Arabella yawned and retraced her steps to the garden to join Bob and Aline. It came to you that moment that you had given me no wedding gift.

"Isn't there anything in the whole world that you want?" you asked me.

And suddenly I knew there was. I was thinking of the thin grey letter upstairs with the foreign postmark. "There's something," you persisted.

"Yes. Terence."

"Terence who?"

"Your uncle, Terence Woode," I told you. "I want him to come live here with us on Palmetto Grove."

"But hasn't he a great estate himself?" you asked in amazement. "I've always pictured him a kind of nabob."

It pleased me to fill in the picture.

"A nabob of dreams, yes," I replied. "He has a great estate; all the stars in the sky belong to him, and the sea is also his. He goes attended by flower troops of 'little red soldiers.' Lucifer's pride is n't a patch on his—and Terence Woode has n't the price of a postage-stamp."

"We'll cable in the morning, when we go to Cottonport to meet the baby," you said; "cable for him to come on the next boat."

"Do you think Pinky Wood-Dove will know me?" I asked tremulously. ***"Really?"***

"You and Pinky Wood-Dove and I," you said impressively, "seem to have one trait in common: ***We know our own!***"

The Codes Of Hammurabi And Moses
W. W. Davies

QTY

The discovery of the Hammurabi Code is one of the greatest achievements of archaeology, and is of paramount interest, not only to the student of the Bible, but also to all those interested in ancient history...

Religion   **ISBN:** *1-59462-338-4*   **Pages:132**
                                                    MSRP $12.95

The Theory of Moral Sentiments
Adam Smith

QTY

This work from 1749. contains original theories of conscience amd moral judgment and it is the foundation for systemof morals.

Philosophy   **ISBN:** *1-59462-777-0*   **Pages:536**
                                                    MSRP $19.95

Jessica's First Prayer
Hesba Stretton

QTY

In a screened and secluded corner of one of the many railway-bridges which span the streets of London there could be seen a few years ago, from five o'clock every morning until half past eight, a tidily set-out coffee-stall, consisting of a trestle and board, upon which stood two large tin cans, with a small fire of charcoal burning under each so as to keep the coffee boiling during the early hours of the morning when the work-people were thronging into the city on their way to their daily toil...

Childrens   **ISBN:** *1-59462-373-2*   **Pages:84**
                                              MSRP $9.95

My Life and Work
Henry Ford

QTY

Henry Ford revolutionized the world with his implementation of mass production for the Model T automobile. Gain valuable business insight into his life and work with his own auto-biography... "We have only started on our development of our country we have not as yet, with all our talk of wonderful progress, done more than scratch the surface. The progress has been wonderful enough but..."

Biographies/   **ISBN:** *1-59462-198-5*   **Pages:300**
                                                 MSRP $21.95

The Art of Cross-Examination
Francis Wellman

QTY

I presume it is the experience of every author, after his first book is published upon an important subject, to be almost overwhelmed with a wealth of ideas and illustrations which could readily have been included in his book, and which to his own mind, at least, seem to make a second edition inevitable. Such certainly was the case with me; and when the first edition had reached its sixth impression in five months, I rejoiced to learn that it seemed to my publishers that the book had met with a sufficiently favorable reception to justify a second and considerably enlarged edition. ..

Reference   **ISBN:** *1-59462-647-2*

Pages:412

MSRP $19.95

On the Duty of Civil Disobedience
Henry David Thoreau

QTY

Thoreau wrote his famous essay, On the Duty of Civil Disobedience, as a protest against an unjust but popular war and the immoral but popular institution of slave-owning. He did more than write—he declined to pay his taxes, and was hauled off to gaol in consequence. Who can say how much this refusal of his hastened the end of the war and of slavery ?

Law   **ISBN:** *1-59462-747-9*   **Pages:48**

MSRP $7.45

Dream Psychology Psychoanalysis for Beginners
Sigmund Freud

QTY

Sigmund Freud, born Sigismund Schlomo Freud (May 6, 1856 - September 23, 1939), was a Jewish-Austrian neurologist and psychiatrist who co-founded the psychoanalytic school of psychology. Freud is best known for his theories of the unconscious mind, especially involving the mechanism of repression; his redefinition of sexual desire as mobile and directed towards a wide variety of objects; and his therapeutic techniques, especially his understanding of transference in the therapeutic relationship and the presumed value of dreams as sources of insight into unconscious desires.

Dream Psychology
Psychoanalysis for Beginners

Sigmund Freud

Psychology   **ISBN:** *1-59462-905-6*

Pages:196

MSRP $15.45

The Miracle of Right Thought
Orison Swett Marden

QTY

Believe with all of your heart that you will do what you were made to do. When the mind has once formed the habit of holding cheerful, happy, prosperous pictures, it will not be easy to form the opposite habit. It does not matter how improbable or how far away this realization may see, or how dark the prospects may be, if we visualize them as best we can, as vividly as possible, hold tenaciously to them and vigorously struggle to attain them, they will gradually become actualized, realized in the life. But a desire, a longing without endeavor, a yearning abandoned or held indifferently will vanish without realization.

Pages:360

Self Help   **ISBN:** *1-59462-644-8*   *MSRP $25.45*

☐ **The Rosicrucian Cosmo-Conception Mystic Christianity** *by Max Heindel*   ISBN: 1-59462-188-8   **$38.95**
The Rosicrucian Cosmo-conception is not dogmatic, neither does it appeal to any other authority than the reason of the student. It is: not controversial, but is: sent forth in the, hope that it may help to clear...   New Age/Religion Pages 646

☐ **Abandonment To Divine Providence** *by Jean-Pierre de Caussade*   ISBN: 1-59462-228-0   **$25.95**
"The Rev. Jean Pierre de Caussade was one of the most remarkable spiritual writers of the Society of Jesus in France in the 18th Century. His death took place at Toulouse in 1751. His works have gone through many editions and have been republished...   Inspirational/Religion Pages 400

☐ **Mental Chemistry** *by Charles Haanel*   ISBN: 1-59462-192-6   **$23.95**
Mental Chemistry allows the change of material conditions by combining and appropriately utilizing the power of the mind. Much like applied chemistry creates something new and unique out of careful combinations of chemicals the mastery of mental chemistry...   New Age Pages 354

☐ **The Letters of Robert Browning and Elizabeth Barret Barrett 1845-1846 vol II**   ISBN: 1-59462-193-4   **$35.95**
by Robert Browning and Elizabeth Barrett   Biographies Pages 596

☐ **Gleanings In Genesis (volume I)** *by Arthur W. Pink*   ISBN: 1-59462-130-6   **$27.45**
Appropriately has Genesis been termed "the seed plot of the Bible" for in it we have, in germ form, almost all of the great doctrines which are afterwards fully developed in the books of Scripture which follow...   Religion/Inspirational Pages 420

☐ **The Master Key** *by L. W. de Laurence*   ISBN: 1-59462-001-6   **$30.95**
In no branch of human knowledge has there been a more lively increase of the spirit of research during the past few years than in the study of Psychology, Concentration and Mental Discipline. The requests for authentic lessons in Thought Control, Mental Discipline and...   New Age/Business Pages 422

☐ **The Lesser Key Of Solomon Goetia** *by L. W. de Laurence*   ISBN: 1-59462-092-X   **$9.95**
This translation of the first book of the "Lernegton" which is now for the first time made accessible to students of Talismanic Magic was done, after careful collation and edition, from numerous Ancient Manuscripts in Hebrew, Latin, and French...   New Age/Occult Pages 92

☐ **Rubaiyat Of Omar Khayyam** *by Edward Fitzgerald*   ISBN:1-59462-332-5   **$13.95**
Edward Fitzgerald, whom the world has already learned, in spite of his own efforts to remain within the shadow of anonymity, to look upon as one of the rarest poets of the century, was born at Bredfield, in Suffolk, on the 31st of March, 1809. He was the third son of John Purcell...   Music Pages 172

☐ **Ancient Law** *by Henry Maine*   ISBN: 1-59462-128-4   **$29.95**
The chief object of the following pages is to indicate some of the earliest ideas of mankind, as they are reflected in Ancient Law, and to point out the relation of those ideas to modern thought.   Religion/History Pages 452

☐ **Far-Away Stories** *by William J. Locke*   ISBN: 1-59462-129-2   **$19.45**
"Good wine needs no bush, but a collection of mixed vintages does. And this book is just such a collection. Some of the stories I do not want to remain buried for ever in the museum files of dead magazine-numbers an author's not unpardonable vanity..."   Fiction Pages 272

☐ **Life of David Crockett** *by David Crockett*   ISBN: 1-59462-250-7   **$27.45**
"Colonel David Crockett was one of the most remarkable men of the times in which he lived. Born in humble life, but gifted with a strong will, an indomitable courage, and unremitting perseverance...   Biographies/New Age Pages 424

☐ **Lip-Reading** *by Edward Nitchie*   ISBN: 1-59462-206-X   **$25.95**
Edward B. Nitchie, founder of the New York School for the Hard of Hearing, now the Nitchie School of Lip-Reading, Inc, wrote "LIP-READING Principles and Practice". The development and perfecting of this meritorious work on lip-reading was an undertaking...   How-to Pages 400

☐ **A Handbook of Suggestive Therapeutics, Applied Hypnotism, Psychic Science**   ISBN: 1-59462-214-0   **$24.95**
by Henry Munro   Health/New Age/Health/Self-help Pages 376

☐ **A Doll's House: and Two Other Plays** *by Henrik Ibsen*   ISBN: 1-59462-112-8   **$19.95**
Henrik Ibsen created this classic when in revolutionary 1848 Rome. Introducing some striking concepts in playwriting for the realist genre, this play has been studied the world over.   Fiction/Classics/Plays 308

☐ **The Light of Asia** *by sir Edwin Arnold*   ISBN: 1-59462-204-3   **$13.95**
In this poetic masterpiece, Edwin Arnold describes the life and teachings of Buddha. The man who was to become known as Buddha to the world was born as Prince Gautama of India but he rejected the worldly riches and abandoned the reigns of power when...   Religion/History/Biographies Pages 170

☐ **The Complete Works of Guy de Maupassant** *by Guy de Maupassant*   ISBN: 1-59462-157-8   **$16.95**
"For days and days, nights and nights, I had dreamed of that first kiss which was to consecrate our engagement, and I knew not on what spot I should put my lips..."   Fiction/Classics Pages 240

☐ **The Art of Cross-Examination** *by Francis L. Wellman*   ISBN: 1-59462-309-0   **$26.95**
Written by a renowned trial lawyer, Wellman imparts his experience and uses case studies to explain how to use psychology to extract desired information through questioning.   How-to/Science/Reference Pages 408

☐ **Answered or Unanswered?** *by Louisa Vaughan*   ISBN: 1-59462-248-5   **$10.95**
Miracles of Faith in China   Religion Pages 112

☐ **The Edinburgh Lectures on Mental Science (1909)** *by Thomas*   ISBN: 1-59462-008-3   **$11.95**
This book contains the substance of a course of lectures recently given by the writer in the Queen Street Hall, Edinburgh. Its purpose is to indicate the Natural Principles governing the relation between Mental Action and Material Conditions...   New Age/Psychology Pages 148

☐ **Ayesha** *by H. Rider Haggard*   ISBN: 1-59462-301-5   **$24.95**
Verily and indeed it is the unexpected that happens! Probably if there was one person upon the earth from whom the Editor of this, and of a certain previous history, did not expect to hear again...   Classics Pages 380

☐ **Ayala's Angel** *by Anthony Trollope*   ISBN: 1-59462-352-X   **$29.95**
The two girls were both pretty, but Lucy who was twenty-one who supposed to be simple and comparatively unattractive, whereas Ayala was credited, as her Bombwhat romantic name might show, with poetic charm and a taste for romance. Ayala when her father died was nineteen...   Fiction Pages 484

☐ **The American Commonwealth** *by James Bryce*   ISBN: 1-59462-286-8   **$34.45**
An interpretation of American democratic political theory. It examines political mechanics and society from the perspective of Scotsman James Bryce   Politics Pages 572

☐ **Stories of the Pilgrims** *by Margaret P. Pumphrey*   ISBN: 1-59462-116-0   **$17.95**
This book explores pilgrims religious oppression in England as well as their escape to Holland and eventual crossing to America on the Mayflower, and their early days in New England...   History Pages 268

QTY

The Fasting Cure *by Sinclair Upton*   ISBN: *1-59462-222-1*   **$13.95**
In the Cosmopolitan Magazine for May, 1910, and in the Contemporary Review (London) for April, 1910, I published an article dealing with my experiences in fasting. I have written a great many magazine articles, but never one which attracted so much attention... New Age/Self Help/Health Pages 164

Hebrew Astrology *by Sepharial*   ISBN: *1-59462-308-2*   **$13.45**
In these days of advanced thinking it is a matter of common observation that we have left many of the old landmarks behind and that we are now pressing forward to greater heights and to a wider horizon than that which represented the mind-content of our progenitors... Astrology Pages 144

Thought Vibration or The Law of Attraction in the Thought World   ISBN: *1-59462-127-6*   **$12.95**
by William Walker Atkinson   Psychology/Religion Pages 144

Optimism *by Helen Keller*   ISBN: *1-59462-108-X*   **$15.95**
Helen Keller was blind, deaf, and mute since 19 months old, yet famously learned how to overcome these handicaps, communicate with the world, and spread her lectures promoting optimism. An inspiring read for everyone... Biographies/Inspirational Pages 84

Sara Crewe *by Frances Burnett*   ISBN: *1-59462-360-0*   **$9.45**
In the first place, Miss Minchin lived in London. Her home was a large, dull, tall one, in a large, dull square, where all the houses were alike, and all the sparrows were alike, and where all the door-knockers made the same heavy sound... Childrens/Classic Pages 88

The Autobiography of Benjamin Franklin *by Benjamin Franklin*   ISBN: *1-59462-135-7*   **$24.95**
The Autobiography of Benjamin Franklin has probably been more extensively read than any other American historical work, and no other book of its kind has had such ups and downs of fortune. Franklin lived for many years in England, where he was agent... Biographies/History Pages 332

Name	
Email	
Telephone	
Address	
City, State ZIP	

☐ **Credit Card**   ☐ **Check / Money Order**

Credit Card Number	
Expiration Date	
Signature	

Please Mail to: Book Jungle
PO Box 2226
Champaign, IL 61825
or Fax to: 630-214-0564

ORDERING INFORMATION

web: *www.bookjungle.com*
email: *sales@bookjungle.com*
fax: *630-214-0564*
mail: *Book Jungle PO Box 2226 Champaign, IL 61825*
or PayPal *to sales@bookjungle.com*

Please contact us for bulk discounts

DIRECT-ORDER TERMS

**20% Discount if You Order
Two or More Books**
Free Domestic Shipping!
Accepted: Master Card, Visa,
Discover, American Express

www.ingramcontent.com/pod-product-compliance
Lightning Source LLC
Chambersburg PA
CBHW080729020726
47503CB00010B/2844